SOMEBODY LIKE YOU

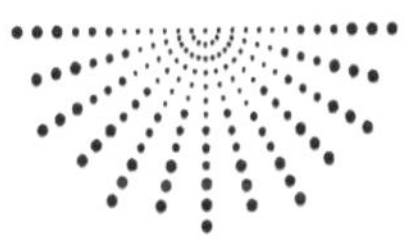

CARRIE ELKS

*A*t first he thought he was asleep in his bed. He was laying on his front, his legs flung out, his hands clutching something beneath him. But it didn't feel like a pillow. And it smelled… different. Letting out a groan, Cam Hartson opened his left eye and all he could see was emerald green.

There was a pause. Like the moment when a baby opens its mouth right before it starts to scream. The kind of silence that has meaning, but you have no idea what it is.

And then the noise came rushing in.

The sound of roaring voices was all it took for him to realize where he was. Not at home on his two thousand thread count bedsheets, but on the turf at Freedom Field, where the Boston Bobcats played their home games.

"Is he conscious?" a voice asked.

"One of his eyes is open," someone else replied. "Cam, can you hear me?"

Cam tried to say yes, but no words emerged. There was some sort of disconnect between his brain and mouth.

"Okay, we're gonna put a neck brace on, just in case. Then

we'll be sliding you onto the gurney. Give me a signal if something hurts."

"No neck brace," he tried to say, but it came out as a grunt. The medics took it as his agreement, because the next minute he felt a stiff plastic brace being clipped around his neck, soft padding holding his chin up.

If he'd had any strength left in his body, he would've mustered it to push them away. But whatever had landed him in this situation had winded him completely. His breath was coming in short, sharp pants, and the pounding in his head was stronger than ever. With gentle hands, they lifted him onto the gurney and he closed his eyes for a moment.

His humiliation was complete.

There was one thing every player in the NFL knew. When you got hurt, you don't let them take you off the field. You swallow down the pain and play, regardless. Because winning was everything.

Only losers left the field.

He'd followed that code since his pee wee football days, and continued with it through high school then college, until his NFL draft nine years ago. And now here he was, being carted off in front of a stadium of seventy thousand people, plus hundreds of millions of viewers watching at home.

And that thought was all it took for his brain to finally connect with his mouth.

"Stop," he croaked. The medics actually followed his instructions. "Let me off, I can walk." From the corner of his eye he could see Dan Motion, the Bobcats' quarterback, running over, followed by a group of Cam's fellow defensive players.

They were his coworkers, his friends, his partners in every play they made. Apart from his family, they were the closest people to him. They knew him inside out, and understood that the pain of being humiliated outweighed any physical ache in his body. Most of them had been here like this – multiple times.

"How is he?" Dan asked, leaning over Cam's stretcher. "Hey, you're awake."

"I'm coming back on," Cam croaked. "Give me a minute." He reached up to touch his throbbing head, and realized his helmet must have come off during the impact.

If only he could remember what the damn impact was.

"You don't look so good, man." Dan frowned. "You sure you're okay to play?"

"He's not playing." Cam recognized that voice immediately. He sat up and swung his legs around, jumping off of the gurney onto the soft grass. A wave of nausea crashed over him, causing Cam to sway. Coach Mayberry had his arms crossed as he stared at Cam with his all-seeing eyes. "I'm putting Rayburn on."

"The rookie?" Dan said. "He hasn't played a game since he joined us. That's a fucking terrible idea."

Coach gave the quarterback one of his famous iron-clad glares, then looked back at Cam. "Hartson, you're off. Go see the doctor and do what he tells you, including going to the hospital if needed. I'll talk to you tomorrow."

"But Coach, I'm fine." Ignoring the jabbing pain in his head, Cam walked toward him. "If I can walk, I can damn well run. There are only twenty minutes left. Let me play."

A flicker of sympathy flashed over the coach's face, and that was worse than seeing his anger. Cam didn't want sympathy. Didn't need it. He was the Bobcats' best paid player. Had been their safety since he was drafted nine years ago, and had played nearly every game in that time. That spot was his. Had been since he was a rookie.

But those years had taught him something else. You didn't argue with the coach during the middle of a game. He was the general, and the players were the soldiers. You kept the discussions for when the battle was over.

"Okay." Cam sighed, nodding his head. He winced at the white hot pain that stung at his eyes. "The rookie can go on for twenty minutes. But he needs to know one thing." His voice was full of determination. "That position is still mine."

———

"You have a choice to make," the doctor said two days later, as Cam sat in his office and looked at the screen in front of him. He'd been in for an MRI scan earlier that day, and they were discussing the results. "You give up football or you end up with a traumatic brain injury. It's that stark, Mr. Hartson."

Cam ran his tongue along his bottom lip. "What about treatment?" he asked. "Something to get me through the season." There was no way he was giving up now. He'd signed a contract. After he fulfilled it, he would consider retirement. Not before.

"There is no treatment. TBIs are permanent. Look at what happened to Junior Seau. Sean Morey. Dammit, Aaron Hernandez if you really want to know the worst case scenario."

TBIs were the dark shadow that followed defensive football players around. The constant collisions as they defended could lead to traumatic brain injuries, which in turn could lead to something worse.

Like the Chronic Traumatic Encephalopathy that footballers like Junior Seau and Sean Morey suffered from. Leading to memory loss, sudden outbreaks of anger, and in Seau's case, suicide.

"Shit." Cam squeezed his eyes shut. The pain in his head still hadn't quite gone away. "It's that bad?"

The doctor's tone softened. "Look, those are worst case scenarios. And hopefully we've caught this in time. You've been having brain scans for a year, and you can see the deterioration in your brain, but it hasn't reached crisis level yet." The doctor cleared his throat. "But if you carry on playing football, it will. Another concussion could be the end of life as you currently know it."

Cam had watched the replay of his collision five times since yesterday. It had been brutal, the way they always were. He'd gone up against the wide receiver, both trying to catch the ball, and their helmets had collided in mid-air. Cam's head had bent back almost ninety degrees, and as he'd suspected, his helmet had flown off in one direction while his body hurled to the ground in the other. He must have been knocked out on impact with the wide receiver, because he hadn't even put his hands out to brace himself as his body collided with the ground. He'd looked more like a ragdoll than a damn football player.

He still didn't remember a second of it. Of course, he knew it was himself he was watching, not only from the number on his back and helmet, but from the way he played. He spent half of his life watching his own football games, he could spot his 'tells' in an instant.

And yet he didn't remember a thing. Not from the play being called to waking up on the grass. He didn't remember going in for the ball, or the sickening thud that must have come from his helmet hitting the wide receiver's. And that scared him more than the scan of his brain on the screen in front of him. He didn't want memory loss to be part of his life. Didn't want to get sudden outbursts of anger like he'd heard from those who suffered from CTE.

He could live with the constant headaches. But not the personality changes.

The problem was, he had no idea how to live without

football. It wasn't just part of his life, it *was* his life. From the moment he woke up in the morning, until the moment his head hit the pillow at night, it was who he was. It was in the breakfast he ate – nutritious and full of protein – to the morning drills he did at the gym to keep his muscles in peak condition. In the drive he made to Freedom Field every day, and the meetings with the coach to discuss tactics.

It was his social life, too. The team tended to stick together in their off-time, hosting parties and dinners and every other kind of get-together. There was solace in spending time with people who understood your lifestyle.

Heck, he'd probably spent more Thanksgivings with the Bobcats than he had with his own family.

And now, he was going to have to leave all that behind? The thought was giving him palpitations.

"I need to think," he said, running a palm across his short hair.

"Of course." The doctor nodded, switching off the screen. "And if you have any questions, call me. I'd like to see you again next week. Make sure you're healing from this concussion."

"Yeah." But Cam's mind was elsewhere. Somewhere in the middle of the turf on Freedom Field. The place he'd called home for the last almost-decade of his life. Giving the doctor a grim smile, he walked out of the consulting room and into the main lobby, swallowing hard when he saw his assistant, Brian, waiting there for him.

"Everything okay?" Brian asked. He'd been Cam's PA for the last six years.

Cam blew out a mouthful of air, then nodded, though nothing was okay at all. "Come on," he said, nodding his head at the exit. "Let's go home. I need to tell you something."

———

"ANOTHER ORANGE JUICE?" Brian asked, pointing at Cam's empty glass. Cam shook his head and stared down at the remaining orange liquid, running his finger along the rim.

"Nah. I think I'll head out of here."

"In the middle of the game? Don't you want to watch the end?" Brian lowered his voice. "You know they were just trying to fill time when they said the rookie was a breath of fresh air, right? You'll always be the Bobcats' star safety. He's just filling your space until you decide what to do."

In the week since Cam's visit to the doctor, he'd had so many meetings his head would be full of wool, if it wasn't already, thanks to the multiple TBIs he'd suffered from. With the coach, with Marty Landsman, the owner of the Boston Bobcats, with the team's doctor, and with some of his defensive team mates, too. And he still hadn't come to any conclusion.

There was still a place for him on the team if he wanted it, Coach had made that much clear. But until he decided one way or the other, Cam needed to take a break and the rookie was going to be played. The guy needed the experience.

"Maybe you could give him some pointers," Coach had suggested. "He looks up to you."

Yeah, maybe. But not right now. Because it felt like he was hitting himself in the face a hundred times every moment he didn't run out onto the turf.

On Friday, before the rest of the team had caught their flight to California, he'd joined them for a party at Dan Motion's house, to celebrate his fiancée's birthday. It had been less than a week since he'd played, but there was already a feeling of being an outsider. He hadn't been able to joke with them about what they'd do in San Francisco on Saturday night, or about the drills Coach had made them run all week. Even when he'd joined in a discussion about the

San Francisco team's weaknesses, he'd felt a pang in his stomach.

Because he wouldn't be able to take advantage of those weaknesses. Or try to intercept the ball and run it up the field. With every day of indecision he was being inched out, and pushed away from the life he knew.

That's why he'd suggested to Brian that they watch the game at a bar. He'd only sulk if he was sitting in his leather recliner at home, watching the oversize screen that had been installed the year he'd bought the house on Beacon Hill. So much better to be surrounded by people than to be alone.

"Hey, is that Cam Hartson?" he heard a woman whisper.

"Jesus, it is," the man next to her agreed. "Hey Cam, what are you doing here? Shouldn't you be playing ball?"

A man to his left lifted his head up. "Saw you take that hit last week. Looked painful. You out of the team now?"

Cam curled his fingers into his palm and forced a smile. "Just resting."

"That rookie though. He's good. You're gonna have a battle to get your place back."

Cam's muscles tensed.

"It's a young man's game," the woman to his left said. "Once you hit thirty, you're pretty much done for."

Brian frowned. "That's not true. What about Brady? He's forty something." Brian drummed his fingers on the table in front of him. His black hair was pulled into a low pony tail.

"He doesn't take the impacts like a safety." The woman shrugged. "Anyway, good luck with retirement."

Cam could tell Brian was getting irate from the way his finger drumming increased in tempo. "It's okay, man," he said, reaching out to calm his assistant's hands. "This is a football town. I gotta get used to it."

"Yeah, well they wouldn't like it if I talked about their job like that." Brian gritted his teeth.

Cam pressed his lips together. "You know I'm still gonna take care of you, right? I'll need you even if I'm not playing football. Or if you want to keep with a player, I'll give you a recommendation."

Nearly every professional player he knew needed some kind of assistant to keep their lives running smoothly while they concentrated on the game. Brian did everything for him, from making sure the bills were paid and the house in order, to liaising with Cam's manager and arranging for endorsements and sponsorships. He'd be nowhere without him.

Brian sighed. "I know. It's not that. I just don't like the way they were talking."

Neither did Cam. But he knew better than to react. The problem was, everywhere he went in Boston he was recognized. This was a football town, the Bobcats were the biggest celebrities around. These kind of questions were going to crop up again and again.

And if he retired, it was probably going to get worse.

"I think I might go home for a while," Cam said, his brows knitting together while he thought about it. "While I'm on a break from the team."

"To Beacon Hill?"

He shook his head. "To Hartson's Creek. Spend a bit of time with my family." He had three brothers and a sister, and all of them were there. Gray, the oldest, who'd spent years touring the world as a singer, but had since settled down with Maddie Clark and had babies. Tanner, the youngest, who'd transformed from a New York computer whizzkid to buying up half the real estate in Hartson's Creek, after he'd reconnected with his childhood best friend. They'd gone on to set up a home together.

And then there was Logan. Cam's twin brother. He'd lived in Boston for years, and though the two of them were always busy, they'd spent lots of time together. But he'd moved back home, too, and become a father to a gorgeous little boy. Cam missed him like crazy every day. Boston wasn't the same without him.

"You want me to book you a flight? How long will you be gone?"

Cam met Brian's concerned gaze. "I think I'll drive. It'll save me renting a car while I'm there."

"You're gonna drive? Won't that take you forever?"

About ten hours, if he kept to the speed limit. Maybe more if he needed to stop. But the good thing about driving was he'd be alone with his thoughts. Nobody to ask him why he wasn't playing football, no reminders of the life he could lose. Just him, some rock music, and the wide open road.

And the truth was, he needed his family. His *real* family, not the one he'd built here. Needed to remember who he was and who he used to be, before he was Cam Hartson, Star Safety.

If he was ever anybody else.

"You're gonna retire, aren't you?" Brian asked quietly. Cam glanced to the couple who'd been showing him interest. They were staring at the big screens hanging over the bar, squabbling over something and paying him no attention.

There was only one answer. It had been that way all along, he'd just been too damn stubborn to admit it. Keep playing and risk permanent injury that would change who he was, or leave the game he loved with his damn head intact.

But he still wasn't ready to accept it.

Giving Brian a tight smile, he shrugged his shoulders. "I have no idea what I'm going to do next."

CHAPTER TWO

Mia Devlin pulled her car onto the driveway and blew out a mouthful of air. Craning her head over her shoulder, she painted a fake smile on her face. "We're here," she said to the two boys sitting in the backseat. Her eldest son, Michael, had his headphones on, and was resolutely staring out of the window at the cracked pavement, as though fascinated by the brilliant pink flowers growing through the gaps.

He'd been this way since they'd left their old home in Kansas City yesterday morning. She had no idea what he was listening to – if he was listening to anything at all – but she sure got the message.

He wasn't happy about this move.

Her youngest, Josh, was asleep. At eight years old, this move to a new town was an adventure to him, like the stories he read in his bed late at night when she'd caught him under his duvet with a flashlight. For most of the journey, he'd had his face pressed against the window, his eyes wide as they traveled from built up metropolis to farm fields and small towns.

"Josh, honey," she said, reaching through the gap in the seats to gently shake his shoulder. "We're here."

"Huh?" He shook his head and opened his eyes. "Where?"

"We made it to Uncle Sam's house."

Michael let out a snort but refused to look at either of them.

"*This* is Uncle Sam's house?" Josh asked, his brows lifting. "Wow. There are a lot of trees here."

Technically, he was Mia's Great Uncle Sam. Her Grandma's big brother. Which made him Josh and Michael's Great, Great Uncle. But she wasn't going to get into technicalities now.

"It's a dump," Michael muttered. "Look at the grass."

"He's old. He can't keep the place up like he used to," Mia said, her patience at a precipice. Any minute it was going to fall off. Yes, it must be dreadful to move states at the start of ninth grade, especially when you had your heart set on going to high school with all your friends. But it wasn't a move she wanted either.

As the responsible adult, she had no choice.

Josh opened the door and jumped onto the concrete driveway. "Hey, Mom, there's a swing in the tree." He ran over to it, pushing the plank that was hanging on ropes from an old branch. "Mikey, we have our own playground. Come and look."

Another grunt, but at least Michael opened the car door and stepped out. Mia followed suit, smiling at Josh as he sat on the swing. At least one of her children was happy. Which made her fifty percent happy, too.

"Come and push me, Mikey!" Josh shouted.

"You're old enough to swing yourself," Michael muttered, running his hand through his thick hair. "Where's this uncle of ours?" he asked his mom. "Shouldn't he be here to greet us?" He lowered his voice. "Or is he as happy to have us as I am to be here?"

Josh jumped off the swing and walked over to them, patting Michael on the shoulder.

"Don't worry. We're only here for a while. Then Dad'll come back and everything will be back to normal."

"Dad's not coming back, you dimwit. He's got a girlfriend. Took all the money from the business." Michael's nostrils flared. "Left us high and fucking dry."

"Don't swear." Mia pressed her lips together. "And cool it. Josh is only trying to cheer you up."

Michael squeezed his eyes shut. "Sorry, Josh." When he opened them again, there was a flash of vulnerability shining back at her, reminding Mia of the little boy her eldest son once was. "This sucks, Mom," he said, his voice low.

"I know." She gave him a half smile. "But we have no choice."

Not when their house in Kansas City was being fore-closed on, and the business Mia and her ex used to run had been stripped bare of assets. She'd tried to find a way to keep them in their home. God knew she had. But when it came down to it, staying with Sam was their only choice.

Her cousin, Joanna, had been the one who suggested it, after Sam admitted to her he couldn't keep the house going like he used to. "He's getting old and his bones are giving out," she'd told Mia. "Thinks he's still a teenager. He should have gotten married and had kids, that way we wouldn't have to worry about him."

Then she'd looked at Mia with a speculative gaze, and rubbed her chin with her thumb, the way she always did when she came up with an idea. "You know, he has a big house. And a bar to run. He could always do with the extra help."

So here she was, standing in front of his old blue

painted Victorian house with a wraparound porch and a cupola that made Mia think of gothic novels and hauntings. She'd never visited this house before, despite it being in her family for generations. When her grandmother had married and moved to Kansas City, that branch of the family had cut ties with Virginia, apart from letters and phone calls.

And now three of them were back.

Twisting her long blonde hair into a bun, Mia opened the trailer she'd rented for the week and pulled their overnight cases out. Sam had assured her there was plenty of space for all of their things, but they'd still left a lot behind.

Michael took two of the bags from her and carried them up the stoop. She flashed him a smile, and he nodded back.

He'd get used to being here. Kids were resilient, weren't they? Even kids who were on the cusp of being men, and angry at the world.

She'd had her fair share of anger, too. In the months since Niall had left, she'd spent evenings pouring over her finances and job postings, trying not to let the boys hear her sobs as she realized there was no way to make things work.

But she'd left that all behind. This was a new place to live, a new start, and she was determined they'd find their happiness here. And if Niall ever remembered he had a family, she'd be civil to him for the boys' sake. Because they needed a father. Even one like him.

"Nobody's answering," Josh said, after rapping with the black iron door knocker five times. "Do you think he's dead?"

"No, I think he's probably at work. He runs a bar in town. Why don't we head over there and check out the town square? He said there's a diner. I'll buy you both a shake."

"I'll just put these bags back in the trailer," Michael said with a sigh.

Her eyes softened, because he was a good kid when he wanted to be. "Okay, then, let's go."

———

"Whoa, this place looks like it should be in a movie," Josh said, as they walked from Sam's house to the town square. All the buildings surrounding the lush green center were old, probably from the same era as Sam's house. Mia looked around at the shop signs. Murphy's Diner, Fairfax Realty, Laura's Dress shop, and a bright pink sign advertising the I Can Make You Beautiful salon. Across the street was a church with a tall spire – The First Baptist Church where her grandmother had gotten married before moving to Kansas City. From the way the steps shone in the September sun, it was well attended and taken care of.

"It looks dead," Michael said. "Where are all the cars?"

"It's a small town. A lot of the residents around here can walk to the shops," Mia told him. Then she pointed at a building in the corner. "Look, that must be Sam's bar. Why don't I head over there while you two grab a table in the diner? I'll get the keys to the house and join you."

"Sounds good." Josh grinned. "I'm gonna have a chocolate shake. Do you think they have whipped cream here?"

"Of course they have whipped cream." Michael ruffled his hair. "Come on, I'll race you there."

She watched as Josh took off first, closely persued by her eldest son, though she could tell by the way he was running that Michael was going to let his brother win. Josh reached the door and threw up his hands in victory, and Michael ruffled his hair again.

It was enough to make her heart melt. At least they had each other. That was one thing she'd always wanted growing up – a sibling. Joanna was the closest she'd had.

And she'd been determined that Michael wouldn't be an only child, even though Niall took some persuading. She'd been a college student when she'd gotten pregnant the first time. It hadn't been planned at all. By the time they had Josh, six years later, their business was thriving and life was good.

And then it had ended with a divorce petition that was still going through the courts.

Pushing the thought out of her head, she walked over to the Moonlight Bar and opened the door, her fingers catching on the flier affixed to the black wood, advertising Karaoke Night every Tuesday.

Inside, the bar was half empty. A scattering of people were at tables, and two workmen were standing at the bar. Every single one of them turned around to look at Mia, who strode up to the counter and smiled at the grizzled man on the other side.

"What can I get you?" he asked, showing no sign of recognition.

Mia brushed a lock of blonde hair behind her ear. "I'm looking for Sam Soper."

One of the workmen whistled. "You got yourself a younger woman, Sam?"

"She's too hot for him," the other man said. "Can't be older than twenty-five."

"Maybe still waters run deep."

"Shut up," Sam told them, then turned back to Mia. "I'm Sam."

She kept the smile fixed to her lips. "I'm Mia Devlin. Your niece. We've just arrived in town."

He gave her a nod. "You'll be wanting the keys then."

"If that's okay. We've got a lot to unload and want to do it before dark."

"I thought you were bringing your kids." Sam frowned.

"They're in the diner." She inclined her head at the door. "I didn't think you'd want kids in here."

He shrugged. "They're family. That's allowed."

"What did you say your name was again, sweetheart," the man closest to her asked.

"Leave her alone, Mack. She's too pretty for you," Sam snapped at him. Then he turned back to Mia and slid the keys over to her. "My bedroom's on the first floor. Your rooms are on the second and third. We share the kitchen and living space, but I'll avoid them first thing. I'm here most of the time anyway."

She curled her fingers around the keys. "We're very grateful that we can stay. And we're here to help, not to annoy you. I'm happy to cook for you, and Michael's fourteen and strong. He can do work around the house and in the yard."

"You said you're looking for a job?"

Mia nodded. "I've sent some resumes out." Not that many people around here were recruiting for a marketing executive. But right now, she'd take anything.

"I can probably give you a few shifts here while you're looking." Sam shrugged. "If you want them."

"That would be great." Her smile was genuine this time. Any money was welcome right now. She'd already had to put the trailer, the gas for moving, and all the new things the boys needed for school on her one remaining credit card. She didn't want to max it out.

"Okay, then. You get on back home and start your unloading. My evening workers arrive at six. I'll be there after that."

"Thank you, Uncle Sam."

"Sam will do. The uncle makes me feel old."

"You are old," Mack said, shaking his head.

Mia bit down a laugh, and waved goodbye, heading back

toward the door and out into the town square. Sam was gruff, but he was kind. She could tell that much from their encounter. She also had a feeling he wouldn't put up with any messing around. Especially from teenagers who thought they knew better than everyone else.

She'd save that worry for another day. Because right now, the sun was shining, she and the boys had somewhere to live, and she was about to buy the biggest strawberry milkshake they had. With extra sprinkles.

If the last few months had taught her anything, it was to enjoy the small things. And that's exactly what she intended to do.

CHAPTER THREE

"I have an interview," Mia called out, waving a white envelope at Michael and Josh who were sitting at the kitchen table, scooping cereal into their mouths. Sam wasn't up yet. After a few days of living here, she still wasn't sure if he always woke late, or if he was avoiding the morning craziness that her two boys brought with them.

"You do? Where?" Josh brightened up. "Is it in Kansas City?"

"No, dumbhead, it's here." Michael shook his head. "We're not going back to our old house, remember?"

Mia shot Michael a look and he had the good grace to apologize. She knew he was anxious. Today was his first day at school. High school, to be more specific. And she knew there was only one thing worse than starting high school, and that was starting it late. When all the other students had already made friends and settled in.

"It's at a whiskey distillery right out of town. There isn't much information, but it's a marketing job." Social Media and Marketing, to be exact. "The interview's on Friday." It gave her a few days to get ready. She'd have to study the whiskey industry while the boys were at school. She placed the envelope on the mantelpiece over the old kitchen fireplace and checked her watch. "Right, we should go. You don't want to be late for your first day."

"Don't we?" Michael asked.

"No, you don't. And remember you have football tryouts later."

"For the freshman team. I would have made junior varsity in Kansas City," he grumbled.

"You *might* have. There was no guarantee. And not many freshmen make junior varsity," Mia pointed out. Though she knew he probably would have. He was good. Had been since Niall first enrolled him in pee wee football. And she hated that this had been spoiled for him, too. "If you work hard, maybe they'll move you up."

"Yeah, maybe." Michael picked up his bowl and walked over to the dishwasher, placing his dish inside. "I'll see you later," he said, kissing Mia on the cheek.

"Don't you want a ride?" she asked him. "Your school's close to Josh's."

"I'll take the bus." Michael shrugged. "I don't want all the guys ogling you like they did when we enrolled. It's embarrassing."

"They didn't ogle me," Mia protested.

"Yeah, they did. One of them asked if you were our sister," Josh said, grinning. "And one of the football players asked Michael for your number."

Her face flushed. How embarrassing. She'd taken particular care to dress conservatively. Since Michael was born, she'd found it difficult for people to take her seriously as a young mom. She'd thought by now that would have gotten better.

But apparently not at Columbus High.

"Can you pick Josh up from after school club for me?" she asked him. "Sam's asked me to work in the bar for him this afternoon."

"Yeah, sure." Michael grabbed his backpack and slung it over his shoulder. "I'll see you later."

"Good luck. Not that you'll need it." She gave him a wave as he walked through the front door.

"Thanks." He swallowed and she saw that flash of vulnerability again. She knew he'd try to hide it at school, but it was there.

"Love you," she told him, her heart full and aching.

"Love you, too." And with that, he was gone.

———

CAM PULLED his car up outside the house and stared at it through the windshield. It had to be the right one. It looked exactly like the listing Brian had sent him, telling him he'd rented it for the next two months.

Thank god for his assistant. It was a shame Brian wouldn't be staying with him in Hartson's Creek, but there really wasn't much for him to do here. Instead, he'd be working on a few things for Cam at his house in Boston, and he'd also be helping one of Cam's teammates, whose own assistant had broken their wrist.

Climbing out of the car, Cam was pleasantly surprised by the warmth in the air. It was harvest time in Hartson's Creek. As a kid, he'd loved the way the smell of corn wafted through the air. Loved going back to school and the football season starting. He'd forgotten that feeling, having had lived in the city for so long. Things like crops and farms and high school seemed like another life.

His brother's life.

"Hey, you made it." The smiling face of Cam's brother,

Tanner appeared at the front door. He walked down the steps and gave Cam's car an admiring glance. "Damn, this is a beauty. Was your drive okay?"

Cam blinked, because he hadn't expected to see his younger brother here. But then realization passed over him. Tanner owned a lot of property in Hartson's Creek – no doubt this house was one of his.

"Why didn't Brian tell me this was your place?" Cam asked, more to himself than his brother.

"No idea." Tanner shrugged. "Maybe he thought you'd try to haggle me out of money. Come inside, let me show you around."

The inside of the house was just as beautiful and sleek as the outside. "This place was only built a year ago," Tanner told him, as he took him into the kitchen. "You see that view?" he asked, pointing out of the window at the creek. The water glistened in the sun as it bubbled and flowed toward the river. On the other side was a copse of mature trees, their leaves green now, but no doubt they would turn gold and red in a few weeks. "Isn't it something?"

"Yeah," Cam agreed. "It's something.

Cam stared out of the window for a moment, letting the peace soak into his skin. This was what he'd come home for, after all. A chance to relax, to think. To work out what the hell he was going to do with his life. Yet the creek was giving him no answers at all.

"You okay?" Tanner asked him. "All this stuff happening. It must have hit you hard. I know when I moved back here, after selling my business in New York, it took some getting used to."

"I'd forgotten how quiet it is here."

"You've visited enough. You must remember."

Cam winced at the mention of his memory. He worried that it was permanently affected. "Yeah, but I'm always surrounded by you guys. And in Boston I'm always at work, with the rest of the team, or watching plays. There's not a lot of time for silence."

"If you stay here for a while, you'll have more than enough of it." Tanner opened a cupboard door, showing him the inside. "Brian sent all your kitchen equipment down. Well actually, he sent everything he couldn't rent for you down. It's all been unpacked by the movers. So you can settle in and relax. And you know where I am if anything goes wrong."

"Do you give this treatment to all your renters?" Cam asked him, grinning.

"Nope. Just family." Tanner hit him on the shoulder and winced at the hardness of his muscles. "It's good to have you home, man."

"Just for a while," Cam reminded him.

"Yeah," Tanner agreed. "Just for a while."

———

HE WAS lucky to have such a nice place to stay while he thought about his next move. And it was good to see his youngest brother, too.

But now Tanner was back at work – as were all of Cam's brothers – and he was bouncing off the walls like a damn pinball. This thinking game was making him crazy.

Grabbing his keys, Cam walked out of the house and looked at his car parked in the driveway.

Of all the things he owned, the Audi coupe was the one thing that made him happy. Like most of his teammates, he'd always been a motorhead. Their cars were the one things they had control over. Their little oasis of calm in the craziness of NFL life. It was where they'd sit and think about plays they should have made, arguments they'd had with girlfriends or wives, or where they'd switch on their top-of-the range stereos and blast out their music to chase the thoughts from their minds.

Cam had bought this car as a gift to himself when he'd signed his latest contract. Sure, he'd been offered a discount, but it had still cost him more than he'd ever spent on a car before. But damn, he loved it.

Running his hands over the metallic blue exterior, Cam opened the driver's door and climbed in. He'd never get tired of the cream leather upholstery and blue detailing that matched the paint. If you asked, he could tell you that it went from zero to sixty in three point eight seconds, and on a private open road, it could hit speeds of two hundred miles per hour.

And yeah, he'd tested *that* out.

Placing the Audi into comfort mode, Cam pulled out of his driveway and took a left, heading toward the main road through town. It was four in the evening, and though the sun was moving lower in the sky, a hint of summer still clung in the warmth of the air. Rather than put the air on, he opened the windows, smiling as that old familiar smell of harvests and corn filled his senses.

He hadn't even made it to the town square when he'd spotted some kids playing in the street, but hadn't really thought about it. His radio was on, tuned to a local country station, and everything felt right with the world.

Until something came crashing against the side of his car.

His first instinct was to hit the brakes hard. The Audi came to a jolting stop, forcing his head forward and down until his brow almost grazed the wheel. His heart started to thud against his chest as he lifted his gaze and tried to work out what the hell he'd just hit.

"Shit! Let's get out of here," a low voice shouted.

"Mikey, wait up. I can't run that fast."

The two kids he'd spotted were like a blur as they ran up the road. Cam climbed out of his car and saw exactly what had hit the side of his car. A damn football, of all things.

"Hey, you two!" he shouted at the running kids. "Come here!"

But they kept running. Cam felt a flash of anger rush through him, because he'd been brought up better than to cause damage and run away. Scooping up the ball in his right hand, he took off after the two boys, one almost grown, the other coming up to his chest if he was lucky.

It was the first time he'd run flat out in two weeks, and his lungs were shockingly unprepared. His breath came in short pants as he rounded the corner and saw the two boys running up some steps. The eldest made the mistake of turning, his eyes widening as he spotted Cam barreling toward them.

"Wait up, you little shits!" A fresh rush of fury washed through Cam. Not just because of the car, though that was more than enough. It was about his damn injury. His career. The whole reason he'd driven down to Hartson's Creek. It made him see mists of red when he should have kept calm.

"Get over here," he shouted from the lawn of a blue-painted house. "Did you see what you've done?"

The eldest boy put his hands up. "I'm sorry. We were playing. I didn't mean to hit your car."

The younger boy looked petrified. "Mikey, I'm the one who hit the car."

"Shut up," the older one – Mikey – hissed. "Go inside. And don't tell Mom."

Before the little kid could do as he was told, the front door opened and a woman walked out, her pretty face pulled into a frown as she took in the situation in the front yard.

"Michael?" she said, looking from the boys to Cam. "What's going on?"

"I can handle this, Mom. Take Josh inside."

Cam blinked, because she didn't look like a mom. Not the kind of moms he'd grown up with, anyway. The kid had to be at least fifteen, and she didn't look much older than twenty-five. His brain might have been addled, but even he knew the math didn't work.

"Your kids threw a ball against my car. It's left a dent," Cam called out to her.

The pretty mom winced and shook her head.

"*You* go inside," she said to Mikey. Her eyes were dark. "Take Josh with you. *I'll* deal with this."

"But, Mom—"

She lifted her hand. "Don't sass me, Michael. Go in *right now.*"

So she didn't look like a mom, but she sure sounded like one.

Michael glanced at Cam, his eyes wide. "Mom, that's…" he started, pointing at Cam.

"*Go inside!*"

The kid recoiled and huffed, then pulled his younger brother through the door with him, slamming it hard enough for the frame to shake. Cam watched as the woman pursed her lips and blew out a mouthful of air, then slowly walked down the steps to come face to face with him.

Close up, he could see how she could be the mom of a teenage boy, though she'd still have had to have been young when she had him. Her skin was smooth, but there were a few worry lines beginning to form on her brow. And though she was slim, there was an enticing curve to her hips that he was trying really hard not to look at.

"Sir," she started, and he immediately interrupted her.

"It's Cam."

She blinked, but showed no sign of recognition. He assumed she wasn't a football fan. "Cam, I apologize for my son's behavior. And of course I'll pay for the damage. Please let me know how much you need once you take it in for repair."

"It's an Audi R8 Coupe. It's gonna cost at least ten grand to get the dent out and resprayed."

She lifted her head up, her expression unreadable. "Send me a quote and I'll write you a check."

He glanced at her clothes. Tight jeans and a flowy white blouse tucked into her waistband, highlighting the svelteness of her body. Her long blonde hair fell over her shoulders in waves.

"You should teach your kids not to run off when they get into trouble," he told her. "I nearly had a heart attack chasing them."

"Do you have children, Cam?" she asked. Her voice sounded strange. As though she didn't come from around here.

"No, Ma'am."

"Then maybe you shouldn't comment on other peoples' parenting. My children know to come home if there are any problems. They did exactly the right thing. They would have come to see you once they told me what happened." She hadn't smiled at him once. For some reason, that annoyed him. He was used to women laughing and fawning, not staring at him as though he was some kind of child chaser.

"I apologize," he said, giving her a slow, easy smile to see if it would melt her icy exterior. But it did nothing.

"Accepted." Her face was still impassive. "Is your car okay to drive?"

"Yeah. Just a dent in the door."

She nodded. "Okay then. Well, I should go in. There are two young men I need to speak to."

He bit down a smile this time, because he wouldn't want to be in her kids' places for all the money in the world. If she was this short with him, god only knew how scary she must be to her kids.

"Can I have your number?" he asked her.

"No." She frowned. "That's completely inappropriate."

He couldn't help but laugh. "I need to send you the invoice. I wasn't asking for a date." Though he wouldn't say no to that. It was crazy how much he wanted to see her smile. She was pretty enough when she was frowning, he'd bet good money she was glorious when she grinned.

A blush stole up her face. "Oh god, I'm sorry. Yes, of course. Do you want me to write it down?"

He pulled his phone out of his pocket. "I'll punch it straight in." He listened as she called out the numbers, then pressed the person icon. "Do you have a name?" he asked.

"Mia."

"Mia?" he repeated, waiting for her surname.

"Mia," she said again.

"Right. So your name's Mia Mia. What are the odds on that?" he said, amused. "I guess your parents really loved the name, right?"

A ghost of a smile passed her lips and damn if that didn't make him want to touch them. "It's Mia Devlin."

He gave her a full blown grin. "Okay, Mia Devlin. I guess I'll get out of here and go back to my car. You'll be hearing from me soon."

"I guess I will." She nodded. "And what's your surname? Just so I know I'm paying the right ten thousand dollar invoice."

"Hartson."

Still no flash of recognition in her eyes. It was weird how he liked that she had no idea who he was. "Okay, Cam Hartson. I'll be going in." She turned on her heel and started to walk back up the path.

"Mia?" he called out, mostly to see what she'd do.

"Yeah?" She whipped her head around to look at him.

"Sorry I criticized your parenting. It was an asshole thing to do."

When her smile came, it felt like the air had gotten ten degrees hotter. It filled her face, making her look younger, softer.

A hundred questions rushed into his mind. Was she married? How old was she? Did she really live in this huge old house? And did she find him as sexy as he found her?

Without thinking, he glanced at her left hand. There was no ring there. Interesting.

"Goodbye, Cam," she said, walking back up the steps to her house, her hips swinging in a distracting way.

"Goodbye, Mia." He grinned to himself and turned away.

CHAPTER FOUR

$\mathcal{M}$ia slammed the front door behind her – a necessary gesture even when she was in a good mood, thanks to the way the wood always got stuck on the frame.

Had Mr. Gorgeous with the designer jeans and cocky smile really just told her it would cost ten thousand dollars to repair his car? She closed her eyes and swallowed down a scream, but instead of blackness she could see him there.

Tall, muscled body. Cropped dark hair. A half grin that made her insides turn into stupid, messy goo. She turned and pressed her eye to the peephole and saw him walking down the path and turn onto the sidewalk. Damn, even from the back he was impressive. Through the black fabric of his t-shirt, his muscles had been obvious. He must work out all the time.

But it had been his eyes that had made her look twice. Hazel with little flecks of green. He'd looked at her like he was trying to work her out, and failing.

Damn if she hadn't liked it.

Just a bit.

Pressing her lips together, she stomped toward the kitchen, clearing her throat as she walked through the door.

Michael was standing at the window, his hand on Josh's shoulder as they both turned to look at her.

"Mom!" Josh said excitedly. "Do you know who that was?"

"His name's Cam Hartson."

Josh's eyes widened and he looked up at Mikey. "She does know," he said, his voice almost reverent.

"I know because he told me," she said, her voice clipped. "But that doesn't matter, because right now I need you to sit down at the table and tell me exactly what happened and why I'm about to get a repair bill for ten thousand dollars."

Ten thousand dollars she didn't have. She rubbed her palms against her eyes and sighed.

"We were playing ball. Mikey got into the freshman team and wanted to practice," Josh said, his voice small. "So I was throwing and he was catching. And I kind of threw it wonky."

"It wasn't his fault. It was mine." Michael pulled out a chair and pointed at it, directing Josh to sit, then he'd sat down in the one next to it. "I was the one that suggested we play in the road."

"You were playing in the road?" Mia's voice rose up an octave. "Why the hell would you do that? You could've gotten hurt. That car could have run you over."

"It was the first car we saw in an hour. There aren't any cars around here, Mom. There aren't many people either." Michael shook his head. "I'm sorry. We should have gone to the park or something."

Mia slumped down in one of the plastic chairs and leaned her forehead on her hands. "You got on the team?" she asked. She'd just come home from a shift at the Moonlight Bar when she'd heard the shouting from the front of the house.

Michael had left her a note telling her that he and Josh were fine and had gone out to practice.

"Yeah." Michael nodded. "They want me to play for the freshman team for a month, but if I'm good enough I might make JV." His voice lifted with excitement.

A tumult of emotions rushed through her. Happiness that something had actually gone right for her son. Sadness that it had been marred by this damn stupid incident. And complete panic at how she was going to find ten thousand dollars.

She looked up at them. Michael and Josh were staring at her, their eyes wide. "We didn't mean for it to happen," Josh said, his lip trembling. "That man was so angry."

"He's an NFL player," Michael added. "Cam Hartson. Safety for the Boston Bobcats."

Mia looked up sharply. "He is? I guess that explains the expensive car." He could probably pay for the repairs himself without blinking. But that's not how she did things. She'd find a way to pay for them, even if it killed her.

It was a matter of pride. And right now that's all she had left.

"Did you have a good day at school?" she asked them softly. Michael shrugged and Josh nodded.

"We had hamburgers for lunch," Josh told her. "They were even better than in Kansas City."

Mia smiled, despite herself. Leaning across the table, she ruffled his hair. "I'm glad it went okay. How about you go and wash up. I think I can see a bit of hamburger still on your lips."

Josh smiled and wiped his mouth with the back of his hand. "Sure. Can I watch some TV?"

Mia nodded, her heart soft as she watched her youngest leave the kitchen.

If only Michael was as easy to keep happy.

"So school was okay?" she asked her eldest.

"Yeah." Michael ran his finger along his bottom lip. "Mom, how are we going to pay for the repairs?"

"I'll find the money. And you can repay me by helping Sam out around the house."

"You don't have the money. I'm not stupid. I know that Dad didn't leave anything. We wouldn't be here if we had any cash." He looked down at the table, shaking his head. "I'm sorry I messed up. This is my fault."

She reached across the table and squeezed his hand. "Sweetheart, you're still a kid. I know you like to think you're an adult, but you aren't. You don't have to worry about how I keep a roof over our head or find money for repairs. That's my job, not yours."

Michael swallowed, but said nothing.

"Okay?" she prompted.

"Okay. But I'm gonna get a job. Help you out around here. You're not alone, Mom."

"The best you can do to help me out is to work hard at school and help out with Josh. Speaking of which, can you go and check he's actually washed his face?"

"Yeah, sure." Michael stood and smiled at her. His teenage mood swings would be the death of her. "Can you believe Cam Hartson was driving through this tiny town? I wonder where he's going. He's miles away from Boston. Though he got injured a couple of weeks ago. Maybe that has something to do with it." His eyes lit up. "Hey, do you think he's getting treatment around here? Is there a big hospital nearby?"

"I've no idea." Mia walked over to the refrigerator to pull out some food. She liked to feed the boys early. That way they had plenty of time to burn off the energy before bedtime. "Hopefully he was driving through and we won't see him again."

Yeah. And she'd keep telling herself that. Because she

didn't have the time to think about sexy NFL players who had a swagger that made her legs feel weak.

————

"CAM HARTSON. YEAH, I KNOW HIM," Sam said later that evening, when Michael asked him about the football player. "His family comes from around here. His dad lives just up the road. And you'll have heard of his brother, Gray."

"His brother's Gray Hartson, the singer?" Mia asked.

"Yeah." Sam nodded. "There are four boys and a girl. All of them live around here."

Five kids? Damn, two were enough to deal with.

"But Cam lives in Boston, so he must be visiting," Michael mused. "I wonder if he's staying with his dad."

"Michael, don't start stalking football players. You have too much school work for that." Mia shot him a look and Michael groaned.

"I wasn't planning on stalking anybody. It's just interesting, that's all. I thought this place would be boring, but it isn't."

"I like boring. Boring is good," Mia said, shaking her head.

Sam chuckled. "Not when you're fourteen it's not. Am I right, Mikey?"

He held up a hand and Michael high-fived him, grinning. "Hell, yeah, you're right."

"Language," Mia reminded him.

"I can't say hell? Seriously?"

"Not in front of me, and definitely not in front of Josh." Mia lifted an eyebrow.

"It's okay. He swears all the time when it's just the two of us," Josh piped up from where he was playing with LEGOs on the floor.

"Tattletale," Michael muttered.

"I am not." Josh folded his arms across his chest.

"It's bedtime," Mia told them. A chorus of groans greeted her suggestion.

"I'm not tired," Josh told her.

Michael crossed his arms. "I'm older than Josh. I should get to stay up later."

"You can go and read to Josh," Mia told her eldest son. "And then maybe read something yourself. Give us all some peace."

And maybe then she'd have some time to think about the ten thousand dollar problem who happened to have eyes that made her breath catch in her throat.

CHAPTER FIVE

$\mathcal{M}$ia waved at Josh as he walked into the school yard, then put her Honda Civic in drive and pulled out of the kiss and ride line. School drop offs were so much more civilized here than they ever had been in Kansas City. Half of the kids here walked to school, and a lot of the moms parked in the parking lot and walked their children into the yard, rather than joining the drop off line. Which meant this morning's drop off had been smooth and fast.

Thank goodness. Because she had just over an hour until her interview at The G. Scott Carter whiskey distillery. She'd spent most of the past two days researching the company and the industry, as well as looking at different marketing campaigns their competitors were using, and making notes on ways they could utilise successes from other industries.

She'd created a presentation to take them through, even though they hadn't expressly asked for one. But she needed this job. There was nothing else that suited her skills so perfectly, or that paid the kind of money she was going to need to get her and the boys back on their feet. If she got this job, she could actually start paying rent to Sam.

Hell, she could even look at getting their own place eventually.

The thought of a little house of her own made her heart clench.

The distillery was on the east side of town, an easy drive through deserted roads lined with farmers' fields and tall trees. She put her foot down on the gas, figuring she could arrive a little early and re-read the notes she'd written down before going in for her interview, but then a loud bang echoed through the interior, and the car lurched to the right, the steering wheel spinning through her grasp.

Adrenaline rushed through her as she realized it was a blow out. For a second, she thought about hitting the brakes, but knew that would only send the car into a skid. Instead, she fought with the steering wheel, trying to keep it as straight as possible as she lifted her foot from the gas pedal, her breath coming fast as the engine creaked loudly and the car slowed down.

By the time she'd came to a stop, the car was off the road and on the soft shoulder, the fender facing a line of trees. With her heart still pounding, Mia climbed out and looked at the front right tire. The black rubber was torn at the seam, gaping away from the metal hubcap. It was completely flat. She stared at it for a moment, her throat dry and scratchy.

She was going to miss her interview. *Dammit!*

Inhaling raggedly, she started to give herself a pep talk. She could deal with this. She'd dealt with worse, after all. She could try to change the tire – she knew for a fact there was a spare in the trunk – and if that didn't work, she'd call the distillery and throw herself at their mercy.

Beg, if she had to.

The spare was heavier than she'd expected, but somehow she'd managed to lift it out and roll it along the ground. It would have been a lot easier if she wasn't wearing a black blouse and tight grey skirt. And these damn heels were a liability.

Kicking them off, she grabbed her phone to bring up a YouTube video on how to change your tire. Her hand shook, causing her to drop her phone. As luck would have it, the device slid beneath the car. It felt like the final straw.

"Why?" she shouted at it. "Why today? Why me?" Why the hell was it that when one thing went wrong, others followed like dominos, until your life was torn to ruins around you?

With a grunt of frustration, she dropped to her knees and started to fish around under the vehicle, but her cell was too far away. She dropped her body flat on the grass and shuffled as close to the underside as she could.

The low rumble of an engine cut through the silence, but she didn't dare look up. Not when she almost had her phone. Just as it was getting louder, she finally curled her fingers around it, letting out a shout of victory as she pulled it toward her.

"You okay, Ma'am?"

With her phone clutched in her hand, she slowly turned her head, all too aware that her skirt was ruched up to her hips, exposing her panty hose, or what was left of them after they'd done battle with the ground.

That's when she saw him. Thick, jean clad thighs. Black t-shirt that clung to his chest, and left her in no doubt that an eight pack was superior to a six pack. And then that face. Handsome, square jawed face, staring down at her splayed out on the ground, shoes kicked off, legs splayed out.

When they'd met a few days ago, at least she'd felt like his equal. For a start, she hadn't known who Cam Hartson was then.

But now, she was at an extreme disadvantage. Not just physically, though that was bad enough. But situationally, too. She had an old, run down car with a blown out tire, and he was either going to find it funny as hell, or he was going to feel sorry for her.

Kneeling, she brushed the dust off her blouse, trying desperately to regain some poise. Her eyes slid to his, and sure enough there was amusement there. But something else, too.

Concern?

Damn he had such pretty eyes. They were way too distracting.

"Mia? You okay?" he asked, sounding genuinely concerned.

She got to her feet, and yeah, there were snags and runs all down her pantyhose. "I'm fine," she told him. "Just a small snafu."

"Did you fall out of the car?" His brows pulled together. "How come you were under it?" He walked around to the front of the Honda and dropped to his haunches, inspecting the tire. "Damn, that's a bad one."

"I dropped my phone," she admitted. "I was trying to find a video on YouTube."

His lips twitched, but to his credit, he didn't laugh. "A video?"

"One that shows how to change a tire. I wanted to do it correctly." She looked at the spare on the ground next to her. "I haven't done it before."

Cam nodded. "You got tools?"

"Um. Probably." There was a bag of them in the car, but she had no idea what was in there. "What will I need?"

"I'll do it."

"Oh no. I couldn't let you do that." She gave him a tight smile. "I'll do it and get on my way."

He eyed her carefully. "You'll need a jack and a lug wrench."

Walking around to the trunk, she pulled the big bag of

tools toward her, and looked inside. Finding the jack was easy. It was the biggest thing in there, bright orange with four castors fixed to it.

The lug wrench wasn't so obvious. There were about ten wrenches in there, all old and rusty. She pulled a couple out, turning them in her hand. They looked like the kind of wrenches you'd use for plumbing.

Cam's body slid against hers as he leaned into the trunk and pulled out a long stick, that looked like something a band major might twirl.

"This one," he said softly, as he stood back up, his arm brushing against hers again. She swallowed hard at the contact.

Even harder when she realized she could smell his cologne. Damn, he smelled good. Like a forest on a rainy day.

It took a lot of effort for her to stand up and turn to face him. "I should have known that's the lug wrench. I don't know why I didn't."

She pulled her bottom lip between her teeth, and his gaze dipped down, his eyes hooded.

"You wouldn't need to know unless you were changing a tire."

Feeling the heat of his gaze on her face, Mia tried to stop her cheeks from flaming. There was something about this man. Not just his confidence, that was too obvious. He had the kind of swagger you only got from being a big deal, multi million dollar sportsman. Not brash or smug, just a pure, masculine assurance that made her throat tighten when she looked at him.

She took a ragged breath and stepped back. Unless she got the spare tire on her car soon, she'd have no interview, and definitely no job. "I should get this changed," she muttered, walking around to the flat tire.

"Loosen the nuts first. If you try to do it when it's jacked up, the wheel will just turn."

She scooted down and slid the wrench onto the nuts, gripping it tight as she attempted to turn it. Her teeth grinded, determined to do this by herself. It wasn't that she wanted to prove anything to Cam Hartson. It was her own fragile confidence that needed the reassurance.

And when the first nut finally came loose, it felt like a huge victory.

"Yes!" She wanted to pump a fist. Behind her, Cam chuckled.

"Those can be tough. You're doing good."

"Thank you." This time her cheeks really did blush.

It took another ten minutes to change the tire. He helped, but she did most of the work. She appreciated the way he let her take the lead, murmuring suggestions and encouragement when her patience got the better of her.

"Don't drive too fast on that spare," he told her, as he lifted the blown tire easily. "Are you headed home?"

She shook her head. "I have an interview." Her body felt like it was in a heady rush. "I need to head straight there."

"Whereabouts? I can follow you, just to make sure there are no problems."

"It's fine, I can—"

"Mia," he said, his voice low. She looked up at him, and his gaze was locked on her face. "I want to make sure you're okay, that's all. For my own peace of mind. So I'm going to follow you. Not because I'm a creeper or a scary guy, but because I'm a man who was brought up to care for women and make sure they are safe. Once you're parked up, I'll turn around and go on my way."

There was something in his voice – a catch – that made her chest tighten. "Okay," she said softly. "Thank you. My interview's at the G. Scott Carter Distillery. Only a couple of miles from here. Do you know it?"

"Yeah, I know it." There was something in his eyes that she couldn't quite make out. But she didn't have time to decipher what the heck it was. So she let him carry the blown tire to his car, and using the Honda to shield her from the road, she quickly shimmied out of her pantyhose and slipped her feet back into her heels.

It wasn't perfect, but when she got to the distillery she'd do what she could to look presentable. Maybe even make a joke about it at the interview. Tell them that she was good in a crisis.

God knew, she'd had enough of those this year to last a lifetime.

"Cam," she called out, as he closed his trunk.

He looked up at her, his head cocked to the side. "Yeah?"

"I'm sorry that you've been inconvenienced again."

He pressed his lips together, and nodded. "It's okay. I've got nothing better to do."

———

As soon as she'd parked outside the distillery, Cam turned his car around and headed back up the road toward the highway. He was late for dropping his car off at the dealership, but he figured they'd forgive him. Brian had booked the car in for him, no doubt dropping his name like a pro. And the delay was worth it, anyway.

His lips curled up as he remembered how much she'd protested against his help. Mia Devlin had fire inside her, and he liked it.

It hadn't taken him long to find out who she was yesterday. One phone call to Maddie, his brother Gray's wife, and he knew that Mia was Sam Soper's great-niece, newly arrived in town with her two boys, but no husband.

And yeah, he liked the no husband bit a lot.

She'd gritted her teeth as she yanked at the lug wrench, muttering to herself until the nut came loose. And all he'd been able to do was stare at her. Take in the soft curve of her slender neck, covered with a dusting of golden hair, swept up into a low bun. Her blouse was slightly transparent in the morning sunlight, revealing the warmth of her skin. And that skirt. Grey and tight and emphasizing the enticing curve of her hip. He'd fisted his hands to stop himself from reaching out to trace the curve of her spine as it disappeared below the waistline.

What had he told her? *I'm not a creeper.* Yeah, right. That's why he couldn't stop staring as she'd pulled her ripped pantyhose down and slid her bare feet into those gorgeous heels, and the blood rushed to a part of him that had no business being part of this.

He sighed and tightened his grip on the wheel. It was pure sexual frustration, that was all. Could have happened at any time. He knitted his brows together, trying to remember the last time he'd had a date, let alone had sex, and he couldn't even remember.

He'd been too busy. With football. With his headaches. With appointments at the hospital. But more than anything, he hadn't even had the inclination. Sure, when he was younger he'd loved being the center of female attention. He'd revelled in the adulation and easy sex. But he was older now. More mature, and if he was brutally honest, easy sex was never as good as his teenage self had thought it would be.

All the best things in life were hard won. That's why he loved playing football.

The sound of his phone ringing echoed through his top-of-the range speakers. He glanced at the dash, raising an eyebrow when he saw his agent's name appear on the screen.

"Accept call," he instructed, and the ringing stopped. "Derek?" he said, eyeing the name on his dashboard.

"You answered. I was beginning to think you were ignoring me."

Cam bit down a smile, because he'd been doing exactly that. "I've been busy."

"So Brian told me. You made it to your hometown, then. Thanks for letting me know."

"I sent an email." Cam merged onto the highway. According to the GPS, the dealership was two exits ahead. "Didn't you get it?"

"A round robin email. I saw your housekeeper was on the list, too. I can't do my job if you don't talk to me. I'm hanging on a limb here." Derek huffed. As long as Cam had known him, he'd been dramatic. And demanding. But he was one of the best agents in the business. If you had Derek representing you, you tried not to piss him off.

"I'm here now," Cam said lightly. "What's up?"

"I want to know what your plans are. I asked Brian how long your lease is, but he said it's a family deal. Your brother? I need to know how long you're gonna be hiding away."

"I'm not hiding." Cam inhaled sharply. "I'm thinking."

"Okayyyy..." Derek huffed again. "How long is the thinking gonna take? Because I've got the Bobcats breathing down my neck wanting to know what's going on. You can't just leave town and not expect a backlash."

"Marty told me to take a break."

"He told you to think. Then you either need to get back on the field or tell them you're retiring. The sooner you do it, the easier my life will be."

Cam almost wanted to laugh. "I can't make a quick decision just to make your life easier."

"Yeah, well while you're staying in your nice house over-looking the creek, I'm being hounded by Marty asking me whether he needs to buy a new safety or not."

Cam licked his lips, his gut clenching at the mention of the Bobcats' owner. Marty Landsman had always been good to him. He treated everybody working at Freedom Field like family. He owed it to him to be honest.

"I'll make a decision soon," he promised.

"Could you not think in Boston? Come and watch some games, show some team spirit? They want you there, you know that."

The memory of that bar in Boston flitted into his brain, and Cam swallowed hard. Watching his teammates on the field while he was on the sidelines physically hurt. He couldn't even be around Boston, let alone sit at Freedom Field while they were playing.

"I have things to do here."

"What things?" Derek was puffing. Probably walking on his treadmill. At almost seventy, he was a fitness freak. "You helping your aunt bake her cakes? Or maybe you're writing a few new songs for your brother. Dammit, Cam, what on earth do you have to do in Nowheresville that you can't do here?"

Sometimes it felt like Derek knew more about Cam's life than Cam did. But that was his job. He'd been Cam's agent for years, and was good at what he did, even if it felt like he was paying twenty percent of his income to a Rottweiler at times.

Cam frowned. "Why can't I just be taking a break?"

"Because breaks are for pussies. I can't tell Marty you're in Virginia because you need the fresh air. Let's see, maybe you can be there because somebody needs you. Any problems with your family?"

"I'm not using my family as an excuse for being here,

Derek." Cam shook his head. Sometimes his agent was an ass. A clever, money-making ass, but an ass nonetheless.

"How about business? No wait... I got it." Derek snapped his fingers, the sound echoing through the car speakers. "Charity. You're doing charity work. Giving back while you recover from your injury. That sounds good. We could even get a Sunday supplement article written. Photos of you surrounded by good deeds. Keep up your profile." Derek sounded almost smug.

"Charity work?" Cam echoed. "What kind of charity work?"

"I dunno. Is there a food bank there?"

"I don't think so." The exit ramp was ahead. Cam merged into the right lane, and followed it, turning into the feeder lane for the dealership. "There's not a lot of homeless here. There's a church that helps out people in need."

"Maybe we should call there. Wait. Is there a high school nearby? You could do some volunteer coaching. We can get the press involved. High profile community work. It'll go down well with the team."

"You want me to coach a high school team?" Cam pulled into a space and hit the brake. Two mechanics heading toward the workshop turned to look at the Audi, their eyes widening as they saw the dent in the side.

"No, I want you to be *seen* with a high school team. Community work, that's the thing. I want your hair cut, your best smile on, and you to continue working out like you're still playing. You need to be a force to be reckoned with on the sidelines, the same way you are when you're in the game. Leave it with me. I'll get my people to speak to some local schools and teams. We can make this work. And in the meantime, keep your nose clean and keep your body in peak condition, okay? I can probably get a lot of sponsorships for us after this."

Cam rolled his eyes. "Sure. Got it. Listen, I have to go. I'm at the dealership."

"You buying a new car?"

"Reparing the old one. It's a long story."

"Okay. Go and get it repaired. I'll call you this afternoon." Derek didn't say goodbye before ending the call. He never did. His time was money, and extraneous words cost dollars. Shaking his head as he turned off the ignition, Cam walked into the dealership and headed for the reception desk, pretending not to notice the staff members staring at him, and elbowing each other as he weaved his way through the cars in the showroom.

"Hi." A young man with a bright smile greeted him. "Mr. Hartson, right?"

"Yeah, that's right." Cam passed him the car keys. "I have my car booked in for repairs. While I'm here, can I ask you a question?"

"Sure, shoot." Another wide smile.

"Do you have a phone number for a Honda Dealership? I need to buy a new wheel for a Civic."

CHAPTER SIX

"Your presentation was impressive," the older woman said. "And your résumé, too." She turned over the piece of paper with Mia's work history printed out on it, placing it on the table. "Why would you want to come work for a company like ours when you've been running your own for years?"

Mia smiled. She'd rehearsed this answer in her head ever since she'd received the invitation to interview. Before that, even. Because it's the same question she would have asked if their roles were reversed. "I ran the company with my ex-husband. I took responsibility for the sales and marketing, while he ran the operations and finance. We dissolved the business last year and agreed to divorce, and now I'm looking for a new challenge here in Hartson's Creek."

"So you're planning to stay here?" the younger man who'd introduced himself as Nathan, asked her. She knew from reading about the business that Nathan was one of four siblings involved in running the distillery, which was owned by their mother, Eliana Scott, who was sitting next to him. Nathan was the operations manager, and if she got the job, he'd be her boss. But she got the impression it was Eliana she really needed to impress.

"Yes. My children are happily enrolled in local schools, and I'm staying with my uncle while I look for a permanent home for us. I love it here, and have no plans to relocate."

Eliana nodded. "Have you applied for any other positions?"

"A few," Mia told her with a nod. "But can I be completely honest?"

Nathan raised an eyebrow, then nodded.

"My heart is really set on working for you. You have an amazing product, and that's a dream for a marketing executive like me. While your whiskey sells itself once somebody has tasted it, I know that I can introduce it to so many new consumers. As I said in my presentation, there are a lot of different strategies we could follow, depending on what you think fits best with your brand. But I'm passionate about making your market share increase. About finding untapped markets not only in the US, but abroad as well. I can make your product stand out and make G. Scott Carter the brand that everybody asks for when they want a glass of whiskey at the end of a meal." She took a deep breath before looking them both in the eye. "You're great at making whiskey, and I'm great at marketing. I feel like this could be a mutually beneficial relationship."

Nathan bit down a grin, and looked at his mother. "Any more questions?" he asked her.

Eliana shook her head. "I think I have all I need."

"You should hear from us within a few days," Nathan told her as he escorted her out of the interview a few minutes later. "But I can tell you I'm impressed. And my mother was, too."

She was? Mia blinked, because Eliana had looked thoroughly unimpressed. But she'd take it anyway. "Thank you for your time. I appreciate it. You have a very special business here."

Once she'd walked out of the building, Mia let out a long, deep breath, feeling her muscles relax for the first time that day. Despite the days of practicing her presentation, and the near-miss thanks to her tire blowing, the interview had gone well.

Or at least, it had felt that way.

It was only as she opened her car door that she noticed a note stuffed between her windshield and the wiper. She pulled it out, the paper flapping in the breeze as she unfolded it.

It was a complement slip, with *Lawson Honda, Shawsville VA* printed in red swirly letters at the top.

DEAR MS. DEVLIN. As instructed, your tire has been replaced, and your spare tire has been placed next to the trunk. Thank you for paying in full over the telephone.

SHE BLINKED AT THE WORDS. She'd been planning to drive to a garage on her way home. Not a dealership, because she knew they charged an arm and a leg. A local garage selling generic brands would be fine. She wanted to feel annoyed, because she was perfectly capable of doing this.

But instead, a little fire sparked deep inside her. Because the tall, muscled football player had gone out of his way to help her. And it made her feel a little gooey.

Yeah, and look where gooey had gotten her. The last time she melted like a chocolate bar on a hot day she'd ended up pregnant as a nineteen year old college student. And it had landed her right here a decade and a half later.

After lifting the heavy spare tire into the trunk, she sat

down heavily on the driver's seat and let her head fall back against the chair. So now she didn't only owe him ten thousand dollars, or for the help he'd given her changing the flat, but for a brand spanking new Goodyear tire that would probably cost more than all the money left in her checking account.

And still the fire didn't go out. Her mouth dried as she thought about those eyes. The ones that kept looking at hers. And his lips, damn they were hot. She'd never really noticed a man's lips before but his were flawless. Soft and parted. Maybe a little too big on anybody else, but perfectly masculine with his square jaw and dark beard.

The kind of lips you'd never want to stop kissing.

She rolled her eyes at herself. Those whiskey fumes had to be stronger than she'd thought. Because she didn't do gooey.

She did strong mom. Determined worker. Woman who wouldn't be messed with.

But gooey? Definitely not that. Because gooey always ended in a big mess.

———

"Look at us," Tanner said, carrying a tray of beers to the table where Cam was sitting with his brothers. "The Heartbreak Brothers together again. I never thought I'd see the day." He handed a bottle to Logan, Cam's twin, and then to Gray, their eldest brother. They'd deliberately chosen a table in the far corner of the Moonlight Bar. With Gray's worldwide fame as a Grammy Award winning singer, and Cam's football career, they were used to attracting attention whenever they got together.

But if they could, they avoided the spotlight. When it was the four of them – or five when their younger sister,

Becca agreed to join them – they wanted to be normal. Shoot the breeze without having to put on a front. Tease each other the way they did when they were teenagers sitting around the kitchen table while Aunt Gina chided them for not washing their hands or bickering over the mashed potatoes.

"Do you know you're the only one of us that calls us the Heartbreak Brothers?" Gray said, shaking his head. "I thought we left that shit behind when we left high school."

"By the time I started high school, it was part of the local lexicon." Tanner shrugged. "It's not my fault we're handsome bastards."

Cam choked on a mouthful of beer. The youngest of the four at twenty-nine, Tanner was the wackiest, too. The family clown who always made them smile. Gray was the protective older brother. Logan, the one who always talked things out. And Cam? He'd always been the strong and silent type. The one who quietly got things done. It was only on the football field that he'd stood out.

Of course, that had changed over the years. It was impossible not to have a certain amount of confidence when you were the star safety of your team. That self-belief was critical to succeeding in his career.

Logan tipped his head to the side, a smile playing on his lips. "I hear you've started going to Lainey's beauty salon to get your nails done," he said to Tanner.

"Yeah. So what?" Tanner shrugged. "A man's hands are important. When I shake on a deal I want to look successful. Maybe you should go. I hate to say it, but you're starting to smell of farm."

Logan blinked. "Farm? Get out of here. I shower every day." He took a swig of beer, then surreptitiously lifted his hand to his nose to sniff it. "Farm," he muttered. "Asshole."

Gray lifted his beer to Cam. "Welcome back. I bet you're

happy to be here talking about beauty salons and pig shit. Beats being in Boston on a Friday night, am I right?"

Cam raised his eyebrows and nodded. "Yep. Just how I wanted to spend my Friday night. If I wanted to talk nail colors, we could have gone to *Chairs*."

Tanner shuddered. "Don't talk about *Chairs*. I hate it. I swear it should be declared a form of torture in the Geneva Convention."

"Didn't you propose to Van at Chairs?" Gray asked, raising an eyebrow.

"Well, yeah." Tanner's brows knitted together. "But that doesn't count. It's still the ninth circle of hell on any night I'm not proposing."

"It's just a Friday night get together," Cam murmured, shaking his head. "How bad can it be?" *Chairs* had been part of Hartson's Creek's weekly tradition for as long as Cam could remember. It took place every Friday night from spring to fall. The townsfolk would drive to the grassy shore along the creek, bringing their own chairs and baked goods, along with pitchers of lemonade and ice tea for them all to share. And of course there was gossip. A whole pile of it.

When Cam was a kid, they'd go with their Aunt Gina and set up games of flag football in the fields. But he hadn't been to *Chairs* for years.

Thank God.

"It's not *just* a get together," Tanner grumbled to Cam. "It's a chance for the whole town to look at you and judge. You can *bet you're* the topic of conversation right now. They're probably all planning on pushing their eligible daughters on you as we speak. Before you know it, there'll be a crowd of them standing outside your house with torches, chanting for you to come out.

"This is Hartson's Creek, not Salem," Logan pointed out. "And won't they be more likely to talk about you?" he asked

Tanner. "I hear you and Van are thinking about starting a family. She's probably describing it in intimate detail to everybody there. Stamina, fertility, and everything else."

Even in the gloom of the bar, Cam could see Tanner blanch. "How do you know we're trying for a baby?"

"Van told Courtney. She wanted some tips." Logan grinned. "I guess some of us have it and some of us don't."

"Why didn't you come to me?" Gray asked. "I've got two kids."

"Because we don't want twins," Tanner told him, his face serious. "One is enough."

"I don't think you get the choice," Cam pointed out, his eyes meeting Logan's. "And what's wrong with twins? I like being a twin."

"Changing the subject, Logan told us you're thinking of retiring," Gray said, his tone turning serious. "Is that right?"

Cam shrugged. "I'm thinking about a lot of things. Not getting many answers though."

Gray's smile was full of sympathy. He'd had to make a few career changing decisions himself. Moving from L.A. back to Hartson's Creek to be with Maddie Clark hadn't exactly been a boost to his career. And yet Cam knew his brother was the happiest he'd ever been, surrounded by his family and running a recording studio on the grounds of his home. "You'll get there," Gray said, his eyes soft. "Just remember that your health always comes first."

"Yeah, I know." Cam returned his smile. "It's factoring into my thoughts."

"It should be your only thought," Logan muttered.

"I think we're ready for another round," Cam said, pushing his chair back with his iron calves and standing. He didn't want to talk about his injuries. Not tonight. This evening was about his brothers. About spending time with the people who really knew him. "Four more beers?"

"Works for me." Gray drained his bottle. "Cheers."

Cam strode toward the bar, weaving around the tables. A couple of customers greeted him, and he gave his usual smile and wave. People around here were typically cool with him. He'd grown up with half of them, after all. And it was Gray who got most of the stares, particularly from his teenage fans. Cam bit down a smile as he remembered Gray's fiancée Maddie, telling them about the time Gray was cornered in the church, unable to escape from a hoard of girls banging on the door.

"Hey," Sam, the bar owner, gave him a half smile. "You boys okay? Nobody bothering you?"

"We're good." Cam smiled back, because Sam always had their backs. Apart from when they tried to sneak in for some underage drinking many years ago. Then he marched them right out of the bar and told them to come back when they were twenty-one. "Can we have four more beers please?"

"Sure." Sam pulled out the bottles he knew they liked the best, popping the caps. As he watched, Cam remembered that Sam was Mia Devlin's great uncle.

Interesting.

"I hear you have some new housemates," Cam said, leaning on the bar.

"Oh yeah, and I heard you had a little problem with my grand nephews." Sam lifted an eyebrow. "I've got my niece and her kids staying with me for a while. Says it's to look after me, but I'm looking after them. Her asshole husband upped and left them high and dry."

"He walked out on his kids?" Cam asked. What an asshole.

"Yep. Disappeared and wiped out their bank account. She lost their house and business because of it, so her and the boys moved down here." Sam grabbed a cloth and rubbed it along the bar. "Good thing he's hiding out somewhere, because if I ever see him, he'll get a knuckle sandwich from me."

Cam bit down a laugh, because Sam didn't look like he'd win a fight against a fly. But the humor dissolved when he thought about Mia being abandoned.

Not your problem, he told himself. He wasn't anybody's white knight. He didn't have a horse and his armor was rusty.

Yeah, so why did you stop to help her change her tire?

The memory of her leaning over the car rushed into his head again. Soft skin, blonde hair, slender neck. Taking a mouthful of beer, he tried to push the image away.

If he thought he had problems, it sounded like Mia Devlin had more. He wasn't going to help with them. If he got involved he'd only pile more on. He was here to think about his next move, to make some life decisions. And they didn't involve an abandoned wife with two kids who liked throwing footballs at cars.

Sliding a couple of bills over to Sam, he told him to keep the change, then walked back to the table with the beers.

And he didn't wonder how her job interview went, or whether she was grateful for the fact he'd gotten her tire replaced. Nope, not at all.

"Next round is whiskey," he told his brothers as he passed them the bottles. "Somebody has to get this party started."

CHAPTER SEVEN

"**I** don't see why we have to go to church," Michael said on Sunday morning, wrinkling his nose as they walked up the steps. "We didn't go every week in Kansas City."

"We went at least twice a month," Mia pointed out, as they walked through the open double doors and onto the parquet floor. The church was almost full, and the sound of conversations and laughter momentarily stopped her from walking. She hated being the new people in town as much as Michael did, but unlike him, she was trying to hide it. "Anyway, it's the best way to get to know people. Sam said most people around here go to church."

"Sam hasn't come," Michael muttered.

"Yeah, why isn't he here?" Josh asked. "If everybody comes?"

"He worked late last night, remember?" Mia pointed to a half empty pew, and Michael sat, sliding down to make space for his mom and brother. "He needs some rest. And we can thank God on his behalf."

"We don't have anything to be thankful for."

She lifted an eyebrow at her older son. "How about having a roof over our heads? A good week at school? You got on the football team." She let out a mouthful of air, because being so damn positive all the time was exhausting.

"And Mom got a job. That's good, too, right?" Josh beamed at them.

"Good if you never want to go back to Kansas City," Michael muttered, taking the hymn book from the shelf on the back of the pew in front of them, and flicking through it. He'd been like this since she'd gotten the call from the distillery offering her the job. She'd taken it, of course. But rather than be happy for her, Michael had rolled his eyes when she'd made his favorite meal to celebrate – chicken pot pies with mashed potatoes.

She knew it was making it all real for him. That even though he'd gone out for football trials, he was still hoping he'd be back at his old school with his friends and team. But she was damned if she'd let that spoil her happiness, because getting this job was a good thing.

The service passed quickly, thanks to an entertaining sermon from Reverend Maitland, who made everybody – even Michael – laugh. When they'd asked for the children to come to the front for a song, Josh had happily gone forward, singing so loud Mia could swear she heard him at the back. He was settling in nicely. He'd already been over to a new friend's house to play that weekend. And from the way he was talking to two of the kids as they walked back to their seats, he'd made a few more.

It was so much easier being eight than fourteen. She wished Michael had found life as simple as Josh did.

As they followed the crowd of worshippers, shaking Reverend Maitland's hand as they left, Mia's gaze landed on the one person she was trying not to think about.

Cam Hartson was standing on the lawn at the front of the

church, talking to a woman who was holding a baby. He was dressed up, wearing a sharp suit and shirt, and his hair was styled differently. Maybe that was why she didn't feel the spark she'd gotten before.

She was both relieved and disappointed. Because that spark was the only thing giving her life right now.

"I'll be right back," she murmured to the boys.

"Can I go play?" Josh asked, pointing at the town square where other kids his age were congregating.

"Sure. But keep within my eyesight," Mia agreed. "You want to go, too?" she asked Michael.

"Nope."

"Okay then. Stay here. I'll be back soon and we'll go grab a shake from the diner." She walked over to where Cam and the woman were laughing.

"Could I have a quick word?" Mia asked him.

For a moment he looked at her, surprised. There was no flash of recognition in his eyes. No soft appraisal of her, like he'd done last week. "Um yeah, sure. You okay, sweetheart?" he asked the woman with the baby.

She smiled at Mia. "Sure."

Sweetheart? So he had a girlfriend and a baby. And she'd sworn he'd been ogling her when she was changing the tire on her car. What an asshole.

Now she was glad there was no attraction. Ugh.

"I wanted to say thank you for the tire," she said quickly, because she wanted to get home and forget about all this. "You didn't need to do it, though. I had it covered."

"The tire?" His brows pulled together. "What tire?"

"The tire you helped me change on the side of the road. You must remember?" Why was he being so weird?

"I didn't change a tire. I'm afraid I don't know who you are." He swallowed, his voice full of politeness.

"You don't remember my sons throwing a football against

your car?" She tried to keep her voice civil, but it was getting tough.

He laughed, recognition finally washing over his face. "You've got me mixed up with my twin. You're talking about Cam, right? I'm Logan Hartson." He held his hand out. "And you must be Mia. It's a pleasure to meet you."

She shook his hand quickly, then closed her eyes, her face flaming with embarrassment. "I'm so sorry. I didn't know you were twins. I never would have…" She trailed off, looking for a rock to hide under.

Logan shrugged. "It's fine. It happens all the time. Most people around here know we're twins, but you're new so you wouldn't." He smiled again, as though trying to put her at ease. "Why don't you come meet my family?" He inclined his head at the woman he was talking to. "Courtney, come say hi to Mia."

"Mia, the car denter?" Courtney grinned and rushed over, passing the baby to Logan. "I've heard all about you. Welcome to town." Instead of offering her hand, she hugged Mia, who despite her surprise, hugged her back.

"Thank you."

"How are you settling in?" Courtney asked. "You're living with Sam, right?"

This was how Mia had thought small towns would be, everybody knowing everyone. And for some reason it made her feel warm.

"We're getting there," she told the pretty woman. "The boys are in school, and I got a job, which is a huge relief. I start next Monday."

"Where are you going to work?" Courtney asked her.

"At the G. Scott Carter Distillery. Do you know it?"

"Of course I do. Logan's sister works there. You need to meet her. Becca!" Courtney shouted out, and a familiar head turned around. Mia remembered seeing her in the offices.

"Come meet Mia Devlin. She's going to work at the distillery."

"Hi." Becca smiled widely. "I heard all about you from Nathan." With her dark hair and hazel eyes she bore more than a passing resemblance to her brothers. But where they were tall and masculine, Becca was petite. She held her hand out and Mia shook it. "I'm Becca Hartson. I'm one of the junior distillers at G. Scott Carter. When do you start?"

"Next Monday, if everything is finalized on time." Mia had already signed her contract and sent it back. The sooner she started the sooner she'd get paid.

Becca gave her a wide smile. "That's wonderful. We need some new ideas. I swear Eliana is stuck in the dark ages sometimes. I mentioned how gin was having a resurgence and that we could take some tips from that industry and she almost bit my head off."

Mia grimaced. "I said the same thing."

"Well hopefully she'll listen to you. You should meet my other brothers. Mind if I steal her?" Becca asked Courtney.

"Be my guest." Courtney smiled at her. "It's a pleasure to meet you. We should have coffee some time. Becca, make sure you get Mia's number."

"Oh, I will." Becca's eyes sparkled. "Did I hear something about you having children?"

"I have two boys," Mia told her. "That's Josh playing in the square." She pointed at a group of children running around the bandstand. "And Michael's over there." He was leaning against the rail of the church steps, his arms folded stubbornly across his chest.

"He's huge. He must be head and shoulders above you," Becca said, sliding her arm through Mia's and leading her over to a circle of people. "Everybody, this is Mia. She's starting work at my place next week."

About ten heads turned, interested eyes taking her in as

smiles welcomed her. Her eyes locked with green-flecked hazel ones, and she felt that familiar rush of blood through her veins. Okay, so the attraction hadn't gone. But she could ignore it. Pretend that she didn't get all fluttery inside when she locked gazes with Cam Hartson.

Weird how she didn't get that way when she looked at his twin. Maybe it was the difference in the way he wore his hair, or the fact Cam was wearing jeans and a black t-shirt that did nothing to hide his defined pectorals.

She tried really hard not to look at the ripple of muscle from his waistband to his ribcage. And those shoulders, damn, they looked almost as big without shoulder pads as they did when he was playing a game.

Not that she'd Googled him. No sir. Not her.

It was impossible to remember everybodys' names as she was introduced to them. There was Gray, the rock singer, and his fiancée Maddie, plus their two boys. Then a younger version of Gray, who was introduced as Tanner, along with his wife Van, who was a gorgeous blonde. Then there was Becca's aunt, and an even older man who was Becca's father. And more people who were either friends or relatives, but Mia couldn't work out which.

As she talked to Becca about the distillery, she found herself looking out of the corner of her eye at Cam. He was staring right at her, and he didn't look embarrassed at all to be caught. Instead, he gave her a lazy smile that did something to her.

It took her a moment to remember to breathe.

"Definitely avoid the coffee machine," Becca was saying. "A few of us get together and order in from a local place. I'll add you to our message group, that way you won't be poisoned during your first week."

"Sounds good," Mia agreed. Becca was a little ray of sunshine. She'd said she was the youngest of her siblings, which must put her in her mid to late twenties, probably ten years younger than Mia. But she could sense they would be friends.

There were some people you just clicked with.

"Will you be coming to *Chairs* on Friday?" Becca asked her.

"*Chairs?*" Mia's brows knitted. "What's that?"

As Becca attempted to explain the town tradition, Mia found her gaze wandering to the left again. Cam was talking to his aunt, but his face turned abruptly and he was staring right at her.

Busted. Mia bit her lip, and looked firmly away.

He was way too good looking. And according to the article she'd read about him, one of the best safeties the NFL had ever seen.

And way out of your league, Mia Devlin. Yeah, she knew that, but a little look didn't hurt, did it?

She was going to be paying ten thousand dollars to the guy, for goodness sake. Or more, if you added the cost of the top end tire. So she'd look if she wanted to.

"So do you think you'll come next week?" Becca asked her.

Mia dragged her eyes away from Cam's. "I wish I could," she told her. "But it's Friday night football at school. I promised I'd take Michael and Josh."

"Do your sons play?"

"Michael does. Josh tried pee wee last year and hated it. He likes going to games, though. For the snacks." Mia laughed.

"I used to like those, too. I remember being dragged along to football at the high school for years. First for Gray, then for Cam and Logan. Even Tanner played, and he hates getting dirty." She tipped her head to the side and looked over at Cam. "Hey, did you know Mia's son plays football?"

"Oh yeah. I've seen him in action."

It was getting stupid how often they were looking at each other. This time, there was a curl to his lips. A kind of half smile that made her legs feel weak. She grinned back at him, and he winked.

Damn it, how could a wink be sexy?

"My son dented Cam's car," she admitted to Becca.

"He's the one?" Becca's eyes widened. "I had no idea. Why didn't you tell me?" she asked Cam.

"Because I haven't seen you. Anyway, it's none of your business, Miss Nosey." He walked over and ruffled her hair. "Now can I steal Mia away from you for a minute? I want to talk to her about the car."

"You can talk here," Becca suggested. "I won't listen."

"Sure. And you didn't rat me out every time I snuck in late at night when we were kids." Cam shook his head. "You forget how well I know you."

"I forgot how much you annoy me." Becca shook her head. "Go on. Steal my new friend. See if I care."

Mia smiled at her. "I'll see you at the distillery."

"Yep. Oh wait, can I have your number? To add you to our messenger group? And Courtney wanted it, too."

"I'll send it to you," Cam told her, his voice impatient. "Okay?"

"You have Mia's number?" Becca's eyes widened. "Why?"

Ignoring her, he inclined his head at Mia. "Shall we go?"

She nodded.

"Bye, Mia. Bye, Cam. Don't do anything I wouldn't." Becca's eyes sparkled, while Cam's rolled as they walked over to an old oak tree, where nobody else was standing.

Finally alone, Mia looked up at him. The sun was shining through the branches, casting a dappled light onto them, making Cam's eyes look almost bronze as they stared down at her.

"Thank you for the tire," she said softly. "But you didn't need to do that. I had it handled."

"I know. But I was going to the dealership anyway."

"Not the Honda dealership."

He shrugged. "They're all connected."

"So you can add it to the invoice?"

"Add what?" Three tiny lines appeared between his brows.

"Add the cost of the tire to the money I owe you for the dent. The ten thousand dollars."

Cam looked at her strangely. "I'm still waiting for the final total. It won't be that much. They said it should be an easy fix. Maybe a couple of thousand. We'll see."

"But you were adamant it was going to cost at least ten thousand." Why was she arguing? This was good news, wasn't it? But she didn't want to be blindsided, not when she still had no idea how to find the money. Better to be realistic than to have hope.

Life had taught her that much.

"I was wrong. And maybe a little hot headed." He gave her that sexy half smile again. "I kind of like my car."

"I got that impression."

Cam bit down a grin at her sarcasm. "Maybe you'd like to come out with me in it once I have it back," he suggested. "You might like it, too."

She stared at him for a few long seconds. "You want me to come out in your car?"

"Only if *you* want to. It'll be kind of part yours anyway, after you pay for the repairs."

She felt the shudders run through her. It was a physical sensation. A little fear, a little excitement, and a whole lot of panic. "I don't... I can't..." She glanced to the side. Michael was talking to a kid his age. Was that actually a smile on his face? "I'm married," she blurted out. Ugh, what an idiot she was. The divorce was almost completed in the courts.

"I heard you were separated."

Her heart was pummeling against her chest. "Who told you that?"

"It's a small town. Word gets round."

"Yeah, well it's complicated. Like the rest of my life. Seriously, you wouldn't want me in your car. Or to do anything with me, come to that. I have two kids, an almost ex-husband, and more baggage than you could fit in the trunk of your Audi."

"I wasn't asking you to bring any luggage." He gave her a wink. "Let me take you out to dinner. That's all. See if this thing between us means something."

"This thing between us?" She arched an eyebrow. "There's nothing between us apart from a ten thousand dollar debt."

No stupid crazy glances. No hot blushes. No Googling and clicking on image searches.

Nope, nothing at all.

He blinked, thick eyelashes sweeping down. "I wasn't asking for your hand in marriage, Mia. Just a date. But I get the hint. You're not interested." He shrugged. "Your choice."

Yeah, it was. But she already felt like a prize asshole for turning him down like that. Sure, he was a player. Maybe in more ways than one. But it never hurt to be polite.

"I should go," she said quickly, looking around at Michael. "I need to get home and cook lunch. I'll see you around. Thank you again for the tire."

"You're welcome." Why was he still smiling? "I'll see you around, Mia."

No he wouldn't, because she planned to hide herself away until he left town. Or maybe join a nunnery. That would work. She wondered if they accepted single moms and their children.

CHAPTER EIGHT

"*Mom!* Guess what?" Michael barreled into the kitchen, his bag slung over his shoulder. Mia looked up from the table where she was helping Josh with his homework, watching as Michael dumped his bag on the tiled floor and walked over to kiss her cheek.

Well, that was new. So was the smile on his face. "What?" she asked, her lips curling.

"Coach asked me to sit with the varsity team tonight. I'm not on the roster, but he says he wants me to sit in with the guys. Get to know them so I'm ready for next year."

"He thinks you'll get onto varsity next year?" Her eyes softened. "That's amazing."

"Yeah. He's already told me to be ready for a JV game next week. There are a few of us who are gonna sit with the team tonight."

"Do we need to be there early?"

"Maybe half past six?"

Mia checked her watch. She hadn't started dinner yet. "Okay. I'll make us some sandwiches and we can go out to eat after to celebrate. How does that sound?"

Michael's grin was huge. "Great."

Her heart clenched – he was finally settling in. With her job starting on Monday, and Josh spending lots of time with his new found friends, they were all making good progress. All those sleepless nights and tears were worth it, if her boys were happy.

Not that her sleepless nights were only related to her kids. Her sleep had been fitful on Sunday night, thanks to her conversation with Cam Hartson. She'd played it over in her mind, again and again, and every time she winced.

Had she really told him no?

Yeah, she had. And she'd been right, because nothing could ever happen between them. Not even if he sent her heart spinning like crazy.

Or maybe because he did just that. She didn't like feeling out of control. She was a strong, independent woman. She was in control at all times.

And she wouldn't let any guy threaten that. Not even one with a smile as sexy as Cam Hartson's.

But sometimes she wished life was a little bit different.

"Mom?" Josh said, his voice cutting through her thoughts.

"Sorry, honey." Mia blinked the memories away. "What did you ask?"

"Can I sit with Noah at the game? His brother's on the team."

"Um yeah, sure." Mia nodded, standing to go make their sandwiches. "But you don't leave the bleachers without asking me, okay?"

"It's not a big stadium, Mom. Not like in Kansas City," Michael told her. "You'll be able to see everybody there."

"And I'm eight now," Josh piped up. "I'm not a baby any more."

"I know." She ruffled his hair fondly. "I just wish you didn't have to grow up. Either of you."

At least they still had this. Homework at the table, meals in the kitchen, and Friday night football. Somehow they were making it through as a family. A smaller one than she'd thought they'd be, but a family nonetheless.

And really, what else mattered but that?

THE SMELL HIT Cam as soon as he followed Coach Hawkins through the double doors and walked into the changing rooms. It was like walking back through twenty years of his life, to the days when he and Logan were kings of the locker room.

The aroma of teenage sweat mingled with the powdery fog of deodorant. Clothes were strewn across the benches, socks balled up in sneakers that were flung on the floor. The squad were all dressed though, in the familiar blue and white uniform that used to be Cam's, along with the white helmets with blue stripes, and the eagle emblazoned on the side.

"Okay, Eagles. You ready for tonight?" Coach Hawkins shouted out. Cam had met with him yesterday, following Derek's request, and the coach had treated him like an old friend. Yes, he was happy for Cam to help out with the teams. More than happy. They'd spent an hour talking NFL and defensive line ups before Coach Hawkins realized he was late for practice.

And now it was Friday night. The atmosphere in the locker room wasn't a million miles away from the better equipped and cleaner Bobcats changing room, where Cam had spent half his Sundays for the past nine years. There was a buzz of electricity, peppered with conversation and laughter, as well as the friendly gibes that were part of being in the team

"Remember, Jackson, you're supposed to catch the ball, not let it sail into the bleachers."

"Hey, Ben. I hear your new girlfriend's coming to the game. Let's hope you don't end up on your ass like last time."

"Like your momma ends up on her ass every Saturday night?"

"Fuck you."

"Eagles!" Coach Carter's voice was louder this time. Enough for the room to quiet and the players to all look at the door where Cam and Coach Carter were standing, the light from the hallway spilling in behind them. "We have a visitor. Best behavior please."

"Sorry, Coach," the curser mumbled.

A rumble of chatter started up as people realized who the visitor was. Cam heard his name repeated, eyes widening as they looked at him.

"Many of you know Cam Hartson, the safety for the Boston Bobcats. He used to be an Eagle, like you. And he's going to be joining us for practice over the next few weeks, to give you some pointers. He'll be working with the Varsity and JV teams, so everybody here will get to meet him. And he'll be watching the game tonight, so give it all you've got and make us proud."

Cam lifted his hand up in greeting. "Hey, it's good to see you all. Good luck with the game tonight. I'm looking forward to cheering the Eagles on again."

One of the players walked forward to shake his hand. "This is Grant Ryerson. Our quarterback," Coach Carter told Cam.

"It's good to meet you," Cam said, his grip strong.

"You too, Mr. Hartson."

"It's Cam. I'm too young to be a mister at a school."

The boy nodded, his expression serious. "Yes, sir."

Ten minutes later, they were walking out to the stadium.

There were a few kids at the back dressed in their street clothes. "They're not playing?" Cam asked the Coach.

"They're mostly JV players. The ones we think will make Varsity next year. The kid at the back is interesting. Joined us this year, but he's good. I put him on the freshman team to see what he's made of, but he'll be moving to JV next week."

Cam followed the coach's gaze to the tall, dark haired boy standing a little apart from the others, and a jolt of recognition went through him. Michael Devlin. The boy's gaze met Cam's and pulled away almost immediately, as though he was embarrassed.

Poor kid. New to the school, the team, and now he had to deal with Cam all over again. "What position does he play?"

"Wide receiver."

Cam nodded and took a seat on the bench where Coach Carter indicated, and glanced around at the bleachers, wondering if Michael's mom was there. He wasn't playing, so there was every chance Mia had dropped him off and would pick him up later.

Either way, the thought of seeing her sent a rumble through him. She'd asked him to leave her alone, and he'd done just that. Maybe he'd even been glad she'd turned him down. She was right, he didn't need any complications. Not even ones that came packaged like her.

With baggage attached.

Yeah, but the packaging was pretty hot.

A drum started playing, then music flooded through the PA system, as the cheerleaders took to the field. Cam swallowed hard, because his memories were so strong. Of being a kid, of having dreams, of knowing that this was the one thing in his life he was good at.

Of having hope that a better life was ahead of him.

Damn, he missed that feeling.

———

MIA TOOK a seat in the bleachers, coiling her hair over her shoulder as she sought out Michael. She finally saw him standing by the fence, talking to the players, his face serious.

What had happened to the big smile he'd been wearing since he'd gotten home from practice? His moods were so mercurial.

The cheerleaders were on the field, doing the kind of tumbles that always made Mia worry they'd end up face-planting, but they were graceful and always ended on their feet. Then they ran to the right, exiting the field and the music faded out, replaced by the announcer.

"Friends, parents, players, welcome to Columbus High. It's Friday night and we're ready for a game! Let's hear a big cheer for the teams."

A loud roar filled the air. Mia joined in, clapping wildly. She couldn't see Michael anymore. Maybe he was sitting on the benches.

"We also have a very special guest tonight. Before he was a Boston Bobcat, he was a Columbus Eagle. Please give a very warm welcome to Mister Cameron Hartson. One of the best safeties the NFL has ever seen."

The roar was louder this time, only heightened by the blood rushing through Mia's ears. She looked down at the sidelines and there he was, waving at the crowds who were shouting his name.

This town was feeling smaller every day. She sat back on the bleachers, swallowing hard, and hoped like hell he couldn't see her up here. It was only when the teams started running out onto the field that she finally allowed herself to relax. She'd watch the game, find Michael and Josh, and head straight home. She probably wouldn't have to talk to Cam at all.

Sometimes life was that easy.

———

AT THE END of the second quarter, the coach gathered the team around him to give them a pep talk. The team was down 12-6, thanks to some impressive plays by the other team. Cam let them talk, wandering over to the refreshment stand lit up with red strip lighting. A line had already formed, and he joined the back of it, but was immediately accosted by one of the parents.

"Mr. Hartson? I'm Renee Mason. My son's a running back. We're so blessed to have you here tonight." The woman smiled and offered her hand. "Is it true you're going to be coaching the team?"

Word got around fast. "Just for a few weeks, ma'am." He took her hand and shook it quickly.

Before long, he was surrounded by a group of people, all wanting to introduce themselves. More than once he tried – and failed – to get away. He was parched – desperate for that soda he'd come over for.

A familiar blonde head was at the counter, paying the cashier. Cam looked at the man in front of him who was asking about the best college for his senior son.

"Sorry, I need to grab a soda and get back to the field." Cam gave him a nod. "Maybe you could make an appointment with Coach Carter. I know he'd be pleased to advise you."

Mia had just turned the corner, heading away from the refreshment stand. He had to run to catch up with her. "Hey," he called out. She turned to look at him, her hands full with a soda and popcorn.

"Um, hi." She gave him a small smile. "I didn't know you were going to be here tonight."

Cam shifted his feet. "Yeah, I just wanted to tell you I wasn't aware your son was on the team. I didn't want you thinking I'm stalking you. Not after last Sunday."

Her cheeks pinked up. "About that. I'm sorry. You took me by surprise and I wasn't very diplomatic." She blew out a mouthful of air. "I'm usually very polite."

"It's okay. You were honest. I can live with that. It was Michael I wanted to talk to you about," Cam told her. "He looked embarrassed when he realized I'll be helping the teams out with some coaching. Do you think it'll help if I speak with him?"

"You're going to be coaching the team?"

"For a few weeks. The JV and Varsity team. He's JV, right?"

"Kind of. He's been on the freshman team, but he was moved up. He was so excited."

He couldn't help but stare at her face. Her skin was so damned perfect. In the harsh light of the floodlamps it was almost translucent.

"He had a sour face when you were introduced over the PA," Mia continued. "I guess he's worried you're gonna be pissed with him."

"I'm not. I'll treat everybody the same. The coach thinks he has a lot of talent. Wants me to work with him, but if you don't want me to, I'll bow out. No hard feelings."

She took a deep breath. Her green eyes looked clouded with thoughts. "You know what?" she said, that smile still ghosting across her lips. "This is stupid. You're an NFL player. He could benefit so much from learning what you have to teach. Let's try to make him more comfortable." She pulled her bottom lip between her teeth, and he couldn't stop looking at it.

"How should we do that?"

"Are you free tonight? After the game?" She swallowed

hard, and of course his eyes were drawn to her throat. Damn, he needed to get a hold of himself.

"Yeah, I'm free."

"The boys and I are planning to eat at the diner. Maybe you could join us if you'd like? No pressure. If you don't want to be seen with us, that's fine, too. Or if you have a better offer..."

"Mia." His gaze caught hers. "I'd love to come to dinner with you all. Michael and I can talk about the game, or whatever else comes up."

Her shoulders relaxed. "Okay. Great. I'll have to wait for Michael, so if you get there before we do, just hold a table, okay?"

A loud roar came from the crowd. "I should get back," Mia said, inclining her head at the bleachers. "I'll see you later."

"Yeah," he murmured, as he watched her turn and walk up the stairs, her golden hair catching the floodlamps. "You will."

CHAPTER NINE

As the game played out, Mia's mind was somewhere other than the football field. Sure, she was staring straight ahead, her eyes fixed on the game, but it was like there was an invisible curtain between her vision and her thoughts. Had she really asked Cam Hartson to join them for dinner? What happened to avoiding him?

She scooped up some popcorn and pushed it into her mouth, but the kernels tasted like ash as they hit her tongue. Wrinkling her nose, she washed it down with a big gulp of soda, then looked at the family next to her.

"Would your little girl like my popcorn?" she asked the mom, who was wearing an Eagles shirt, a blue stripe of paint smeared across her nose. "There's nothing wrong with it, I'm just not that hungry."

"Can I, Mom?" the little girl asked, a smile bursting out on her face.

"Okay. But be sure to say thank you."

The girl took the carton in both hands, holding it like it was some kind of prize. "Thank you," she whispered.

"You're welcome." Mia winked at her.

As the Eagles made a play, her mind was still a mess of thoughts. How could the man get more attractive every time she saw him? It was so unfair. Her body needed to be put in a time out. Because she had no time or inclination to deal with this attraction she felt toward him.

Not even if her body heated up every time their eyes met. He was so damn tall it was stupid, dwarfing her five foot three frame. For a moment, she pictured him sliding his hands beneath her, hitching her body against his. She could almost feel the iron of his muscles against her soft skin.

Stop it! He's your son's coach.

When the game finally ended – with the Eagles winning 26-20 – Mia rushed down the steps and waited at the bottom for Josh. Families filed past her, young children hitched on their dads' shoulders or clinging to their moms' hands, laughing and talking as they made their way to the parking lot.

For a moment, her heart clenched, because that had been her family once. The four of them, walking away from Michael's games, talking about where they'd be going out for dinner.

She pushed the thought away. That was old news. And the good times had been so few and far between, anyway. Instead she painted a smile on her face, nodding at the friendly glances she was sent.

"Mom! Mom!" Josh came barreling down, and her smile widened. "Noah says I can stay over at his house tonight. They're getting pizza. Can I go? Please?"

"What does his mom say?" Mia asked dryly. She was too experienced a parent to think that plans made between kids were set in stone.

"It's fine by us." Noah's mom put her hand on her son's shoulder, offering the other to Mia. "I'm Alice Rickson. We live on Shawson Circle, about a ten minute walk from your place. I'll send you the details if you give me your number."

"Please, Mom?" Josh said again.

Okay, so it would just be her and Michael with Cam. That was fine.

"Sure. Do you need me to drop some things off?" Mia asked Alice.

"No, we have everything. Josh can borrow some PJs from Noah, and we have spare toothbrushes. We can drop him off in the morning on the way to Noah's pee wee practice."

"That would be wonderful. Thank you." Shooting Alice a grateful smile, Mia hunkered down in front of her son. "Be good, and make sure you brush your teeth before bed, okay?"

Josh sighed. "Okay, Mom."

She leaned forward to kiss his forehead. He wrinkled his nose, but submitted. She knew it was only a matter of time before he started rejecting her public displays of affection. She could remember the first time Michael stepped away from her, telling her he was too old for kisses.

Why did they have to grow up?

She waited in the car for Michael, listening to a country station as she watched boys spilling out of the door, talking and laughing. Not that you could really call them boys. They were men in all ways but age. Tall, strong, and most of them had at least some kind of facial hair.

She wasn't sure she was ready to admit her son was becoming a man.

It was ten minutes later that her phone lit up. She looked at the screen, her brows dipping when she saw Michael's name. "Hey honey, everything okay?"

"Yeah, all good. A couple of the guys are heading over to Mark's place to grab some food. They asked me if I could go."

"Who's Mark?"

"He's on the JV team. Can I go?" Michael's tone was short. She wondered if somebody was listening to him.

"How are you going to get there?" There was no way she was letting him ride in another teenager's car. At least not without vetting them first.

"Mark's mom is here. She's driving us. Is it okay?" he asked quickly.

"You'll keep your phone on at all times. If I call, you pick up. This is your chance to prove to me that you can be responsible, okay?"

Michael sighed. "Whatever you say."

"I mean it, Michael. If anything goes wrong, that's it. You'll be spending every Friday with me and Josh for the rest of your life."

"Nothing will go wrong. I promise." His tone was more conciliatory.

"Okay." It was her turn to sigh. "Call me when you want me to pick you up. Have fun."

"Thanks, Mom."

Putting her phone down, Mia let her head fall back onto the car seat behind her. She was pleased her boys were making friends. But there was a little chunk of her heart that disappeared every time they were away.

A sudden thought over took her. Cam! They were supposed to be meeting at the diner. Oh lord. She ran her tongue over her dry lips, because the thought of sitting alone with him and having dinner made her tense up all over.

She'd cancel. Simple. He wouldn't want to eat with just her, anyway. Dinner was supposed to be about putting Michael at ease, and Cam couldn't do that if Michael wasn't there.

Picking up her phone again, she unlocked it, then let out a grunt of annoyance when she realized she didn't have his number. She'd given him hers, but he hadn't messaged her yet. She thought about texting Becca, whose number she did have, but what would she say?

Hey, can I have your brother's number?

Hell no. That wasn't going to happen.

She was resigning herself to the fact that she'd have to walk into the diner and call the whole thing off when she saw a large, familiar frame stroll into the parking lot. *Thank you, Jesus.* Unbuckling her seatbelt, Mia flew out of the car, reaching Cam right as he was unlocking a black SUV.

"Hey," she said breathlessly. Cam looked up, his brows lifting.

"Hey. Everything okay?" He glanced over her shoulder at the Honda. She'd left the door open in her haste to catch him. "Are you having problems with your car again?"

She shook her head. "No. It's all good. I just wondered if we could take a raincheck on dinner. The boys have both gone to friends' houses to eat. They're new and I didn't have the heart to say no when they're still in the friend-making stage. I'm sorry. I hope I haven't inconvenienced you."

He looked at her for a long moment. "But *you* still have to eat."

"I'll make myself something at home."

"Why don't we go anyway?" he suggested, his voice light. Then seeing her expression, he added, "As friends. Nothing more. Maybe you can tell me a little more about Michael. Give me some insights into his psyche."

"He's a teenage boy, I'm not sure I have any insight."

Cam laughed. "Maybe I can give you some insights, then." His smile was slow and sexy, and it was only by force of will that she didn't blush.

"I'm not sure…" she trailed off, because it was hard to find the right words. "I'm new in town, and if people see us eating at the diner alone, they're going to talk. Even if we both know it's innocent, they'll still talk. And my kids don't need their mom being gossiped about."

"Yeah." Cam nodded. "I can understand that." He ran a finger along his bottom lip. "How about you come to my place?"

Her mouth dropped open.

He squeezed his eyes together. "Shit. I didn't mean anything by it. We can eat, talk about Michael, and then you can head home. I'll grab us something on the way."

That was such a bad idea. Not just because people would talk, but because something inside of her that had been dormant for so long had come to life, warming her, making her skin tingle and her heart race.

Michael. She was doing this for Michael.

Blowing out a mouthful of air, she lifted her gaze until it clashed with his. "Maybe for an hour…"

"An hour sounds good." He smiled at her. He had a dimple in his cheek. *A damn dimple*. Dear lord, could he get any sexier?

She had a horrible feeling the answer was yes.

"I'll text you my address. There's a key locker on the side of the house, I'll send you the code to it. Let yourself in, and I'll grab us some food from the diner. Burgers okay?"

Nothing was okay. She was about to have a heart attack.

"Burgers are fine. Thank you."

"No problem." He flashed those dimples again. "I'll see you at my place."

———

"You're in an NFL player's house? Shut up!" Joanna laughed down the phone line, then cleared her throat. "Just a minute, I need to close the living room door because the guys are playing a damn card game and they're all sore losers."

"You don't need to close the door," Mia whispered, even though she was alone in his house. Maybe he had surveillance cameras. Or hidden microphones. "There isn't any more to tell you."

"Oh come on. Tell me his name at least. I might've heard of him. There has to be some kind of silver lining to all those times Grant made me watch Sunday football with him."

"Cam Hartson."

"Oh. My. God." Joanna let out a little squeal. "There's no way you're in *his* house. He lives in Boston, doesn't he?"

"Not anymore, apparently." It was weird how Mia's cousin knew more about Cam than she did. But there was nobody else she could think of to call when she walked into his huge, opulent house that overlooked the creek. And she had to call somebody because she was freaking out.

Big time.

"I can't believe it. Damn, he's hot. He dated Soraya, didn't he?"

"Soraya?"

"The supermodel. She's from Iran, I think. Beautiful brown glossy hair and shining skin. She did that perfume ad where the guy sniffs her and practically comes in his pants."

"Oh god. You're disgusting." Mia winced. And not just because Joanna was gross. She was used to that. The two of them were cousins, but they'd practically grown up together, thanks to their grandma being their child minder. Mia was three years older than Joanna, and that had seemed like a lot growing up. Not so much now though. "He really dated a supermodel?" Her voice was small. She so didn't belong here. Not even as a mom asking for his help with her son.

She'd eat with him, and tell him a little about Michael's background. That would be more than enough to make sure there was never anything between them. Men like Cam dated supermodels. They weren't interested in soon to be divorced women with two children.

And that was a good thing. It really was.

"So are you gonna do it?" Joanna asked, her voice low.

"Do what?"

"Have sex with him, dumb dumb. I mean, he's a football player. He has the moves, right? I bet he's amazing in bed. You don't date somebody like Soraya without being able to please a woman."

"Stop it. I think I'm going to vomit. And no, I'm not gonna *do it.* I'm here as a parent, to talk about Michael. Then I'll go home and let him get back to his supermodels."

"Model. Singular. He's not Leonardo DiCaprio. She's the only model he's dated as far as I know."

Yeah, and one was enough. Because it told Mia all she needed to know. Cam Hartson wasn't just out of her league, he was out of her stratosphere.

"Even if I was interested, which I'm not, I'm not his type. And technically I'm still married."

"Technically, you're almost divorced and your husband is living with another woman, which means the marriage is over in all ways but name," Jo reminded her. "You can do exactly what, or who, you like. Please promise me if he makes a move you'll let him."

"Jo…"

"You haven't had sex for eons. Niall was your one and only. It's time to get yourself back out there and start over. Cam Hartson could be your rehab guy."

"My rehab guy?" Mia echoed, confused.

"The guy you get under to get over your separation. The one who teaches you to be comfortable being naked with a man again. It's like going to a therapist or something. A few nights with him and you'll be ready to jump on anybody."

Mia bit down a laugh, because Jo was so damn crude.

"Stop it," she said, but even Jo could sense the humor in her statement.

"I bet he has a big dick. You can tell by looking at him. Wait, let me check him out in his uniform."

Mia could hear clicking. "Are you Googling him?"

"I'm watching him in action. Hang on…" Jo trailed off for a moment, before saying, "Oh yeah. He's hung. Dayum." Her voice held a note of reverence.

"Can you stop? I don't want to be thinking about his penis while I'm talking about my kid."

"Then don't talk about your kid. Not everything has to be about Josh and Michael."

"Right now it does."

Mia's phone pinged against her ear.

"I sent you a link to a video," Jo told her. "Watch it, and pay particular attention to the area beneath his waistband as he runs. You'll be mesmerized. *Seriously.*"

"I'm not watching the damn video," Mia told her. "This whole conversation is horrible. Imagine two guys having a discussion about somebody's boobs like this."

"Honey, that's *all* guys have discussions about. That and football. I'm just evening the score," Jo told her.

The rumble of an engine echoed from the driveway, and the security lights flashed on. Mia looked over her shoulder at the window. "He's here. I gotta go."

"Okay, but call me tomorrow. I need all the details."

"There won't be any details."

Jo laughed. "Of course there will. Guys don't just invite you back to their place to talk about your son. They invite you because they want to see you naked."

Mia paled. "Tell me that's not true."

The sound of the keypad beeping made her heart start to speed. That and Jo's suggestive remarks. She felt lightheaded, like she'd stood up too fast, even though she was sitting on a stool at his breakfast bar.

"Mia?" a low voice called out. "You here?"

"Is that him?" Jo asked. Mia ended the call without replying and shoved her phone in her pocket. If it wasn't for the boys, she'd switch it to silent, because she had a feeling Jo was going to keep hounding her until Mia told her every last thing that happened tonight.

Nothing's going to happen. You'll eat, talk about Michael, and leave. Simple.

"Yeah, I'm here," she called out, blowing out a mouthful of air.

Here went nothing.

CHAPTER TEN

"Would you like a drink?" Cam asked her, pulling open his oversize refrigerator. "I've got beer and sodas. Oh, as well as a really good Chardonnay that'll blow your mind."

"A soda would be good. I'm driving." She was pulling two plates from the cabinet he'd pointed to, her long blonde hair falling over her shoulders.

Cam poured their drinks and carried them to the granite breakfast bar. Everything in this house was high quality. His brother was building himself a reputation for top class renovations all over the local area, and this one was no different. "You should at least take a sip," Cam suggested, offering Mia his glass. "It's good. You won't regret it."

"Are you some kind of wine connoisseur?" she asked him, a tiny smile playing on her lips. She looked completely different when she smiled. Young and carefree.

He was all too aware that every time they'd come into contact until now, something had gone wrong. His car. *Her* car. Him asking her on a date. It was good to see her face without those tiny furrows between her brows.

"Not really," he admitted, as she lifted the glass to her face and inhaled the aroma. "Logan's the one who knows all about wine. He buys it, I try it. Only off season, of course."

"You don't drink during season?" She pressed the glass to her soft lips, and closed her eyes as the crisp Chardonnay coated her tongue. "Oh boy, that *is* good. Your brother has good taste."

"It runs in the family. And no, I don't drink when I'm playing. I have a nutritionist who'd whip my ass if I didn't keep to the plan she gives me. The older I get, the more I realize how much my performance relies on what I put in my body."

Her gaze flickered down to his torso. She swallowed hard. "I guess she'd have a fit if she saw these burgers," Mia said, sliding his plate to him.

The burger was still on the foil wrapper, the fries covering the rest of the plate.

"I guess I'd better make the most of it."

"Will you be going back to Boston soon?" she asked him, her voice light. She took a bite of her burger, washing it down with her soda. He liked the way she smiled with the pleasure of it.

"I don't know. I'm still trying to figure out what happens next." He didn't want to talk about his injuries with her. Didn't want to see any pity on her face. "In the meantime, I'll be coaching the Eagles and relaxing for a few weeks. I guess I'll go back after that."

"It must be hard, leaving the team behind. You've played with them for years."

For a woman who hadn't known who he was when they first met, she seemed to have a good knowledge of his playing career. Had she been Googling him? A little pulse of satisfaction rushed through him.

"I guess I could say the same about you. Coming here with your kids must be tough. Where are you from again?"

"Kansas City." She popped a fry between her lips. "And yeah, it's hard, but other people have it harder. I'm lucky the boys are settling in. Even luckier to get a job that suits my skills. So I'm not going to start complaining."

He liked that about her. "Sam said your husband left you without warning. Cleaned out your bank account."

Mia dropped the fry she'd been holding. Her gaze that had been steady on his slid away. She swallowed hard, before tucking her hair behind her ear.

"Sam should keep his mouth shut."

"For what it's worth, I think your husband's a damn fool."

She took a deep breath, still looking down at her plate. For a moment, there was silence. Cam wanted to reach for her chin, to make her look at him again. Because when she looked at him, it felt like he knew where he was.

Maybe even felt like he belonged.

"Can I ask what happened?" Cam's voice was soft.

"It's old news," Mia finally said. Her cheeks plumped as she forced a smile onto her face. "Boy and Girl meet. Girl gets pregnant when they're too young and they're forced to grow up together. Except she grows up and he thinks he's Peter Pan. He wants to relive his twenties, and she and the kids don't fit in there anymore." She caught his gaze. "And I wouldn't want to. I don't want a guy who hasn't grown up. I don't want my kids to get hurt again. I just want to build somewhere safe for us all. I guess that's why I'm here."

"How old were you when you met him?"

"Eighteen. Freshman year of college. We were both business majors. I got pregnant during our sophomore year, and dropped out. He carried on while I waitressed or worked in shops or did whatever it took to pay the rent and save some money. We agreed that I'd go back to college once he had a job and the baby was a little older."

"And did you?"

She nodded. "But only part time. It took me seven years to get my degree. I worked for our business, and took care of the kids, so trying to fit in school was difficult."

"But you did it."

"Yeah. I guess I thought the hard part was done, you know? I was ready to enjoy life, to finally relax, spend time with my family, really throw myself into the business. And then he left."

"Like I said, he's a damn idiot."

"Maybe I was the idiot for believing we had an unwritten deal. For thinking that good things came to those who put in the work."

"Life's a bitch like that, isn't it?" Cam said, taking a mouthful of wine. He held the glass out. "You sure you don't want another sip?"

She bit on her lip. "Maybe just a little one."

Grinning, he passed her the glass, watching as she lifted it to her lips. The same glass he'd touched against his own. For some reason, it felt erotic.

Forbidden.

"Oh god." She sighed. "So good."

The blood shot right between his groin. He crossed his legs, trying to hide his growing erection.

"Have you dated since the breakup?" he asked her.

Mia looked up, her face a little flushed. "Nope. Haven't had the time or the inclination."

She was eighteen when she met her husband. Pregnant within a year. "How old is Michael again?" he asked her.

She tipped her head to the side, her hair gleaming beneath the lights. "Nearly fifteen. He's old for his year."

"Which makes you, what, mid thirties?"

"I don't know whether to hit you or congratulate you on your math. Didn't anybody ever tell you it's rude to ask a woman's age?" From the amusement in her voice, he could tell she was kidding.

"So you haven't been with another man for fifteen years?" He blew out a mouthful of air. "Wow."

Her eyes sparkled as she leaned forward. "That's normal. It's what people do. Or what they're *supposed* to do. Meet someone, get married, spend the rest of their lives only sleeping with them."

"Not the people I know." Cam shrugged.

"That's because you're all too busy chasing supermodels."

So she *had* been checking him out on the internet. *Interesting.*

"You really haven't touched anybody else since you were eighteen? No kisses, no gropes? Nothing?"

"I believe that's how marriage works." She lifted an eyebrow.

"Yeah, but you're not married anymore. Aren't you curious to know what it would feel like to be with another guy? You're young, are you planning on living like a nun for the rest of your life?"

She pressed her fingertip against her lip, her brows dipping as though she was remembering something. "I hadn't really thought about it. Kisses aren't on the top of my priority list."

He looked at her, taking in the intensity of her green eyes, and the softness of her blonde hair as it cascaded in waves to her shoulders. "If you were mine, kissing would be right at the top." He gave her a wicked grin. "No, make that second from the top. Sex would take first."

"It's a good thing I'm not yours then," she said lightly.

She was playing the game. Flirting. And damn if that didn't make him harder than ever. Cam took the last bite of his burger, ate the final handful of fries, then wiped his face with one of the free napkins the diner had put in the bag, before dropping it on the empty plate. Taking a long, cool sip of wine, he looked at her again. She'd already finished eating.

"You're fast."

"I come from a family of quick eaters. If you didn't eat what was on your plate, somebody else would." She shrugged.

He gave her a speculative glance. "You should kiss someone. Get it over with. Like riding a bike or something."

Mia laughed, her eyes crinkling. "You sound like my cousin."

"What did your cousin say?" He smiled back at her, and a blush stole up her face.

"It doesn't matter."

"Oh, come on." He turned in his stool, so he was directly facing her. "You can't tease me like that and not follow through."

"It was stupid, and she has a big mouth. You'll laugh at me."

He leaned forward, his eyes catching hers. "Now you have to tell me. Come on, just spit it out. I can guarantee I've heard worse in the locker room."

Mia sighed. "You're not gonna let this go, are you?"

"Nope. I'm a sportsman. I never let anything go. If I want something, I go for it. And I don't give up until I get it."

She was silent for a moment. The air crackled between them. She looked at him through those thick, pretty lashes.

"She said I need to get under a guy to get over the breakup. That I should use…um…somebody as a rehab guy. To get me ready for dating."

"A rehab guy?"

"She's stupid. And young."

"Like sex rehab?" He grinned at her, propping his chin on

his elbow as he leaned closer. He rested his foot on the rung of her stool. "I get that. Kind of like when I get an injury." Or most injuries, but he wasn't going to think about that. "We go to physio, keep working it until the injury's gone, then we get back on the field."

"I guess that's what she meant. As I said, she's an idiot." Her hair fell in front of her face again. This time he reached out and tucked it behind her ear, his fingers trailing along the soft skin of her neck.

Her breathing hitched and she looked up at him, her pupils dilating.

Yeah, she felt this. Whatever it was between them. The air around them was so thick he could almost touch it.

"You want to try it now?" he asked softly.

"What?" Her voice was thick. Low.

"A kiss. Just one. See if you're ready to move on." He played with the ends of her hair, rubbing the glossy locks between his fingers. "Nothing more than that. Unless you want more."

Her gaze dipped to his lips, and she bit down on her own. "It won't mean anything?"

"Nothing at all. Just a little rehab. That's all."

"Okay." She blushed. "Yeah, I could do that."

He slid his foot around the leg of her stool, and pulled it closer, until their knees were touching. "I gotta warn you," he told her, cupping her head with his palm, "I'll probably ruin you for anybody else."

She laughed, and the tension around her dispelled. He grinned back at her, liking the way her giggles sounded. A little rough, a little breathy, and a whole lot of sexy.

He leaned closer, his thumb drawing tiny circles on her neck. Her lips parted, and he could feel the warmth of her breath against his cheek. She tipped her head back, the movement almost subconscious, as though she was opening herself up to him, ready for his mouth.

The pulse between his thighs was strong. Constant. He brushed his lips against her jaw, and she sighed. Her fingers curled around his neck as he kissed and sucked at her skin, her body arching on the stool as his lips slid up to hers.

He paused for a moment, tasting the anticipation in the air. Her chest was rising and falling rapidly, pulling his gaze, making him admire the curve of her breasts as they pushed against the thin t-shirt.

He pulled her against him, pressing his mouth to hers, groaning loudly when he felt how soft they were. How pliant. She curled her arms around his neck, arching her body against his, and he swore he could feel the tightness of her nipples against his chest.

With a sweep of his tongue against the seam of her lips, he encouraged her to part them. His fingers flexed around her neck as their tongues slid together, sending a pulse of electricity through his body. Mia moaned as he deepened the kiss, his fingers tracing her spine, until his palm pressed against the small of her back.

Her breath escaped in small pants. He slid his hands beneath her behind and hitched her off her stool, sliding her along his legs until she was straddling his lap. She rolled her hips, her body grinding against his, and the sweet friction made him want to strip her right here, right now. Her hips were moving rhythmically, her arms tight around his neck, her mouth taking everything he had to offer.

And then her phone rang.

Abruptly, she pulled away, leaving only cool air against his lips. He touched them, and watched as she pulled her phone out of her pocket with shaking fingers, swallowing hard as she read the screen.

"I need to take this." Her voice sounded ragged.

Cam nodded, because he had no idea what else to say. His hardness was thankfully abating. No longer a teasing ache as she ground herself against him.

"Hey, honey." She sounded breathless. Like she'd just been thoroughly kissed. Cam bit down a smile.

"Sure, of course. I'll be there in twenty minutes." She paused, and he noticed how swollen her lips were. Damn, he wanted to kiss them again.

"No, no problem. I wasn't doing anything. I'll be there, sweetheart. Okay then, bye. See you soon. And don't forget to thank Mark's parents for inviting you."

She ended the call and blew out a mouthful of air. "That was Michael," she told him, keeping her face resolutely turned away from his.

"I got that impression."

"I need to go pick him up. I said I'd give his friend a ride home, too." She looked around for something – her purse by the looks of it, as she grabbed it from a stool on the other side of the breakfast bar. "Thank you for dinner."

"It was a burger. Not exactly dinner."

Pulling her keys out of her bag, she dropped her chin to her chest. He couldn't see the expression on her face, but he could imagine it.

"It's okay," he told her. "It was just a kiss. A rehab kiss. Nothing more."

When she lifted her head up, her eyes were wide and shiny. "Can we forget it ever happened?" she whispered.

"I might find that a bit difficult." Considering he was planning on thinking about it tonight in bed. Planning on thinking about her, too.

"Please?" Her lips turned down. "You're Michael's coach. I was supposed to be talking about him with you. And then, this happened." She swept her arm across the breakfast bar, her hand pointing at him. "I don't know what came over me."

He grinned. "Nothing came over you. That's the problem."

"This isn't funny. It really isn't. I've embarrassed myself." She pressed her palms against her face, and let out a little groan. "I should leave. Before I make it worse."

"Your problem is that you put too much meaning on everything. It was just a kiss, Mia. A really nice, sexy kiss that made me hard as hell. Nothing more. It doesn't mean Michael will be affected at all by it. We kissed. It was good. It's done."

"We're done?" She looked up at him. And damn if she didn't look a little disappointed.

"I get the impression you want us to be," he pointed out.

"We're just different. Too different." She rubbed her face again. "The last time I kissed somebody I ended up married for fifteen years. You eat supermodels for breakfast."

He coughed out a laugh. "I think you have me all wrong. And I can guarantee that you won't end up married to me. I'm your rehab guy, remember? Think of that kiss as your stepping stone to your Mr. Right. If you want to invite me to the wedding, I'll be there with bells on."

He ignored the pang in his stomach at the thought of her with another guy. But one thing was true – he was nobody's Mr. Right.

"Are we okay?" she asked softly.

"Yeah, we're good."

"And you won't tell anybody?"

He mimed a zip across his lip. "Our secret."

"Okay. I really should go. Are you okay cleaning up without me?"

He wanted to laugh. He'd just kissed the hell out of her, and now she wanted to do the dishes. "I think I can manage," he said dryly.

"Okay. Bye." She walked around the breakfast bar and

turned toward the door. As if she had a change of mind, she swiveled on her feet and walked over to him, pressing her lips to his cheek. "Thank you for being so nice about this." She quickly scurried toward the door.

"Mia?"

"Yeah?"

"If you need any more rehab, you know where I am."

She didn't respond. He heard the tap of her shoes against the wooden floor of the hallway, then a moment later the door opened and then slammed closed.

Cam took a sip of wine, then laughed to himself. Tonight had been interesting. He'd felt a rush of adrenaline like he hadn't in a long time, even when on the field. His body liked it. Liked her. And he'd completely lied that it was just a kiss.

Because he knew he wanted more.

CHAPTER ELEVEN

ood luck today BB – you got this! Joanna xx

Mia smiled down at her phone as she locked her car and walked to the distillery's main entrance. It was her first day of work and the nerves were setting in. It didn't help that she'd barely slept that weekend, thanks to a certain NFL player who had lips to die for. She'd spent way too many hours thinking about that kiss. About what might have happened if Michael hadn't called.

Thanks honey. I'm going in now! Will call you later. Mia xx

She sent the message then pressed the buzzer on the front door, giving her name to the receptionist who answered almost immediately. Nathan – her new boss – had asked her to arrive at 9:30am, then she'd be taken through orientation by an assigned member of staff. This afternoon she would have her first strategy meeting with the board.

She was nervous and excited, and every other feeling she could think of. Taking a deep breath, she smoothed down her skirt and pushed the door open, letting out a sigh when her phone pinged again.

If you get any free samples, remember your favorite cousin, okay? I'm a whiskey convert ;) Joanna

Mia laughed as she walked down the hallway toward the reception desk. An older woman with pretty blue eyes and a white bun was sitting there. A smile lifted her lips as she saw Mia.

And then Mia's phone rang. Dammit. This thing was a liability.

"I'm sorry," she told the woman, who hadn't yet said a word. "I have to have my phone on. I have two boys at school and I'm the only contact for them. Let me just check who it is."

The woman's smile didn't falter. "No problem."

It wasn't a number she knew. She didn't dare reject it, in case it was one of the boys' schools or teachers. "Hello?" she said, putting the phone to her ear. "Mia Devlin speaking."

"Hey."

Her mouth went dry. Just one word and she knew who it was. She'd been thinking about him all weekend, after all. And Cam Hartson had a distinctive voice. Low, almost sexual. Like the whole world could wait while he spoke.

"Um, hi. Can I call you back later? I'm about to start work. Is it about the invoice?" She shot a smile at the receptionist. Sandy, according to her badge.

"It's not about the invoice. I just wanted to wish you a good first day. But you *can* call me back later." Humor curled through his words. "Make sure you do, Mia."

He disconnected before she could protest that she wasn't planning on calling him at all. Pushing down the aggravating warmth in her chest that appeared whenever she was near him, Mia slid her phone in her bag and turned back to Sandy.

"Sorry about that."

"No problem. I know how hard it is to juggle work and family. My three girls are grown up now, but when they were younger, oh boy." Sandy widened her eyes. "I'm still surprised I have any hair left." She pulled a file from beneath the counter and slid a plastic pass out. "Here's your I.D. You'll need to wear it around your neck at all times while you're here. It'll let you through the doors, including the front one, so you won't have to buzz to get in tomorrow. And your buddy will be down soon to show you around and take you to your meetings with HR and Security. Oh, and has anybody warned you about the coffee?" She lowered her voice, as though it was a huge company secret. "Try and avoid it at all costs. It's terrible."

Mia laughed. "So I heard. I've already been added to the take out coffee Whatsapp group."

"That's good news. I had to find out the hard way. My taste buds have never been the same since." She looked over Mia's shoulder, and her grin widened. "Oh, your buddy's here," she told her. "You'll be in safe hands with this one."

Mia turned to see Becca Hartson walking toward them. She was wearing black pants and a cream shirt, her hair pulled into a high pony tail. "Hi!" she said, leaning forward to hug Mia. "I hope you don't mind me being the one to take you through orientation. When they sent out an email looking for volunteers, I hit reply immediately."

There was something so warm about Becca. "Of course I don't mind. I'm happy to see a friendly face."

"Great. You got everything you need, Sandy?" Becca asked her.

"Yep." Sandy nodded. "You can take her now."

"How was your weekend?" Becca asked after Mia said goodbye to Sandy. "You watched the football game, didn't you?"

Becca had a good memory. "Yeah, that's right. Varsity at the school. My son wasn't playing, but he was asked to sit with the team."

"Go Eagles." Becca gave a fist pump. "Man, I spent way too many Friday nights shouting that at my brothers. What else did you do this weekend?"

I straddled your brother's thick muscled thighs and writhed against them as he kissed me.

Mia blinked that thought away. "Nothing much. I'm helping Sam around the house, trying to keep it clean and the yard tidy. So we mostly did that."

"Ugh. I hate yard work. Come on. We'll head to HR first, then I'll show you the kitchen and all the places Nathan probably left out when he took you around last week. Then we'll order some coffee."

Becca led Mia through the security doors that led to the distillery itself. The air was heavy with the sweet, thick smell of brewing whiskey, as they passed the huge metal washbacks that stretched from the ground to the high vaulted ceiling, then through the cooperage – G. Scott Carter still made their own barrels – to the offices beyond. Becca introduced Mia to every member of staff they passed.

"There are only fifty of us working here," Becca told her, "so you'll get to know everybody quite fast. I'm not going to give you my opinion of anybody, because I don't want to influence you, but nearly everybody is lovely. Even Eliana, as long as you do what she asks of you. And Nathan is pretty great, too."

"Is it the two of them who own this place?"

"No, but only the two of them are working here right now. Nathan has an older brother, who runs a distillery in Scotland of all places. From what I hear, that's a good thing because when he was here he was a bit of a tyrant. And they also have a sister and brother from their dad's first marriage, who sit on the board, but they live in New York. Eliana and Nathan are the ones you'll deal with the most."

They'd made it to the HR department, which turned out

to be one part time HR Manager. "I'll leave you here," Becca told her, after she'd made the introductions, "and I'll pick you up in half an hour. You'll need that coffee after all the forms you have to complete. Just be glad they're on a computer now. When I joined they were all paper. I couldn't move my hand for a week." She laughed. "How do you take your coffee? I'll add it to our list at the local coffee shop."

"Americano with hot milk please," Mia smiled at her.

"Got it." Becca nodded. "Now good luck, be strong and I'll see you on the other side."

"Thank you so much for everything," Mia told her.

"It's not a problem. I'm so happy you're here."

So was Mia. And wasn't that a good thing?

———

CAM WAS CRAZY BORED. After his abortive phone call with Mia, he'd spent the next hour lifting weights in the basement gym that Tanner had fully equipped for him, then had gone out for a run that had done nothing to clear his head. If he was in Boston – still playing – he'd be running drill after drill right now, shooting the breeze with his teammates in between, laughing and ribbing each other like they always did.

A few more weeks and he'd lose the fitness that was getting harder to maintain each year. He had to run harder, lift heavier, and go longer than he had than when he was twenty-three. And if he was honest, it all hurt more now.

He was about to call Logan to offer his help at the farm – that's how bored he was – when his phone rang. Cam smiled when he saw Brian Lockharte's name flash across the screen. He hadn't spoken to his assistant since the day he'd moved into this house.

It was funny how much Cam missed his face and voice.

"How's the new place?" Brian asked after Cam had accepted the call.

"Pretty good. Tanner's done a great job on the renovations," Cam told him, leaning on the kitchen counter as he pressed the phone to his ear. Glancing to his left, he could see the stool he'd sat on for dinner on Friday. The same one he'd dragged Mia onto, letting her body straddle his as he'd kissed the hell out of her.

Pulling his gaze away, he blew out a mouthful of air. Damn, he needed to get that woman out of his mind.

So why did you call her, dumbass?

"How's Boston?" Cam asked, walking to the refrigerator and grabbing an ice cold bottle of water from the door. Along with everything else he did to make Cam's life easy, Brian had arranged a weekly food delivery for him from the local grocery store.

"It's good. Weather is still warm, so we're making the most of it before winter hits."

"And the team?"

"Yeah, they're all good, too." Brian spent a lot of time at Freedom Field. "Did you watch the game yesterday?"

"Yeah." It was a lie; he still couldn't bring himself to watch the team play without him. It physically hurt to watch them play. "Good result."

"There's talk of making the playoffs. Hey, maybe you'll be back if we do. Though the rookie is doing pretty well. Coach Mayberry likes him."

Cam inhaled sharply. "Yeah, I heard that."

"That's kind of why I'm calling." Brian's voice lowered. He cleared his throat. "Um, Coach has suggested I help out the new guy while you're away. He needs to get some things for his apartment, and he's hopeless with shopping. Kind of like you, I guess." Brian laughed awkwardly. "I said I'd ask you first. I don't want you to think I'm going behind your back or anything. But I do have a lot of time on my hands while you're not here."

Weird how that question hit him right in the gut. It wasn't like Brian was cheating on him. Just trying to fill in some time with some work to do.

Cam knew how he felt. "Yeah, sure. Whatever Coach wants."

"Do you know when you'll be back?"

"Not yet." Cam kept it short, because he didn't want to talk about it. Didn't want to admit he had no idea how to get back on the field. Not without causing himself greater harm. But he still wasn't ready to let football go.

Because then what else could he do?

"I guess you'll be coaching the high school team for a while. How is it going?"

"Yeah, pretty well." Cam felt the tightness in his chest lessen. "They're a good bunch of kids. Enthusiastic, talented, they just need some honing. I guess I'll keep doing it for a few weeks."

"It's good you're keeping yourself busy. And football's football, right? You can come back when you're ready."

"Yep. The football is good. And they have so much stamina. I'd forgotten how much unharnessed energy teenagers had." His thoughts turned to Michael – and of course from there they leapt to Mia. He swallowed hard as he remembered how soft her long hair was as it brushed against his cheek. "Anyway, I'd better go. Lots going on here." Lies, all lies. "I'll catch you later, okay?"

"Sure. Take care. Glad you're doing well."

Cam disconnected and grabbed his car keys, heading out to the SUV that the dealership had loaned him. He climbed inside and pressed the ignition, turning the stereo to high. Loud music blasted out – a new track Gray had sent him yesterday to check out. The pumping bass somehow calmed him, making his breath slow and easy.

Glad you're doing well.

Yeah, he was doing great. His career was hanging by a thread, his teammates were moving on without him, and he had a boner for a woman who was completely uninterested in him.

He turned the car around and drove down his driveway, eyes blinking at the reflection of the sun shining up from the creek.

Two of those things he had no control over. The third? She was a challenge, and she intrigued the hell out of him.

And he wanted her. Maybe too much.

CHAPTER TWELVE

"Hey, Mom, come and look!" Josh called out from the living room. Mia put the last clean glass away and closed up the dishwasher, wiping her hands on the kitchen towel as she walked through the doorway.

Josh was sitting with Sam in front of the coffee table, the two of them leaning over a half-finished jigsaw puzzle. "We've done all the edges," Josh told her, a beaming smile on his face. "I did most of it, didn't I, Uncle Sam?"

"Yep, you did." Sam nodded. "But the edges are the easy part. It's the middle pieces that determine the men from the boys. See this bit?" he said, pointing at the picture on the puzzle lid. "We have to find all these different shades of blue and somehow put them all together. That's where the skill is."

"I can do that," Josh said, his eyes lighting up. "Mom, do you want to help?"

Mia shook her head, shooting a grateful look at Sam. He and Josh seemed to have a natural affinity, and it made her life so much easier.

She may be able to start paying Sam some rent when she

105

got her first paycheck, but it wouldn't be market rate. That's why she was already planning on painting the living room during her free weekends, and why she'd written up a schedule of repairs for the kitchen and bathrooms.

She owed Sam a lot. They all did.

"I have some work to do," she told Josh. "You can carry on with the puzzle until eight, then you need to shower and get into your pjs, okay? If you do that, we'll read some Harry Potter together."

"Sure," Josh said. "It's a deal."

Sam looked up at her again, his grizzled face pulled into a frown. "Are they working you too hard already? It's only your first day."

"Says the guy who only takes one day off a week."

Sam shrugged. "Yeah, but I own the business. Your extra work is lining somebody else's pockets."

"I want to make a good impression," she told him lightly. "And I enjoy working. I always have." She'd spent the afternoon in a conference room with Nathan and Eliana, talking about a secret project they were working on with Eliana's other son in Scotland. They were creating an international blend, with whiskey from four different distilleries across the world, and had tasked Mia with creating a marketing plan for the new product.

"We've always outsourced our marketing before," Eliana had told her. "But Nathan and Daniel persuaded me that we need a dedicated resource. That's where you come in. You'll work on our other brands, too, but I want this to be your top priority."

It was exciting, and scary, and Mia knew this was her chance to make an impression. If the Carters liked her work, then her job would be safe, which would mean she could start paying her way and even saving for the boys' futures.

In a few years, Michael would be going to college, and as

much as she hoped he'd at least get a partial scholarship, she needed to have enough money to help pay for everything else.

And then there was Josh. He didn't have a lot of expensive hobbies, but he did suffer from asthma. His prescriptions would be covered by this job, too, minus the copay.

For the first time in what felt like forever, she was starting to relax about money and their future. And it was good to be challenged professionally. She'd always been good at her job, even if she sometimes felt like a failure at everything else.

"Hey, Mom?" Josh said, as she went to head back to the kitchen, where her laptop was set up on the table.

"Yes, honey?"

"Noah's mom says she's going to call you about pee wee football. There's a place on Noah's team I could join."

"I thought you didn't like football." Okay, so maybe he wasn't as cheap as she thought.

"I didn't like it in Kansas City." Josh shrugged. "Dad would always shout at me when I dropped the ball. Noah says nobody shouts at his games." Josh gave her a hopeful look. "Noah's mom says she can take me to practice every Saturday. She says if it's okay with you, I can stay over on Fridays after the game at the high school."

"Oh. Okay." Mia nodded. "I'll call her."

"Two footballers in the family." Sam shook his head. "I worry for the cars of Hartson's Creek."

"Uncle Sam." Josh rolled his eyes. "I'm not going to hit any cars again. I'm gonna be a good footballer."

Mia bit down a smile and walked back into the kitchen, grabbing a soda from the refrigerator.

———

IT WAS ALMOST midnight by the time she climbed the stairs to her bedroom. Josh had been asleep for hours, and Michael had come home from a friend's house just before eight, muttering something about an assignment. She assumed he'd gone to bed at some point, because there was no light spilling out from under his door. Carefully, she peeked in, and sure enough he was curled beneath the covers, his face resting on his hands.

She'd just finished brushing her teeth when her phone vibrated.

I thought you were calling me later. It's later.

She didn't need to look at the number to know who it was. Shaking her head, she brushed her hair and pulled the covers back off her bed.

The screen had faded, but the memory of the text remained. If she didn't reply, he'd call her tomorrow.

It's late. And I was only going to call because I thought you had the invoice for the repairs. M

There, that should put an end to it. She climbed into bed, and turned the light out. A moment later, her screen lit up the room.

If I have the invoice you'll call me? C

She rolled her eyes. *Yes, if you want to discuss money, I'll call you. M*

I want to discuss money. C

Now? M

Yeah now. C

But it's almost midnight. I'm tired. M. That was a lie. She'd never felt so awake, thanks to the rush of blood around her veins.

Damn Cameron Hartson. Why did she react like this to him?

You're the one who didn't call when she was supposed to. I've been sitting by the phone all night. I feel rejected. C

She smiled in spite of herself. Dammit, he was flirting. And it felt nice, so nice, to be flirted with. Her finger hovered over the phone. Turn it off, or call him? For a moment it all hung in the balance. Then she pressed her finger on the screen.

———

"Hey." He answered the phone almost as soon as his screen lit up. Didn't want to give her a chance to disconnect. "You okay?"

"I'm good."

He smiled at the sound of her voice. Everything about her made his body tense up in the best of ways. He blamed it on his furlough from football. His mind was bored and his body was restless and she filled all the blanks where a ball used to be.

"How was your first day at work?" Keep it clean, Hartson. He leaned back on the sofa, propping his feet up on the coffee table made out of driftwood that had probably cost Tanner more than most people made in a month.

"You know what? It was great." Her voice lifted up with enthusiasm, and it made him smile. "Everybody was so lovely, and I have this amazing project to work on. I just need a few more hours in the day."

"I got a few if you want them."

She laughed. "If only it was that easy. I don't suppose you know anything about marketing?"

"I know how to look sultry in a magazine campaign to sell watches."

Another laugh. Each one felt like winning a game. "I bet you do. What watches were those again? Just so I can check out the competition."

"You're not selling watches," he reminded her. But damn, he liked it when she flirted back with him.

"No, but somebody in a marketing department or advertising company came up with it. They're my competition. The product is just the thing we play with. The ball, if you like. So give me a name, Hartson."

"Depuis."

She let out a whistle. "They're expensive."

"I got three if you want one. They do nothing other than sit in my top drawer. I don't even wear a watch." He imagined clipping the oversized silver strap around her delicate wrist, and damn if that didn't make him hard.

Everything about Mia Devlin made him want her.

"Sure. Just give me a twenty thousand dollar watch. Add it to the invoice for the car. I have a spare thirty thousand sitting around." She laughed. "And I'm not even going to mention the fact that you have sixty thousand dollars worth of jewelry sitting in a drawer. What else do you have? A Matisse in the closet? A Rolls Royce in the basement?"

It was his turn to laugh. "I always meant to do something with them. Then I thought I'd save them for my nephews, but they're still too little, so they're just waiting."

"You should put them in a deposit box at the bank or something. Anybody could steal them." She sounded concerned.

"Since I only have a cleaner come in, I think I'm safe there. Unless you're planning on putting on a catsuit and sneaking into my Boston apartment." And now he wanted to see her in a catsuit, dammit.

"I was thinking more about burglary. Or a home invasion. People know you're a football player, you're an easy target."

His voice lowered. "Are you worried about my safety, Mia? Because I don't know if you've seen me, but I'm two hundred and twenty pounds of brick wall. And I have a baseball bat under my bed and I know how to use it."

"You don't take a baseball bat to a gunfight. And you're not even in Boston. Please put them in a safety deposit box."

His chest tightened. When was the last time anybody worried about him? "Okay," he said softly. "I will. If it'll make you sleep easier at night."

"Thank you. Though I haven't been sleeping at all for the past few nights, so you don't need to worry about that."

"Why not?" Cam always slept like a log. Didn't matter what bed he was in, or which state for that matter. His head hit the pillow and he was out. The thought of not sleeping made him wince.

"Too much on my mind. My job, the boys, everything. I can't relax."

"I know how to help you with that." His voice was gritty. Low.

"I bet you do."

"Come here on Friday night. Let me give you some therapy. I promise I'll work you so hard you'll sleep for days."

"I can't." She sounded almost regretful. "I have the boys. Or Michael, at least."

"Then another day. You name the time, I'll be here." He wanted to see her naked. To kiss her everywhere until she was gasping. He wasn't lying about working her out. He had more energy than he knew what to do with.

And he wanted to use it on her.

"It's not a good idea, Cam." Her voice was soft. It curled around him like a blanket.

"Why not?"

"I told you. The kids. They don't deserve having their mom talked about in town. And I'm trying to build up a reputation at work. I don't want it to be for the wrong reasons."

"And if I promised you nobody would find out?"

"Somebody *always* finds out."

His lip quirked. "That's because people are stupid. Come just once." He laughed. "I mean, come *here* just once. I'll make sure you come plenty more times than once."

Her breath hitched. "Cam, I…"

"Don't answer now. Think about it. I'm gonna hang up and go to bed, because I'm not the kind of man who begs."

She didn't respond, but he could hear her breathing soft and low.

"Touch yourself tonight. Think about how good I'd feel inside you. I know I'll be thinking about that."

Her breath was heavier now.

"You still there?" he asked, though he knew she was.

"Yeah."

"Are you touching yourself?" Jesus, he was aching. It was his turn to feel breathless.

"Not yet."

Not yet. Which means she was planning to. If one of her laughs felt like winning a game, this admission felt like winning the damn Superbowl.

"Good night, Mia. Sleep tight." he said, adjusting himself because right now he could drill a hole through a rock. He needed a cold shower. *Stat.*

There was another long pause, then a sigh. "Good night, Cam."

CHAPTER THIRTEEN

"Okay, team, we're done for tonight." Coach Hawkins clapped his hands together. "Go home, get some food inside you, and I'll see you tomorrow after school."

Cam nodded at the defensive team, who'd been running drills with him. Sweat was dripping from his head – he'd never ask them to do anything he wouldn't do with them. "Good work," he told them. "Those tackles are getting better." They'd been working on creating turnovers from offensive running plays. It had been fun to play offense for a change, letting the team try to block his runs toward the end zone. Like them, he was exhausted now. He really needed to up his training.

Tomorrow he'd go running twice. If he couldn't keep up with a high school team, he was definitely losing it.

"Before you all go, I need a couple of volunteers," Coach called out at the team's retreating backs. "The local pee wee team is short a couple of coaches, and I thought it could be a chance to give back. You'll be needed Saturday mornings at nine. Anybody up for it?"

There were a few murmurs about Saturday jobs, and

wanting to sleep in, before one of the Varsity players put his hand up. "I guess I could help. My kid brother's on the team."

"Thanks, Leon." Coach gave him a wink. "One down, one to go. Come on, show a little spirit here. Coaching will be good for your play. You get to learn how to spot weaknesses and work with others on them. Plus it'll earn you points with me."

"I can do it. My brother's joining the team, too."

Cam turned to see Michael with his hand up. He'd been running drills with Cam, though avoided talking to him.

"We can go together," Leon said, slapping Michael on the back. Michael looked pleased to be noticed by the older player. "You're Josh's brother, right? Noah won't stop talking about him. I think he wants my mom to adopt him."

"She's welcome to him," Michael mumbled, and Leon laughed.

Coach nodded at them both."Great. I'll email you all the details. Okay, team, help me collect up the equipment and then hit the showers."

Half an hour later, Cam was walking across the parking lot when he heard somebody call out his name. He turned to see Michael running toward him, holding his hand up as though trying to get Cam to stop.

"Everything okay?" Cam asked, as Michael reached him, his breath coming in short spurts. Michael looked over his shoulder at Cam's dark blue Audi.

"You got your car back," he said, swallowing hard. "I guess that means you got the invoice, too."

"Yeah, I got it." He'd paid it, too.

Michael shifted his feet. "And you plan on sending it to my mom?"

No he wasn't. Cam wasn't *that* much of an asshole. "I don't think that's your concern."

"But it is. It wasn't my mom's fault your car was dented. I'm the one who should pay for it, not her."

"You got a spare eight thousand hanging around?" Cam had been pleasantly surprised at the cost. Two thousand less than he'd anticipated.

"Um, no?" Michael raked his fingers through his hair. "But maybe I can work it off or something. Make a payment plan with you. I'm hoping to get a weekend job as soon as I turn fifteen. Until then, I can do stuff like cut your lawn or tidy your yard or something. I do it for my uncle and he's happy with my work."

"You want to make a payment plan?" Cam repeated. "How long do you think it'll take you to repay eight thousand dollars?"

Blowing out a mouthful of air, Michael grimaced. "A while. But I'm a man of my word, sir. The money will come back to you."

Cam tipped his head to the side and stared at the boy. He'd been avoiding Cam ever since he'd started working with the team. It was understandable, as they hadn't gotten the best start after all, but he could still remember Mia's request to try to mend some bridges.

"Does your mom know about this?" Cam asked him.

"No. And I don't want her to. She'll only tell me not to worry about it, but that's a crock of sh—, I mean a load of trash, because she's the one who always worries about money."

"You shouldn't keep secrets from your mom."

Michael sighed. "I'm a teenage kid. That's practically my job. But seriously, she'd go ape on me, and I'm only trying to make her life a little easier. She works too hard and has too much to worry about already." He lifted his gaze to Cam's. "Please, can we work this out between us? Man to man?"

There was something in his voice that made Cam stop in

his tracks. He knew enough about what Michael had been through this year to understand why he wanted to take control of something. Anything. And he had a lot of time for a kid that wanted to repay his debts. As much as he didn't need the money, maybe Michael needed to feel like a man.

"What do I tell your mom when she asks for the invoice?" Not that he was ever planning on giving it to her. But if Michael had a good idea on how to stop her from going apeshit about it, he was all ears.

"I don't know." Michael screwed up his nose. "Maybe you can stall her for a while. Tell her you're still waiting for the final amount. Give me time to think about something better."

Cam bit down a smile. "If she finds out, it's your funeral."

"Yeah, I know. But it'll be more of a cremation. When my mom gets mad, it's like a nuclear explosion."

His smile was threatening to break through. Cam turned to his car and pressed on the fob, the locks unclicking instantly. "You heading home now?" he asked Michael.

"Yeah."

"You want a ride?" Cam inclined his head at the car.

Michael's eyes lit up, as he stared at the sparkling blue coupe. "Seriously?"

"I figure it's safer when you're *in* the car." Cam gave him a grin.

"Okay then." Michael rubbed his hands together. "Let's go."

IT HAD BEEN A GOOD DAY. Mia had spent the mornings in meetings with Scotland and Tokyo to discuss the new international blend campaign she'd be working on, then the afternoon doing more research and starting to sketch out some ideas. It would be weeks before the plan was good enough to present to the board, but it was progress, and it felt good.

Even better, the sun was shining, golden beams illuminating the changing leaves on the trees, their red and orange hues reminding her so much of fall as a child.

Turning the corner onto Ash Street, she immediately pressed the brake when she saw three people in the road. Josh was running toward her, a football in his hand. Turning, he threw it hard at Michael who was at the far end. But before he could catch it, another person intercepted it.

No, not another person. *Cam Hartson.*

Cam Hartson was playing ball with her kids.

It felt like two worlds were colliding. Memories of her late night conversation with Cam rushed into her brain. His low, sexy voice, with his intriguing offer. The way her body responded to his words.

And now he was here with her children.

"Mom!" Josh called out, his face lighting up when he spotted her car. He ran toward her, his face bright red with exertion. She lowered her window, and he leaned on the sill, his breath catching.

"Mikey's gonna help coach my pee wee team, and Cam's been running drills with us. How cool is that?"

She forced a smile on her lips. "Way cool."

"Wanna come and play?" Josh asked her.

Glancing down at her skirt and heels, Mia shook her head. "I need to get dinner started. And you boys need to come in and do your homework."

"Oh mom." Josh sighed. "I need to practice. Cam says that all games are won in training."

"Yeah, well even Cam had to do his homework when he was a kid. Let me park, and I'll watch you throw a couple."

"Yes!" Josh did a fist bump, and Mia tried not to laugh, because he looked so damn happy.

Climbing out of her car after she'd parked it in the driveway, Mia looked over to where Michael and Cam were standing. They were talking about something, and Michael laughed and slapped Cam's back.

When had they become best friends?

"Hey, Mikey, I'm gonna throw the ball again. Mom, are you watching?"

"Yes, honey, I'm watching. Five more minutes and it's time to come in."

"Okay." Josh sighed, then looked over his shoulder at Michael. "I'm gonna run," he told his brother. "Yell at me when you throw. And then I'll throw it back to Cam."

Sitting down on the top step of the stoop, Mia kicked her high heels off, and watched her son as he ran down the street. She'd tell him off for playing in the road, except she was the only one who ever drove down here. Michael yelled and threw the ball, and Josh kept running until it landed in his hands.

And then she made the mistake of looking at Cam Hartson, and her heart started racing.

He was staring right back at her, his eyes narrowed, his mouth slightly parted. Everything about that look made her shiver.

Come here just once. I'll make sure you come plenty more times.

She'd been thinking about those words ever since he said them. Late at night, when she still couldn't sleep. At work when her mind drifted.

And now, when she was feeling angry because he shouldn't be here with her kids.

"Okay," she shouted, when the five minutes were up. "It's time to come in."

"Oh, Mom…"

"I mean it, Josh. Go inside, wash up, and get your school work out on the kitchen table. You too, Michael."

"You want me to do my homework, too?" Cam asked, a stupid lopsided smile pulling at his lips.

"Nope. You can stay out here." She put a mom-voice on, ignoring his smirk. "I want to talk to you."

Michael shot her a look. The kind of look he used to shoot her when he was a tween and she'd ruffle his hair in front of his friends. "Mom, I asked Cam to come play football."

"It's okay." She forced a smile on her face. "Just go inside."

Josh walked up the steps, the football still grasped between his hands. "Did I do good, Cam?" he asked, glancing over his shoulder.

"You did great, kiddo. You're gonna knock them dead on Saturday. Just remember what I said, eyes on the ball. Nowhere else."

Josh nodded, his face serious. "Got it."

"Thanks for the ride," Michael mumbled, following Josh through the front door. "Sorry about my mom."

Mia closed the door behind him, then turned to face Cam. He was leaning on one of the wooden struts holding up the porch roof. His eyes were still narrowed, his gaze set on her.

"Hi," he said, giving her a lazy smile.

She didn't smile back. "Let's talk around the side. That way Michael and Josh won't hear us." She walked down the steps, her arm brushing against his, then followed the path to the side of the Victorian house. When she was around the corner, she stopped, turning to see Cam right behind her.

It was an effort not to jump at his proximity.

"Are you going to tell me off?" he asked, that stupid sexy smile still playing around his lips. "Because you need to know, it'll turn me on."

She put her hands on her hips. "Is this a game to you?"

The smile slid from his mouth. "Is what a game?"

She gestured at herself then him. "This. Us. Flirting with me then playing with my kids behind my back. What are you trying to achieve?"

His eyes flickered to her lips. "What makes you think I'm trying to achieve anything? I gave Michael a ride home from football practice, and Josh was dropped off at the same time. He was so excited about Michael being his coach that he asked for us to practice with him. That's what we were doing when you got home." He lifted an eyebrow. "I'm not trying to corrupt your kids. We were just having fun."

Her chest was so tight it was hard to breathe. Of course he wasn't doing anything underhanded. "I'm sorry," she said, her voice thin. "I'm just…" She exhaled. "So confused."

"About what? Throwing a football." He gave her another smile. It shot right through her.

Pressing her lips together, she shook her head. "No, the football's the easy part. It's life that's harder. The last time I talked with you, we were talking about sex. And now you're with my boys. The two don't mix. Not ever. Not in my family."

She leaned her head back against the stuccoed wall, and Cam cupped her face with his warm, strong palm. "Mia, there's nothing going on. What you see is what you get. Yes, I want you. I've made no attempt to hide that. But I'm also Michael's coach and you asked me to build some bridges with him. So here I am, building bridges."

"I'm an asshole." Mia shook her head. "God knows why you'd want a mess like me."

"Because you're fucking beautiful." His words echoed through her ears. "And sexy, and funny, and you make me hard, especially when you're angry with me." He gave her a crooked smile. "I want you because I know I can make you feel so damn good you won't stop thinking about me for days. And I know you want me, too."

Her lips parted, her eyes shadowed as she stared up at him. Her cheeks were stained pink. "It doesn't matter what I want. This can never happen. I'm not the woman you need in your life."

"I'm not asking you to marry me. I'm offering nothing more than a few hours together to make you feel good. To make us *both* feel good. Don't tell me you haven't thought about our kiss. The way our bodies moved together without us even thinking about it." He curled his fingers around her neck, the rough pads caressing her skin. "Don't tell me you haven't imagined me inside you."

Her body clenched at the thought. "Stop it." She didn't sound convincing.

"I said it before. There's something here. Either we can keep fighting it and end up like this every time, or you can come to my place and we'll try to douse this damn flame together." He brushed his lips against her jaw, his breath warm and tantalizing. "Let me be your rehab guy. Let me make you come so hard you forget your name."

He pressed his body against hers, so hard and strong. She blinked, trying to focus, yet finding it impossible. His lips slid away from her jaw, his tongue flicking at her ear, then he pressed his mouth against the corner of hers.

"Say no and I'll walk away," he murmured, those teasing lips still hovering against hers.

"Cam, I…"

"Say it." He curled his hand around her waist.

"It won't work. The boys… I can't just disappear one night."

"Michael's coaching on Saturday morning. Come over then." He brushed his lips against hers, so softly she could barely feel it. But her body responded anyway.

"You want to have sex on Saturday morning?"

He grinned against her skin, his eyes flickering up to hers. "I believe it's legal in all fifty states."

"What happened to dinner?" she asked him. "To seduction, to wine, to soft touches and long glances?"

"I'll take you to dinner," he murmured. "Just say the word. You're the one who doesn't want anybody to know about us. I'd happily parade naked with you around town." He pressed his cheek to hers. It was rough and warm.

All she knew was that she liked the way he was holding her. As though he never wanted to let go. Loved the way she could feel his desire pressing against her. He was so tall, so broad, so muscled. He could dominate her if he wanted to.

Did she want him to? The catch in her breath told her she did.

"Saturday…"

He gave her a half smile. "Yeah."

"And then? What happens after that?"

He ran his thumb along her bottom lip. "I don't know," he told her. "Does it matter? I want you, you want me. And on Saturday we both get what we want."

She shouldn't want him. And she definitely shouldn't do this. Yet there was an inevitability to it. It started from the moment they met. She could fight it, try to push it away and forget all about Cam Hartson. But she'd been trying to do that for weeks, and all she'd had were sleepless nights.

"Nobody has to know," she whispered, her hand clutching at his arm. She could feel the hard steel of his bicep flex as he held her.

"It's nobody's business but ours. I'm not going to tell anybody, and I'm pretty sure you won't either."

Running the tip of her tongue along her bottom lip, she lifted her gaze to his. Among the darkness and desire, she could see the truth there. He wasn't playing games. He wasn't offering her something he couldn't give.

He wanted to give into his desire. The same way she wanted to submit to hers. It was so simple.

And so damn complicated.

"Okay," she breathed, and a huge smile lit up his face.

"Okay?" he repeated.

"Yeah. I'll see you on Saturday."

He pushed himself off the wall, and the sudden rushing of air between them sent a shiver down her spine. "Until Saturday, then."

Two tiny lines formed between her brows. "Aren't you going to kiss me?" Because right now she really needed to feel him again. When his body was against hers everything seemed so easy.

"Nope." He shook his head, and his eyes crinkled as he stared down at her. "I'm going to leave you wanting. If you want a kiss, be at my place by eight-thirty on Saturday."

He turned on his heel and strode easily back down the path. Mia watched him, her mouth dry, her heart galloping like it was trying to win the Kentucky Derby.

Saturday. It was way too soon and too far away.

She had no idea how she'd make it through until then.

CHAPTER FOURTEEN

"Hey, Mia, over here!" a female voice called out as she walked up the steps of the bleachers. Josh had already run off to sit with Noah – his overnight bag already safely stowed in Noah's mom's car, along with his clothes for practice in the morning.

Mia looked up to see Becca Hartson waving madly at her from a bench in the middle of the stand. She was surrounded by her family. Mia recognized Cam's twin, of course, and his gorgeous wife with a baby strapped to her chest, his head lolling as he slept. And everybody knew who Gray Hartson, their older brother was. Next to him was a pretty woman with a brunette pony tail who was swapping small children with the rock star. Maddie? Yeah, that was her name.

Next to Gray, was the youngest brother. Mia couldn't quite remember his name, though she knew Becca had introduced him at church that Sunday.

"Tanner, stop hogging the damn popcorn," Gray said, grabbing the bucket from him.

Well that solved her problem.

"Hi." She shot Becca a smile as she came level with the bench they were all sitting on.

"Come and sit with me." Becca tapped the bench next to her. "Where's your son? Josh, is it?"

"He's sitting with a friend. And Michael is down there with the team."

"So you're on your own." Becca's smile was huge. "Then you *have* to sit with us. You remember everybody, right?"

"Yeah." Mia gave them a shy wave. "Hi."

"Hey!" Logan's wife said, grinning over the top of her baby's head. "It's good to see you again."

"Likewise." Putting her purse between her feet, Mia pulled her hair out of her hoodie. "What are you guys doing here?" she asked Becca, who was slurping from a huge cup of soda. "I thought you went to that Friday Night Chairs thing."

"We thought we'd come and support Cam. And it's kind of fun to watch Friday night football. I feel like I'm a kid again, watching my brothers get kicked to pieces on the field." She wiggled her eyebrows at Mia. "I had to get my fun vicariously in those days."

Mia bit down a grin as Logan and Gray hurled friendly abuse at her. They were such a nice family. It made her feel warm to watch them.

"Look, there's Cam," Becca said to her brothers. She stood up and waved like crazy. Cam looked up at his sister, lifting a large hand to wave back at her.

And then he spotted Mia sitting on the bench.

His head tipped to the side, as he gave her a long, speculative look. Then his gaze dipped, his eyes hooded, before he noticed the rest of his family sitting there. He shook his head, a smile ghosting his lips as one of the boys standing at the sideline whispered something in his ear.

He grabbed his phone from his pocket and quickly tapped his fingers on the screen.

The next moment, Mia's phone vibrated in her pocket. Her breath caught, because she knew exactly who had messaged her. A sideways glance at Becca told her the younger woman was too busy playing with one of her nephews to notice Mia surreptitiously pulling her phone from her pocket to glance at the screen.

Look at you sitting on the bench surrounded by my family. What are you trying to achieve? C xx

She bit down a grin at him reflecting her words from the other day back at her. When she glanced back down at the field, he was still looking up at her.

I figured I should get to know them. You are going to ask me to marry you after we have sex, right? M

Cam laughed out loud, and looked back up at her. Damn, he was hot as hell. Wearing a pair of dark training pants and a grey sports top, she could see the outline of his chest through the elastane fabric. His shoulders looked broader than ever, his arm muscles glistening in the glow of the floodlights.

Tomorrow she'd feel that body pressed against hers.

She shifted in her seat, and turned to Becca who had one of Gray's children sitting on her lap, pointing at the field as the Eagles ran out onto the turf.

"Is your boy one of them?" Becca asked her. "I can't tell when they're wearing their helmets."

"You could never tell which ones we were either," Logan pointed out. "No matter how many times we told you our numbers."

"To be fair, I couldn't tell the difference between you when you were in your normal clothes, let alone your football gear." Becca shrugged. "It's not my fault you two are so alike."

"All four of them are alike," Maddie said, smiling up at

Gray. "It's scary. When I talk to any of the brothers on the phone I can never tell who it is."

"Of course you can." Tanner grinned. "I'm the friendly one. Logan's the talkative one and Cam just grunts."

Mia stole a look down at the sideline again. Cam was talking to one of the players, demonstrating some kind of move. His shoulder muscles rippled as he moved his arm to mimic a throw. The player nodded, his face set with concentration.

"I'm so glad he's home," Becca said, noticing Mia watching the field. "It's like our family is back together."

"Don't get too used to it," Logan told her. "He's determined to get back to football one way or another."

"Do you think he'll play again?" Becca asked.

"I've told him he should get into coaching. Look at him down there." Logan pointed at Cam. "He's a natural. He still needs to accept that his playing days are over."

"He needs to stay here with us," Becca said, shaking her head.

"Not gonna happen. Unless an NFL team decides to move to Hartson's Creek." Logan shrugged. "Can't you be happy with having the rest of us here?"

"I want *all* of my brothers nearby. Call me greedy if you like."

Logan gave her a gentle smile. "Yeah, well I'd like him to be around more, too."

Mia swallowed hard, scanning the group of boys for Michael. He was talking to one of the players, then Cam walked over and Michael looked up at him with a grin. Mia's stomach contracted as Cam ruffled her son's hair.

So he wasn't staying around very long. That was good, wasn't it?

I'm not asking you to marry me. I'm offering a few hours together to make you feel good.

His words from the other day echoed around her head. He wasn't making promises, and she was glad about that. In the eyes of the law, she was still a married woman, after all.

Sure, her divorce was progressing, but if you wanted to get technical, there it was.

This moment felt like being on a precipice. She wanted to throw herself forward and take a leap in the dark. She was still young, even if some days her body ached from running on fumes. She still had desires, the kind that kept her awake at night, remembering Cam's hot stare as he whispered against her lips.

And she wanted him. That was the truth. She wanted to know she was still desirable after fifteen years of marriage and two kids. That a man as sensual and attractive as Cameron Hartson wanted to have sex with her. From Becca's conversation with her brothers, there was no possibility of this becoming anything more than one morning together.

They lived two very different lives. There was no chance of either of them getting attached.

"That's Michael, right?" Becca leaned in, following Mia's gaze.

"Yeah."

"He and Cam look like they're getting along well. That's nice."

Mia nodded, but said nothing. She could compartmentalize the two different sides of him. Cam the coach who dealt with Michael was different to the Cam who'd pressed his body against hers and left her in no doubt about how much he desired her.

Then the PA system crackled, and the announcer came on, his voice blasting across the field as he called out the names of the teams. Mia sat back and let out a long, deep exhale.

She needed to stop thinking about him, or she'd never have the guts to turn up at his place tomorrow morning.

And that would be something she'd regret forever.

———

It was right after eight-thirty when she rapped her knuckles on Cam's door the next morning. There was something so deliciously wrong about presenting herself on his doorstep while the sun was rising in the sky.

And yet it sent shivers down her spine. She wasn't hurting anybody, she wasn't doing anything wrong.

She was doing something for herself for the first time in forever.

Just once. That was all. Then she'd be able to live her life without fear of sleeping with a new man after all those years as a married woman. It was rehab, pure and simple.

People went for physical therapy sessions and back massages on Saturday mornings. This was no different, right?

The door opened. Cam stood in the hallway, a pair of low-slung grey sweats clinging to his hips, his hair wet from what must have been a shower, and no top to be seen. Just a deliciously rippled chest that made her realize exactly how mismatched they were.

"That's not fair," she told him. "If I'd have known we were starting like this I would've knocked on your door in just lingerie."

He laughed. "Next time you can do it naked."

"There is no next time, remember?" she said, stepping into his house as he held the door open for her. "This is a one time rehab session."

He looked at her through thick lashes. "There's nothing one off about what I'm about to do to you." He closed the door behind her. "Okay, you can strip here. Leave your clothes by the front door."

Her eyes widened. "Now?"

This time his laughter filled the hallway. "I'm kidding. Keep your clothes on for a while longer. I've made some coffee." He walked toward the kitchen, inclining his head for her to follow. "To be honest, I wasn't sure you'd turn up."

"Really? You doubt your prowess that much?"

He looked over his shoulder at her. "You're a smartass, you know that?"

"There's nothing smart about me being here."

He stopped in the kitchen doorway, his body almost filling the frame. Mia went to squeeze past him, but he hooked his arm around her waist and pulled her against him. The warmth of his bare chest radiated through her t-shirt, his strong, thick arms circling her tightly.

"Hey," he whispered, pressing his lips against her brow. "I'm glad you came."

Mia lifted her head up, a smile ghosting her lips. "Did you mention coffee?"

"It's coming right up. Sit down over there." He inclined his head toward the breakfast bar. The infamous location of last week's kiss. She did as she was told, sliding onto a stool and leaning her chin in her hands as she watched him froth the milk and pour it into two small cups.

She didn't really need the caffeine. She'd been up with the birds, long before Michael left at the crack of dawn to meet Leon, Noah, and Josh for practice. She'd showered, shaved, and taken way too long looking at the parts of her nobody had seen – let alone touched – in a long while.

Would he expect her to be fully bare? Or just trimmed? What did supermodels do?

Of course they'd be bare. Hair was probably the enemy in

their world. But she didn't have time to do that. Not unless she'd used a razor.

And there was only one thing less sexy than hair down there, and that was cuts all over her soft skin.

Nope. He was going to have to cope with a little hair. That's all there was to it.

She'd stepped out of the shower and taken a look at herself in the old mirror that hung over the basin. She was pretty good from the chest up. Her breasts weren't too saggy, and her arms were toned thanks to all the yoga she used to do when she had the time and money back in Kansas City.

Below was a little trickier. She had stretchmarks, of course, and loose skin where her body had never quite gotten back to normal after two pregnancies with big babies. Even if she sucked in, that skin was still there.

The thought of him seeing her naked made her feel sick. The last time a guy saw her fully bare for the first time she'd been eighteen, with a body she wished she'd appreciated at the time.

Now she was almost double that age. And right now she felt it. Cam was used to supermodels. How the hell could she compete with that?

She should just go home and hide before she embarrassed herself.

"What are you thinking about?" Cam asked, leaning across the breakfast counter, his elbows resting on the granite surface.

"I'm thinking I'm way too old to be a booty call on a Saturday morning, when I should be doing laundry or something."

He laughed. "You can do my laundry if you'd like. I'll tell you what, we'll carry it down together and I'll bend you over the machine while it washes."

An image of Cam's muscled body pressed against her

back flashed into her head. "You can try all you like to make laundry sexy, but I'm not buying it."

He shrugged, looking amused. "I was only trying to kill two birds with one stone. And if you want my opinion, there's nothing sexier than being inside a woman at a time when everybody else is going about their daily lives. I've always been a morning sex kind of guy."

"I can tell you've never had kids."

Another laugh. "I guess they can ruin the mood. But there are no kids here now."

No, there weren't. It was just the two of them, and this lingering promise between them.

"Come here," he said softly, tipping his head to look at her.

Mia swallowed hard. "Now?"

"Yeah." His voice was honey sweet. Damn, it did things to her. She walked around the counter to where he was standing. He immediately turned her around until her waist was pressing into the breakfast bar, his firm body hot against her back. "You're so tense," he said, his breath warm against her ear. He started to massage her shoulders, his fingers strong and firm. She groaned at how good it felt. "You need to relax. There's nothing to be scared of. We're two adults doing what we want to do. It's nobody else's business." He circled a finger to release a knot in her muscle.

Mia groaned. "If you keep doing that, I think I'm going to come anyway."

Cam chuckled, the air tickling her neck. "Come upstairs with me."

She looked down at the counter, her eyes tracing the patterns in the stone. This was it. There was still time to leave. To do the damn laundry waiting for her at home or the grocery shopping or whatever else she really should be doing right now.

But she didn't want to. She wanted to be here. Wanted to know what it felt like to be with another man. It was a milestone she needed to pass on her way to the new Mia. The kick-ass independent woman who took care of herself and her family.

He was holding his hand out to her. She slid her palm against his, feeling the roughness, the callouses, and the strength as his fingers curled around her. He pulled until her body was pressed against his. "Come on," he said, his lips barely brushing against hers. "It's time for a little therapy."

CHAPTER FIFTEEN

*H*is bedroom was bigger than the entire ground floor of her old place in Kansas City. The shining light oak floor was covered with huge white rugs, which matched the walls and the bedding, along with the full size leather sofa and easy chairs at the far end of the room.

"This feels like walking into heaven," Mia said, shaking her head as she looked around. "Why is everything so white?"

Cam shrugged. "Not my décor. But it's nice and easy on the eye. Though every time I take my clothes off and throw them on the floor I feel like I'm making things a mess."

"Imagine what it'll feel like with my clothes on the floor," she teased.

"Dirty," he said, a grin pulling his lips. "Really dirty."

At least his bed looked normal. *Big,* but normal. He'd made an attempt to tidy the covers, but it was a guy kind of attempt. She could see some cushions and a throw folded over the back of the sofa. No doubt they were supposed to be on the bed, making it the main feature of the room.

"You wanna take a shower?" Cam asked her.

Mia looked up at him. "Now?"

His lip quirked up. "Why not?"

"You just took one, didn't you? Your hair's still damp." Her brows pinched together. "Are you worried that I'm dirty? I showered this morning."

He traced his finger down her spine. "Relax. I don't think you're dirty. I just thought it might make things easier. You can close your eyes, let the hot water soothe your muscles. Get used to me being with you." He shrugged. "Just an idea."

Internally rolling her eyes at herself, Mia nodded. "A shower sounds good."

His bathroom was as impressive as the bedroom. Pale marble tiles covered the walls and floor. A large tub was on the left side, and on the right was a double sink, with a huge mirror above it, surrounded by lights that would make putting make up on a cinch.

But it was the shower that she was focused on. The tray was sunk into the marble floor, a glass screen stretching the length of the wall with an opening at the end to walk into.

Naked.

With wide eyes she looked up at him, then back to the vast shower.

Cam traced her bottom lip with his index finger. "Don't be scared."

She swallowed hard. "It's just been… a really long time since I've had sex."

He slid his finger to her jaw. "How long?"

"I can't even remember."

"This year?"

She shook her head.

"Last?"

"Possibly."

His gaze dipped to her neck, as he traced a line down to her chest. "So I'm the first man to touch you this year."

"Yeah." Her breath caught as he pressed his palm against

the top of her chest, his fingers splaying out as they pushed under the neck of her t-shirt.

"That's fucking hot."

"It is?"

He gave her a lopsided smile. "Every man's dream. To be the one to reawaken you." Circling his hands around her waist, he lifted her onto the marble counter where the basins were inlaid. Then he pushed himself against her, leaving her in no doubt as to how hot he found it. Her body clenched at the sensation of his hard thickness pressing exactly where she needed it.

Curling his free hand around the hem of her t-shirt, he looked down at her with needy eyes. "Can I take this off."

She nodded, and he tugged at the white cotton until it reached her arms. She lifted them to help him, feeling the neckline scrape her hair as the t-shirt came off.

He threw it on the ground and looked at her body, taking her in with a hot stare. "Damn, you're beautiful." He cupped her breasts through the lace of her bra, his hands so big they spanned the entirety of them. The warm pressure made her nipples peak against his palms.

Lowering his head, he pressed an open mouthed kiss against her shoulder, and rolled his hips, his erection so hard. Sliding his lips down her sternum, he kissed the swell of each breast, then reached around her to unfasten her bra.

When it was off, he held the weight of her breasts in his hands, his thumbs softly brushing against her nipples as he swallowed hard. "Fucking gorgeous," he said, sucking one of them between his lips, grazing it with his teeth, then soothing it with his tongue.

Mia arched her back, letting out a soft cry. He wasn't gentle. But then she didn't want him to be. They weren't going to be making love. They'd be having sex.

Hard, dirty morning sex.

When he released her nipple, his eyes were dark as he gazed up at her. Then he curled his hand around her neck and kissed her lips with a hungry need. She kissed him back, her fingers raking through his short hair, as desire lit up her body like a night parade. This time it was her rolling her hips, seeking the friction only he could give her. He pinched her nipple between his thumb and forefinger, pleasure and pain mixing together until she was breathless with longing.

"You need to get in the shower," Cam told her, his voice gritty. "Before I take you on the damn sink." He pulled back, blowing out a mouthful of air as he adjusted himself, wincing as if it was painful. "Take the rest of your clothes off."

"Now?" She was still giddy from his touch.

"Yeah." He nodded.

With her eyes on his, she unbuttoned her jeans, shimmying them down her hips and legs until they were bunched on the floor. Stepping out of them, she hooked her fingers into her lace panties and a realization washed over her.

She wasn't afraid anymore. She felt strong. Powerful. Enough to make a man like Cam Hartson palm himself through his sweats as he watched her strip. Running her tongue along her bottom lip, she flipped her long, blonde hair over her shoulder, then turned and looked at him with a smile. "Are you coming?"

"I will be."

He opened the bathroom drawer and grabbed a packet of condoms, pulling one out and placing it on the counter, then pulled his sweats down. He was hard and thick, and she tried not to stare at him too long.

"Press the button on the wall," Cam told her, as she walked toward the shower. "Then stand under the spray. I want to watch you."

She did as he told her, walking across the marble tiles and into the shower. It came on as soon as she pressed the button, steam radiating from the shower head as a cascade of hot water fell onto the floor. Mia moved under flow, feeling the spray hard against her skin, wetting her hair, her body, warming her up.

"Touch your breasts."

She looked up at him. He was still standing outside the shower. When she hesitated, he nodded. "Touch them like you'd touch them if I wasn't here. To give yourself pleasure."

She curled her hands around them, pulling her nipples between her fingers, and a pulse of pleasure shot down between her legs. Cam walked into the shower and lowered his head to kiss her again. She gasped at the sensation of his wet, naked body against hers.

His mouth set her pulse racing. Slowly, he slid a single finger between her legs, until it was barely touching where she needed him the most. Mia let out a gasp, as he traced a lazy circle around her, making her body clench with need.

Sliding his finger inside her, he curled it, searching for her pleasure points, his lips smiling against hers when he found it and she let out a moan. He circled inside her, his thumb teasing her until her mind was a swirl of pleasure and need. His kisses were hot, his movements rhythmic, and her body felt like it was burning from the inside out, water cascading over them as he brought her to the peak.

"Oh god, I'm going to…"

The words barely escaped her lips before he was pulling his finger out of her.

"Not until I'm inside you," he whispered, pressing his lips to hers once more. He reached through the gap at the end of the shower, grabbing the condom and rolling it on. Then he was lifting her, turning their bodies until her back was against the tiles, his sheathed erection sliding against her wetness as the shower drenched them both.

She was shocked at how easily he held her. As though she

weighed nothing at all. But then she looked at the corded muscles in his arms, and remembered that he was an athlete, trained to peak performance.

And damn, what a performance it was.

"You ready?" he asked, his gaze capturing hers. Mia let her head fall back against the tiles as he pulled her tighter against him, tucking her curves into his hard contours. He was there, the thick head of him pressing against her. She could feel as they connected, feel herself open up to him, and the hard ridged thickness of him as he slowly slid inside.

His eyes didn't waver from hers. She felt captive in his gaze. She felt full, so full, that it took a moment for her to adjust.

Then he pulled back and slid forward again, and warmth pooled at the pit of her belly, making her thigh muscles tense, and her body clench around him. Cam let out a growl, then rolled his hips again, moving in a steady rhythm that set her on fire.

She could feel it building inside her. That teasing, aching delight that made her breath shorten and her back arch. She grasped tightly onto his shoulders, fingers digging into his warm skin, and he kissed her again, his tongue sliding against hers as he sent her soaring.

She was on the edge, barely holding on.

"So good," he rasped, taking her harder and faster against the wall. Then she felt it. The storm breaking inside of her, as she shattered into tiny pieces, her body clenching around him.

He was the only thing holding her up, as her muscles loosened into a honeyed mess. He kissed her hard, swallowing her cries, his thrusts relentless until he let out a low groan as he emptied inside her.

She expected him to collapse with her on the floor, or pull out and walk away, but instead he pinned her against the wall, his eyes drilling into hers. For a moment they were silent, enough for her to hear the rush of blood through her ears as the pleasure continued to pulse through her.

"You okay?" he asked softly, brushing wet strands of hair from her face.

She nodded, afraid if she actually said anything she might start crying. Not because she'd hated it, but because it had been *so* good. Being held by this man was the first time in forever she'd felt safe. Not alone.

Sliding his nose against hers, he kissed her again. This time softly, slowly, as though he had all the time in the world. Her throat felt thick as she kissed him back, using the moment to blink back the tears before they started.

Tightening his arms around her, he lifted her from the wall and gently set her on her feet. "Come on, let's go to bed."

CHAPTER SIXTEEN

"Iknew it! I read somewhere about athletes making the best kind of lovers. They have stamina, energy, and they always want to win." Joanna sighed. "I'm so jealous I could spit."

Mia put the phone a little closer to her ear, even though she was alone in her room and the boys should be fast asleep by now. But Joanna had a loud voice, and she didn't want to take the chance that they'd be overheard.

"So what happened after the shower?" Joanna asked. "You can't leave me hanging."

"That's what *I* said." Mia bit down a grin.

Joanna giggled. "I've never been with a guy strong enough to hold me up for that long. I don't suppose you can introduce me to his teammates."

"Your boyfriend might have something to say about that," Mia pointed out. "And anyway, I haven't met any of his teammates. And I'm not likely to. This was a one time thing, remember? Get under him to get over the separation."

"Ah, but you didn't get under him." Jo paused. "Or did

you? What happened next? Come on, I'm living vicariously through you."

"He carried me back to his bed, and we made out for a while. Then he… ah… went down on me." And damn if her face didn't flush with that memory. Cam Hartson had more than football skills. "After that, I had to leave to meet the boys at the field." Mia leaned her head back on the bedframe. "Oh, he did dry my hair for me. I couldn't turn up at pee wee practice with wet hair in October. I was going to just towel dry it, but he made me sit on a chair and he dried it for me." She swallowed hard, remembering how gentle his fingers were as he aimed the dryer at her long hair. How good they'd felt as he raked them against her scalp. It had felt strangely intimate – more intimate than the act of sex.

And yeah, she'd liked it a bit too much.

"He dried your hair?" Jo's voice was full of disbelief. "Seriously? And now I'm swooning. Do you think he has a thing about hair? Not that yours isn't gorgeous, but no guy's ever done something like that for me."

"I think I did something to my shoulder when we were in the shower," Mia confessed. "When I lifted the dryer up my muscles did a weird ping and I groaned a little." Or a lot. She never was great with pain. "So he took it from me and told me to hold still."

"Have you heard from him since?"

"Just a text this evening to ask how my shoulder was." Today had been too busy to even think about him. "After practice, we went out to lunch with Josh's friend's family, and then they insisted on taking us to the local farm that's just opened their pumpkin patch. Even Michael enjoyed it, I think. They have an older son, too. A junior at Michael's high school, and the two of them get along pretty well. Which meant fitting all our chores into about two hours this evening."

"So the boys are settling in. That must be a relief."

Mia blew out a mouthful of air. "You have no idea how much. I've been wondering if I made the right decision coming here, but today it really feels like I have."

"That's because you got *some*."

"Stop it." Mia laughed. "It has nothing to do with that." Okay, maybe it had a little something to do with her good mood. She had a good time with Cam this morning, and from the way he kissed her before she left, he did, too.

There were no regrets, and she was determined not to second guess herself. She'd done that for too long. As he'd said, they were two single adults having sex. It was nobody's business but theirs.

And it was over. Done. She'd gotten back on the horse and she knew her body still worked. If one day she went on a date, maybe she'd have that extra bit of confidence.

"So what did you say when he texted you?" Joanna wasn't giving up.

"I haven't replied. I haven't had time."

"Don't bullshit me. You always reply to messages. Even when I send you stupid memes of cats licking their own genetalia. The fact you haven't replied to him tells me volumes."

"It tells you I'm not interested in anything long term with him. It was a polite enquiry. He probably doesn't even expect a reply."

"Mmhmm."

Mia shook her head. "You know I hate it when you do that. It reminds me of Grandma Maisie. She used to sound exactly like that when I told her I hadn't stolen the last cookie from the jar."

"Yeah, well Grandma Maisie would be saying the same thing as me. You can lie to yourself but don't lie to me. If you'd have said you replied to tell him your shoulder was feeling better, I'd have known you weren't interested in anything more. But the fact you didn't reply… girl, you need to ask yourself why you're not following the Mia Devlin rulebook of polite texting etiquette. But don't bother telling me, because I already know the answer."

"Which is?" Mia didn't know why she was playing the game with Jo. But they'd been so close for as long as she could remember. More like sisters than cousins.

"That you want more of that big footballer d—"

"Okay! I get it. And in another life, sure I'd like to see him again. He's funny, sweet, and great in the shower." Not to mention his skills out of the shower. "But not in this life. I'm too busy with work and the boys to think about a relationship with anybody. And he's leaving town soon. I'd rather not risk my children's happiness for a booty call. Not after all they've been through."

Joanna sighed. "Ah, but what a waste. If I lived any closer I'd be jumping on the guy like a shot."

The sound of flushing came from the bathroom. One of the boys must have gotten up to use it. "I have to go," Mia whispered. "I'll talk to you soon, okay?"

"Okay. Take it easy, sweets. Rest that shoulder up."

"I will."

When she ended the call, Mia stared at the fading screen, her brows knitting together as she thought about Cam's message. Her cousin was right, it *was* rude not to reply. If she was a suave, sophisticated woman of the world, she'd reply without a second thought. She was going to see him every Friday at football, after all.

The shoulder is still a little achy. I'm thinking of suing you for $10,000. Do you have good insurance? ;) M xx

She swallowed as she saw two green ticks appear.

This can happen in rehab sessions. Once sometimes isn't

enough. I'll book you in again for next Saturday morning. See if I can iron out some kinks. C xx

She stared at his words for a moment, frowning at the way her heart leapt at the offer of another meeting. No, not a meeting. A sex session. She might as well be honest with herself about what it was.

Her phone started to buzz. His name lit up the screen as she swiped to accept, lifting her phone back to her ear.

"Hey. Is your shoulder really hurting?"

Her lips curled up. It was nice that somebody cared. "It's not that bad. Just twinges when I roll it backward. I think my days of pretending to be a windmill are over."

Cam laughed. "You need to do some cold compresses. Do you have an ice pack in the house?"

"I think so. My son plays football, remember?" She had a whole first aid kit full of things to mend his scrapes and bumps. Plus Josh wasn't exactly Mr. Graceful. "I just can't remember if I put it in the freezer when we got here, or if it's still in the box."

"You can use a pack of frozen peas or beans instead. Wrap it in a thin towel and ice for twenty minutes. Do it a few times and see how it is in the morning. I can come over and look if you'd like."

"I bet you could."

He laughed again. "I'm being serious. I know a little about muscle injuries. And for the record, I'm fantastic at massages."

"It'd be fun explaining to Michael why his coach is in my bedroom rubbing me down."

"I could do it quietly." Cam's voice was sugary low.

"I'll go with the peas. But thank you." How the hell did he always manage to make her smile?

"Okay, but I was serious about next Saturday. I think we

should schedule in a recurring appointment. It's going to take a few sessions until you're fully rehabilitated."

"Are you scared I'm really going to sue you for ten thousand dollars?" Mia asked him, leaning back on the headboard, then wincing when her shoulder twinged.

"No, Mia, I'm not scared of being sued. And if I'm honest, you'd be worth every cent. Not that I'm planning on paying."

"I wouldn't take it anyway. This morning was a mutually beneficial transaction." She pressed her lips together, remembering how good he'd felt inside her.

"Yes, it was. And I think we should do it again."

"That's a really bad idea," she whispered.

"Why?"

"Because today was a one off. If we do it again, it means…" She sighed. "I have no idea what it would mean."

"Maybe it means we had a good time and want to do it again," Cam said, his voice soft. "And I know it's just semantics, but technically you didn't get under me." He echoed Joanna's words. "You were against me. Between me and the tiles, but not under me. So maybe we should remedy that. I'd hate for the rehab to fail."

She was silent for a moment. The only sound in the room was the soft cadence of her breath.

"Mia? You still there?"

"Yeah. Sorry, I was just thinking."

"What about?"

"You," she admitted.

"That's good, because I've been thinking about you all day." The low tone of his voice sent a shiver down her spine. "You want to know what I've been thinking?"

"I guess I do."

"I've been thinking about how fucking beautiful you looked in my shower. How amazing you felt when you came all over my cock. And I've been driving myself crazy remembering how sweet you taste. I want to do it all over again."

She felt a hot pulse of need shoot through her.

"Tell me you've been thinking about me, too."

She opened her mouth, her breath catching in her throat. "I have," she told him. "I've thought about you a lot."

"Then come over again next Saturday."

"Cam, I…"

"Don't over think it. Just say yes. Same rules as before. Nobody has to know."

Her nipples were hard and achy, pressing against the soft fabric of her pajamas. She thought of how he'd sucked and teased them with his tongue. He was a man who knew how to please, how to coax pleasure out of her.

Her thigh muscles clenched at the memory of him teasing her *there*.

"I'll think about it."

He let out a chuckle. "Okay. Think about it, and then say yes. Because we're good together, you know we are."

"I should go to sleep."

"Are you in bed?"

"Yeah."

"What are you wearing?"

It was her turn to laugh. "Good night, Cam."

"'Night, Mia," he replied, his voice good natured. "And just so you know, when I want something, I always get it."

"Yeah, but you've never been against me before."

He laughed. "No, I haven't. You might have raised the stakes, but I'm still playing to win. I want you and you want me. This needs to happen."

"We'll see." She ended the call with a smile, because it felt damn good to be chased. Especially by a man like Cam Hartson. Her self confidence had taken a knock over the past few years, and it felt like it was slowly being rebuilt, brick by brick.

The boys were happy.

She'd gotten a job and was making progress with it.

And now a man who could have any woman he wanted was chasing her. Whatever happened, she was determined to enjoy the feeling.

She lay back on the pillow, a smile pulling at her lips. She'd ice her shoulder in the morning. For now, she wanted to enjoy the warm, pleasant feeling breaking over her body.

And think about Cam Hartson for a little while.

CHAPTER SEVENTEEN

"You wanna tell me why you've got some kid from your team pushing a lawn mower out there?" Logan asked, lifting his mug to his lips and swallowing a mouthful of coffee.

"He's paying off a debt. That's the kid who dented my car. He asked me if he could work off the invoice instead of his mom paying it. I said yes." Cam shrugged and poured himself a cup, glancing out of the window at the yard. "To be honest, I'm running out of work to give him. Any ideas?"

"You could send him to the farm. I've always got work there."

Cam lifted his eyebrows. "That's not a bad idea."

"How old is he?" Logan asked, leaning his long arms on the breakfast bar. "He'd need to be over eighteen, or have his parents' permission."

"Fourteen. And he doesn't want his mom to know he's doing this. So the permission thing is a no go."

Logan gave a low whistle. "You're going behind his mom's back? Isn't that gonna cause some problems? Imagine if we'd done something like that to dad. He would've whooped our asses."

"We *did* go behind dad's back," Cam pointed out. "How many parties did we go to when we promised him we were staying at a teammate's house? And all those times when we pretended to be each other so one of us could sneak out to meet a girl? Lying to your parents is practically a requirement of being a teenager."

"Tell me that again when you have kids of your own." Logan's smile was wry.

"Yeah, well we don't have to worry about that any time soon."

Through the window, Michael stopped pushing the lawn mower and wiped his brow with the back of his sleeve. "Shouldn't you give him a drink or something?" Logan asked.

"I'll give him a soda."

"Invite the kid in. Let him sit down," Logan suggested. "Give him a break."

Grabbing a can of Coke from the refrigerator, Cam opened the back door and hollered Michael's name. Looking up from the grass, Michael looked almost scared he'd been caught taking a break.

"Sorry. Just catching my breath."

"You want a soda? Come inside for a bit. Take the weight off."

Michael's face lit up. "That'd be great." He kicked the grass from his boots and walked over to where Cam was standing in the doorway. "I'll leave these by the door," he said, toeing his boots off. "Thanks, man."

"No problem. This is my brother, Logan."

Michael looked over his shoulder and gave Logan a nod. "You're twins? Cool."

Logan patted the stool next to his. "Come and sit down. I

need to apologize for my brother. He's an asshole and has no idea how to treat employees."

"I treat Brian just fine," Cam pointed out.

"No, *Brian* treats Brian fine. You forget all about him. He messaged me the other day to check that you were still alive."

Cam swallowed. "I might have missed a couple of calls." Maybe a few more. Not just from Brian either. But some from Derek as well.

"Can you put the kid out of his misery? He thinks you're ignoring him because he asked if he could work for another player."

"I'll call him." Cam rolled his eyes. "Brothers, right?" He grinned at Michael.

"You got a brother?" Logan asked him.

"Yeah, my kid brother. He's eight." Michael went to sit down on the stool, but then reached out for something. He lifted his hand, a long strand of blonde hair pinched between his thumb and forefinger.

Logan started to laugh. "You been bringing women home, bro?" Taking the hair from Michael's hand, he held it up and inspected it. "Let me guess, a twenty something. Blonde, of course, though probably not naturally. Curvy, pretty, and won't stop blowing your phone up which is why you won't answer it."

Cam pressed his tongue against his cheek, sweeping his gaze over Michael. There was no recognition on his face, even though Cam knew the hair had to be one of Mia's.

"Yeah, something like that."

Logan turned to Michael. "Take a tip from me. Don't grow up and be a manwhore like my brother."

Michael laughed. "If Soraya fell at my feet wearing that swimsuit, I'd probably head that way, too."

"And now you're corrupting minors," Logan said,

elbowing Michael in the arm. It was clear from Michael's smile that he was enjoying being one of the guys.

Logan was still holding that damn hair. Sunlight glinted off the strand, highlighting the soft waves that exactly matched Mia's style. Cam snatched it out of Logan's grasp and walked over to the trashcan, pushing his foot on the pedal and depositing the hair inside.

Sliding his gaze to Michael again, Cam's jaw twitched. If Mia found out he'd seen her hair she'd probably go crazy.

Best not to tell her. Because if she knew, she almost definitely wouldn't come over to his place on Saturday.

And he really wanted to see her. *Needed to.* Since yesterday morning, he'd felt more alive than he had in years. She was a beautiful enigma he wanted to solve. A game he wanted to win more than anything else.

He'd always loved games, and he'd always been a winner. Until his latest injury. But injuries didn't matter when he had her pinned against the shower wall. Nothing did. Just the sweet sensation of her lips against his as his hand curled around her ass, giving and taking all at the same time.

Damn, he needed to stop thinking about her, especially with her son sitting six feet away. "You want something to eat?" he asked Michael, clearing his throat to stop his voice from sounding so low and thick. "I have a few bags of chips in the cupboard."

Michael shook his head. "I'm trying to cut down on saturated fat."

Logan laughed again. "Kid, you don't have an ounce of fat on you. You're too young to worry about putting on weight."

Michael shrugged. "I read an article about macros." His eyes flickered up to Cam's. "I heard you try to follow them when you're playing."

Cam blinked. Michael had been reading about him? That was weird. And maybe a little flattering. "I do try to eat better when I'm training or playing," Cam agreed. "But a few chips never hurt."

Michael shrugged. "I'm still good."

"You know what?" Cam drained the last of his coffee. "I think you've done enough yard work for today. Why don't we go throw the football instead?"

"Seriously? Yeah, that'd be great." Michael grinned.

"If you can put the mower away, I'll grab a ball," Cam told him.

Michael was out of the kitchen like a shot, leaving his half-drunk Coke on the counter.

"He's a nice kid." Logan gave Cam a strange stare. "I think he has a bit of a hero complex about you, though."

"Are you going to come play ball?" Cam didn't want to think about any kind of complexes.

"Yeah, I'll throw a few. But first you need to tell me who this blonde is. Somebody I know? Or did she come visit you from Boston?"

Cam looked away from his twin, in case he could read the truth in his eyes. "It was nobody. Just a one time thing." Grabbing a ball from the closet, he hitched it under his arm and headed toward the yard. "You coming?"

———

How's your shoulder? – C xx

Holding up. I'm thinking it might only be $5000 worth of damage. – M

That's reduced by 50% in a few days. By next week I'll owe you nothing ;) – C xx

That's not how reducing something by 50% works. It'll be reduced to a quarter by next week. Then an eighth after that. Do you need a math refresher? – M

You can give it to me on Saturday morning. After I've made you come. – C xx

Who says I'm coming on Saturday morning? In either respect? – M

You'll be there. – C xx

So sure of yourself. – M

Yep. And sure of you, too. I'll see you on Saturday. – C xx

Not if my shoulder's still hurting, you won't. - M

———

"COFFEE'S UP." Becca craned her head around Mia's office doorway. "You want me to bring it in, or are you joining us in the kitchen?"

Mia shut the lid on her laptop and pushed herself up to standing. "I'll drink it with you guys. I could do with a break. I don't think I've moved from my desk since I got in this morning."

"That's why I could never do a desk job." Becca wrinkled her nose as they walked down the hallway. "I can't sit still for five minutes. If I do, my legs start twitching."

Mia laughed.

"It's true," Becca told her. "When I have to do any kind of desk work, I have sleepless nights. I prefer standing and doing something."

That was something Becca had in common with Cam. Mia had noticed how he didn't like sitting still, either. He'd called her last night while he was running, his breath as regular as the sound of his feet hitting the pavement. She'd asked him how far he was running, and he'd told her he was doing a half marathon.

"And you can still talk?" She'd widened her eyes in shock. "How is that possible?"

He'd either called or texted her every night. And if she

was honest, she liked it. Maybe too much. Especially when he asked if she was coming to his place on Saturday, and she demurred.

The chase was fun. So was he. And she was enjoying it for a while. It didn't mean anything, and it damn sure wasn't going anywhere. But it made her feel desirable, and she was going to enjoy it while she could.

"Hey!" Naomi, one of G. Scott Carter's accountants, smiled as Becca and Mia walked into the kitchen. It was full to bursting. There were eight of them in the coffee syndicate and the kitchen was pretty small.

"Hi, how's it going?" Mia asked her.

"This is making it better," Naomi said, lifting up her coffee cup. "We got donuts, too. They're on the side over there." She gestured at the far end of the counter. "Make sure you take one before you leave, because if the guys see them, they'll steal them all.

"Not if I have anything to do with it," Becca muttered. "They know they're *our* donuts. If they want some they can buy their own."

Mia bit down a smile. The rivalry between the coffee syndicate and non-members was legendary in the distillery. The guys had refused to join, yet bitched every time the coffee arrived that nobody had asked if they wanted to order.

"They can make their own damn group," Naomi muttered. "Donut stealing assholes."

"Mia?"

She looked up from her coffee, a smile still threatening her lips. The receptionist was standing in the hallway, and behind her was a woman wearing dark training pants and a white polo shirt.

"Hi Sandy, everything okay?" Mia shot her a smile.

"I tried calling your office, but you weren't there. This

lady has been asking for you." Sandy pressed her lips together. "Did you order a masseuse?"

Becca burst out laughing. Behind her, Naomi choked on her coffee.

"Um, no." Mia shook her head. "I really didn't."

"Mia Devlin, right?" the masseuse asked. She looked like she was barely out of college. "I have you down for a shoulder massage. Sports injury?"

"You play sports?" Becca asked. "I didn't know that."

"It's your left shoulder, is that correct?" the masseuse asked. "Suspected pulled ligament. Injury happened on Saturday. If you give me thirty minutes of your time, I can make it feel a lot better." She smiled widely. "It's already paid for."

The penny dropped. She knew exactly who'd arranged this. "I really don't have time," Mia told her. "I'm working all day."

"You have lunch coming up soon," Sandy said, trying to be helpful. "Why not take it a little early?"

"Girl, if you don't want a free massage, I'll take it." Naomi grinned at her. "My shoulders are stiff as heck. I keep leaning too far over my keyboard."

"That's really bad for you," the masseuse told Naomi. "You should think about getting some ergonomic advice."

Mia finished her coffee. "Can you stay here for one moment?" she asked the woman. "I need to make a quick phone call."

"Sure."

"I'll leave you here," Sandy said, giving the masseuse a nod. "I shouldn't leave the front desk unmanned for too long."

Pulling the door to her office closed, Mia picked up her cellphone, taking a deep breath as she pressed the call sign next to Cam's name. He picked up on the second ring.

"Hello?"

"Seriously? A masseuse?"

"You said your shoulder was still hurting. Fifty percent pain, wasn't it? I figured a massage could get it down to, say, twenty. Have you been icing it like I told you?"

"No."

"You need to ice it, Mia. And keep it rested as much as you can."

"A massage isn't exactly rest."

"The therapist I sent is the best in the area. She works with professional teams. Let her massage you, and then tell me if it hasn't helped."

"Cam…"

"What, baby?"

His endearment sent a shiver down her spine. "You can't be sending masseuses to my workplace. I have a reputation here, and I'm trying to keep it."

"I'm just trying to make you feel better. So you can have a good time with me on Saturday."

Damn, he was persistent. She hated that she liked it. "I still haven't said I'll be there," she reminded him.

"Yeah, but you will. And this way you can leave with no pain. Just pleasure. Now hang up and get that massage, okay? I'm busy."

She laughed. "You are not."

"Yep I am. I'm trying to work out how I'll take you first. In the kitchen, maybe? But I'm not sure I'll be able to wait that long. Maybe in the hallway as soon as you've walked in. Then we can save the second time for the bedroom."

Mia shook her head. "You're incorrigible."

"If I knew what that meant, I'd agree."

"I'm going now. Some idiot sent a masseuse over. I'm going to have to let her touch me all over."

"You can tell me all about it on Saturday."

"You're annoying, you know that?"

There was a grin in his voice. "So I've been told. See you Saturday."

"Maybe."

"I like maybe. It's better than no."

She shook her head. "Goodbye, Cam." Throwing her cellphone on the table, she rolled her neck and headed back to the kitchen.

The masseuse was leaning against the counter, sipping a coffee that one of the ladies must have given her. She looked up with a smile as Mia entered. "Are you ready?"

"Yep. Shall we do it in my office?" There was no point in sending her away. And though she'd exaggerated the pain to mess with Cam, there were still twinges that shot through her every time she raised her arm.

"Great. Lead the way."

———

"So how was school?" Mia asked, as they ate dinner at the kitchen table that night. It was a rare evening when Sam wasn't expected at the bar until later, so he'd sat down to join them, shoveling the spaghetti Bolognese into his mouth with gusto.

"Fine." Michael twirled his spaghetti around his fork. She could remember teaching him how to do it at their favorite Italian restaurant in Kansas City. Niall had laughed at them, telling Michael he should just cut the damn noodles like everybody else did.

Josh, on the other hand, was hacking at his pasta with his knife, then using his fork to shovel it into his mouth.

She had some work to do with him.

"I have a project to do," Josh announced, a piece of pasta flying out of his overstuffed mouth.

"Try not to speak with your mouth full, honey," Mia reminded him. When he'd swallowed the food and had taken a sip of water, she asked him, "What kind of project?"

"Science. We have to make a life size human, then add in all his organs and bones and stuff. We're getting the supplies this week and it's due next Friday." He grinned, and loaded more spaghetti on his fork, lifting it to his mouth. Then, remembering he wasn't supposed to eat and speak at the same time, he dropped the fork to his plate. "We get to draw all the blood and guts and stuff. And then we have to present it to the class."

Mia pressed her lips together. If there was one thing she didn't need right now, it was a school project. She was already working hours each night on her proposals, plus they had football and church on the weekends, not including the work they were doing together on Sam's house. Over the next few weeks they were going to paint the hallway.

"Maybe you should miss pee wee practice this week," Mia suggested. "So we can get a headstart on the project."

"No!" Josh frowned. "I really want to go to football. Noah says I can stay over again. Can't we do it on Sunday?"

Mia sighed. "I don't think we can complete it in one day."

"I'll work on it every night next week," Josh promised. "Please, Mom." He looked over at his brother. "Michael will help, won't you? If Mom's busy with her own work?"

Michael twirled another forkful of spaghetti. "You don't need my help. You're big enough to do it on your own."

Mia caught her eldest's eye. "It would really help me if you could work with Josh," she told him. "I have a presentation next Friday I need to prepare for."

Michael rolled his eyes. "What about my assignments?"

"You told me you had hardly any homework," Mia pointed out.

"Okay, I'll help him. But he has to listen and do as he's told."

"I will." Josh's face lit up. "I promise."

Mia gave them a gentle smile. "Thank you," she said softly. "That will help a lot."

"You eating the rest of that?" Sam asked, pointing at Mia's plate. She blinked because she'd almost forgotten he was there.

"It's yours," she said, passing her plate to him.

"Did practice go okay tonight?" she asked Michael.

"Yeah. I'm officially in junior varsity." Michael beamed proudly. "I get to play in the game next week."

"That's wonderful." Mia leaned across the table and hugged him. He took it good naturedly, his face flushing with pleasure. "Congratulations, I'm proud of you."

"I… ah… got a call from dad, too," Michael told her, looking down at his plate as though it was the most interesting thing on Earth.

"Your dad called you?" Mia swallowed. Niall hadn't spoken to either of her sons since he'd left. Hadn't spoken to her, either. Only through their lawyers.

"Yeah. He's called a couple of times." Michael shrugged. "He wanted to know if he could visit soon. I told him about being on the football team, and he wants to see me play."

"Is he coming to see me play, too?" Josh asked, his voice small.

Michael glanced at his little brother. "I didn't tell him about your pee wee lessons. I should have. Sorry, kiddo. I'll tell him next time he calls."

Sam put his silverware on his plate and looked over at Mia. Running his finger along his bottom lip, he gave her a questioning look.

She shrugged at him.

"Did he say when he was coming?" she asked Michael.

"I dunno. He asked me to send him the game schedule. I guess he'll see when he can fit it in."

"Is he still living in our house in Kansas City?" Josh asked.

"No, dummy. We sold it, remember?" Michael rolled his eyes. "He's living in Wichita right now." He glanced up at Mia. "He's still with his girlfriend." His voice was wary, almost afraid.

She smiled at him. "I know, sweetie."

Michael's shoulders visibly relaxed. "Do you think it'll be okay if they come watch?"

"It'll be fine," she reassured him. Whatever happened with her and Niall had nothing to do with the children. He'd always be their father, and they deserved to be noticed by him.

If that meant putting up with him while he was here, she'd do it. As long as her boys didn't get hurt.

"Did I hear somebody say something about ice cream?" Sam asked. She shot him a grateful smile.

"Ice cream sounds good," she told him, standing up and collecting the plates, as the boys cleared away the rest of the dinner. "I think we all deserve a double scoop."

———

How's your shoulder? – C xx

A little better, thank you. – M

How much better? Give me a percentage? Has the doctor cleared you to play on Saturday? – C xx

Mia stared at the screen, the sound of her pulse loud in her ears. These snatched messages with Cam, his little gestures of caring, and the way he was chasing her – they were tiny pinpricks of light through the dark of the night. She wanted to see him again. Not just across a football field while they were both playing their roles, the way they would on Friday. But the real him. The Cam who knew how to make her body sing.

Who knew how to chase all the melancholy away and make her feel good.

A smile curled at her lips as she tapped out a reply.

Okay, but I'm bringing breakfast. – M She stared at it, then added two ***xx***s. He'd been sending kisses in all his messages, but it was the first time she'd returned them.

Would he notice? Pressing send, she watched as the two blue ticks appeared.

And she didn't feel afraid or guilty or anything she thought she would. She just felt alive.

Yes you are. And I can't wait to eat you. I'm starving. C xxx

He'd added an extra kiss. It was stupid how much that made her smile.

"Are you close?" His breath was hot and heavy in her ear. She could feel a sheen of perspiration clinging to her skin, mixing with his as their bodies moved in unison. Mia swallowed a gasp as he moved his lips to her throat, scraping his teeth along her skin as he rocked his hips against her.

"I can't… not again." Her words were breathless. She felt like a ragdoll, limp beneath him. As he'd promised, they'd started in the hall, the breakfast she'd brought discarded on the polished wooden floor, where he'd dropped to his knees and pressed his face against her thighs, leaving her in no doubt how hungry he was.

That's where her first orgasm had happened. Hot and fast, like a firework rushing through her body. The second was on the stairs, as he'd pulled her onto his lap and made her ride him, his circling hips squeezing every last ounce of pleasure from her as she'd clamped her body around him.

He'd tried to press his mouth against her center again, even though he hadn't come. She'd squealed, feeling so sensitive, and had managed to run away from him, laughing loudly as she scrambled up the stairs, his loud stomps behind her.

Then he'd captured her, lifting her easily into his arms and throwing her onto his bed. This time, when he'd tried to pull her legs apart, she crawled across the mattress and taken him into her mouth, swirling her tongue around him as he knotted his fingers into her hair.

"Touch yourself," he'd rasped. "As you suck me."

She'd done as she was told, letting out a cry as she'd reached another peak. And though he'd swelled inside her, he still hadn't come.

But now he was close. She could tell from the shortness of his breath against her throat, from the arrhythmic thrust of his hips as he tried to stop the inevitable pleasure. Sliding his hand between them, his fingers sought her out, circling against the intense part of her that made her gasp.

"I can't…" she told him again.

"Yeah, you can," he rasped out. "Feel it. Let it wash over you. I'm not coming until you do."

This time, when it came, the intensity of her orgasm left her breathless as Cam stilled his body, spilling inside of her. He let out a low groan, his lips capturing hers, kissing and scraping against her mouth as though he couldn't get enough.

He dug his fingers into her behind, pulling her closer as his climax heightened. "Look at me," he said, his fingers biting harder.

She tipped her head back, her green eyes meeting his hazel, as he slid his hands up her spine and raised her to him, his chest hot against hers. Her back was arched away from the bed, her breasts and stomach flat against his chest, their skin sticky and sweaty as he throbbed and emptied inside of her.

Letting out a mouthful of air, he slowly lowered her back

to the mattress, pressing his brow against hers as his eyes captured her gaze again.

"Jesus." He blew out again. "I think you broke me."

She grinned up at him. "You broke me first."

Laying back on the mattress, he hooked his arm around her, pulling her body against his. "Send me the massage bill."

She smiled softly against his chest. "Maybe you should be the one doing the massaging. You're pretty talented with your fingers."

"You'd like that, wouldn't you? Me showing up at your work and giving you all my massage skills?"

"Um, no." She shook her head. Her whole body felt light, like somebody had pumped her full of helium. "It'd be better if you hid under my desk and came out when I need you."

He pressed his lips against her hair. "When do I start?"

She nestled closer to him. Another hour and she'd have to leave. But she was too tired and way too comfortable to think about that now. "You'd be too distracting. I'd get fired within a day."

"Yeah, but what a way to go. With me stashed between your knees."

She burst out laughing. "Can you imagine the scandal? No, I think I like you right here. In bed, waiting for me whenever I need some more rehab."

"Speaking of rehab. I see some definite improvement, but a full recovery is going to take longer than I thought. I'm not sure if you gave it your all today."

Her eyebrows lifted. "I gave it everything."

"You ran away from me."

"That's because you were going to kill me with orgasms."

His smile was crooked. "Is that a thing? Is it even possible?"

"I don't know, but I've got no desire to find out." She

traced her finger over his chest, her lips curling when his pectorals flexed. "What if I'm busy next Saturday?"

"Cancel it."

"I'm supposed to be having coffee with your sister," she told him.

"Meet her on Sunday," he murmured, trailing his fingers down her spine. "Saturday mornings are mine."

"Until you leave town," she said, because she was a masochist.

"Yeah, until then." He was quiet for a moment, as though deep in thought. "Can I ask you something?" He tipped his head to catch her gaze.

Her brows dipped. "Okay, but I won't promise to answer."

"If I was staying, would you come out on a date with me?"

"Are we talking hypothetically?"

"Of course." His hand reached the dip of her back, his palm pressing against it.

"Possibly. Though not right away. I'd need to prepare Michael and Josh for me dating anybody."

"Their dad is dating, right?" Cam asked. "Michael said something about that."

"Did he tell you Niall is going to visit? To watch him play."

"He might have said something."

"Yeah, well I'm not holding my breath. Niall says a lot of stuff that he doesn't follow through on. But for Michael's sake, I hope he does. He misses his dad."

"How about you?"

She tipped her head to the side. "What about me?"

"Do you miss him?" His voice was low.

She had to press her lips together to stop herself from laughing. "Oh god, no. I really don't. Sometimes I'm wistful about the boys when they were babies, and the life we had in Kansas City, but I don't miss Niall at all." She looked down at her hands, inspecting her fingers. "Can I tell you something?" she whispered. "Something I've never told anybody else."

His eyes flashed. "Yeah, you can tell me anything."

She took a deep breath. "Do you know how I knew it was over?"

Cam blinked. "How?"

"I took the boys away one weekend. Niall couldn't join us because he was working. We stayed at an amusement park. Had so much fun without him, and the boys seemed to bloom. But it was that Sunday night, when we got back and the boys were in bed that I found out."

"What did you find out?"

"Niall told me he'd met somebody else. That he was leaving me. I was getting into bed when he'd told me. And I realized that the photo I have of the boys on my bedside table had moved, so I asked him if he'd brought her to our house."

"Had he?"

She nodded. "Yeah. And do you know what the first thing I thought was?"

"That you wanted to pull his balls off?"

Mia laughed. "No, though that would have been good, too. It was that I hadn't cleaned the bedroom that week, and she'd slept on dirty sheets. Can you believe that? That's how I knew we were over. I was more embarrassed about the state of my house than the fact my husband was leaving me?"

"Yeah, I can believe it. The mind does strange things. So why isn't he around more? Doesn't he want to see the boys?"

"I think he was going through a midlife crisis. I told you before, we got together young. Too young. When he left, I think he was pretending he was eighteen again and there was no place in his life for a teenager and an eight year old."

"You think he got over his crisis? Is that why he wants to see Michael?"

She shrugged. "I don't know, and honestly, I don't care. As

long as he doesn't hurt them, he's entitled to see them. He's their dad."

"And if he wants to see you?" Cam murmured, two tiny lines appearing on his brow.

She lifted her gaze to his. "Are you asking if I want him back?"

The corner of his lip curled. "I guess I am."

"No. I definitely don't want him back. I think we were over long before he cheated, and I was just fighting against it. I don't like the way he left, and I'm furious about what he did to our business, but I wouldn't go back to him for any reason."

Cam's muscles relaxed as he breathed her in, her hair tickling his nose.

"How about you?" she asked him, inclining her head to capture his gaze.

"What about me?"

She pulled her lip between her teeth. Damn, she was sexy. Even sexier when she looked uncertain about something.

He loved the way she always kept him guessing.

"What ended your last relationship?"

"I haven't had one in a while." He shrugged.

"You dated that supermodel. Soraya." Mia swallowed. "She's very beautiful."

"We saw each other a few times. I wouldn't exactly call it a relationship. I think the press was more invested than we were."

Mia rolled onto her front, resting her hands on his chest and propping her chin on them. "Why didn't it go any further?"

He screwed his nose up. "You really want to talk about this? It's old history."

"I guess I just want to know more about you. You know

all about my marriage breakdown. You've spent time with my family. You're an enigma compared to me."

"You could just Google me," he suggested. "I'm not exactly a closed book. What you see is what you get."

"I don't believe that for a moment." She smiled at him. "Your online presence is probably managed to death. And anyway, there's nothing on the internet that tells me why you aren't still dating Soraya."

"So you *have* been Googling me," he murmured, tracing his finger down her spine. "That's kind of hot."

"I notice you keep avoiding my question," she said, tipping her head to the side.

"Okay. We met when I was doing a cologne commercial. I was the big brawny football player, she was the woman who stopped me in my tracks. You might have seen it. All dark with stupid music playing." He'd never lived that one down with his brothers. And of course, he got at least one bottle of cologne from them every Christmas. It was like a thing now.

"And you fell for each other?"

He laughed. "We didn't exactly fall. We talked and she was fun. We went out on a few dates. And then she got busy with her work, I got busy with the season, and it felt too hard. Neither of us was invested enough to coordinate our schedules. That spoke pretty loud. So we stopped seeing each other."

"Did you have sex?"

He blinked, surprised by the question. "Yeah."

"I guess you've had sex with a lot of people." She smiled. "It's alien to me, you know? You're only my second."

There was a wobble in her voice that belied her calm expression. Just the merest hint of insecurity. Somehow it made her even more attractive, more real.

He liked that she showed her flaws. He had enough of his own, after all.

"I'm thirty years old, so I've had a few partners. But probably not as many as you think." And never one he wanted to see as much as her. He loved the way she made him laugh. The way she challenged him, made him work for what he wanted.

She shifted on his chest.

"What's wrong?" he asked. He knew they were walking a tight line in this conversation. The most confident of people felt exposed when talking about their sexual history, after all. And she'd taken one of the biggest knocks of all.

"I'm being stupid." Her eyes were warm, even though her voice was wary. "I just keep thinking about you being with supermodels, and then, me."

"You think I compare you to them?"

"Honestly? I don't think you do. But *I* compare me to them. And maybe that's worse."

He hooked his arm around her waist, pulling her against his naked body, until she was laying over him. Running his hands down her back, he pressed his lips against her throat. "You're the most beautiful woman I've ever met," he told her, sliding his palms over her behind. "You may not think it, because you've been through a lot these past years, but somewhere inside you have to know it. Because I knew it from the moment I saw you standing at the front door, your eyes flashing fire at me because I was chasing your kids. Do you know how fierce you are when you're in protection mode? It was hot and scary at the same time."

She laughed, running her hands over his short hair. "Come over any day at about six. You'll see me really losing it then."

"I'd come over to your place any time."

"I know you would. And in a different life, that would work. But not this one."

No, not this one. And it made his stomach feel tight,

because for the first time in forever he could see another kind of life for himself. One where he had a kick-ass woman always beside him. With two kids who weren't his but who were funny and clever, and saw him as something more than a coach.

A life that made him feel like he finally belonged somewhere off the field, the way he hadn't in more than twenty years.

But he didn't want to think about what he couldn't have. He wanted to enjoy the moment, having her in his arms. Because her soft, sweet body felt amazing against his.

"We have an hour until you have to go," Cam whispered, hitching her against him, as he kissed his way up her neck. "Let's see if I can make you scream my name this time."

CHAPTER NINETEEN

*I*t was almost six. How the hell had it gotten so late? Mia saved the document she'd been working on and searched through the papers on her desk for her phone. She was supposed to have left half an hour ago – to make dinner and finish working with Josh on his project. Like her, he had a big presentation tomorrow. And they were both as nervous as hell.

As she grabbed her jacket, she typed up a quick message to Michael.

Running late. Just leaving work now. Can you grab a pizza from the freezer and turn the oven on? Mom xx

She was rushing down the hallway when his reply appeared.

It's okay, we're going to order in. It's all under control. You still like Hawaiian, right? – Michael xx

Okay, but check if there are any coupons before you order. – Mom xx

Chill. It's all under control. See you later. Michael xx

Unlocking her car, Mia let her muscles relax. Michael was growing up. He wasn't a man yet, but he was definitely more responsible than he'd been in Kansas City. Maybe the move had done him good after all. As promised, he'd helped Josh with his project this week. The three of them had sat at the table every evening, Mia working on her own presentation and her sons bent over Josh's life size man 'with his guts spilling out'.

Josh's words, of course.

It had been sweet watching the two of them together. Not squabbling or ignoring each other, but actually having fun as they glued body parts and identified them with black sharpies. Now the body was complete, and tonight was all about working on Josh's presentation.

And hers. Because tomorrow was a big day for her, too.

She was loving working on the new blend. Everybody at G. Scott Carter was excited about the potential of their new product, and she was determined to make the marketing plan shine. Eliana had even nodded her head when Mia had given them a run down at the last board meeting, looking impressed at the first draft Mia had made.

She hoped her boss was as impressed tomorrow. The whole board would be there – including Eliana's other son, Daniel, who was Skyping in from Scotland, and her two step-children. They wanted to start moving forward with their plans, ready for the big launch next year, and Mia's project was an important part of that.

She was excited and anxious as well as every emotion in between. Thank god for Cam and the way he made her smile. Thinking about Saturday was one of the things that was keeping her going. His body was an amazing stress reliever.

The house was quiet when she opened the front door, dropping her briefcase on the floor as she kicked off her heels, feeling the warmth of the wooden slats against her stockinged feet.

"Hello!" she called out. "Where are you guys?"

"We're in the living room," Josh piped up. "We've been waiting for you. Hurry up, I want to show you something."

A smile flittered on her lips as she walked down the hallway. "Okay, I'm coming."

In the living room, Josh was standing next to his project. The diagram of a man had been mounted onto thick cardboard with a stand at the back since she'd last seen it. It was complete, each part of his anatomy labeled, and of course in true Josh style, there was a lot of blood splattered around his body.

"Do you like it?" Josh asked, clapping his hands together. "We finished it. I've even been practicing my presentation. Cam says I'm a natural."

Cam? Mia turned her head to the sofa, where Michael and Cam were sitting, their body positions mirror images of each other. Leaning back on the cushions, their long legs sprawled out, with matching grins on their faces.

Mia swallowed. "Hi." Her eyes were wary as they met Cam's. "I didn't know you were coming." Ugh, could she sound any less welcoming?

"I gave Michael a ride home from practice. He was telling me about the project, so I thought I could help." Cam gave her a grin. "I know a lot about anatomy."

She bit down a smart retort. "That's really kind of you. Thank you."

"Cam ordered some pizzas, too," Josh said. "Isn't that cool? He said you shouldn't have to come home and cook every night."

Cam lifted his eyebrows, that smile still ghosting his lips. She rolled her eyes at him, and it widened.

"That's very nice of Cam," Mia said. "But I don't mind cooking."

"I just heard that things got dicey around here at six," Cam told her. "I kind of wanted to experience it for myself."

"Mom shouts a lot when she's cooking," Josh told him. "But she's always better after she eats."

"She's probably hangry." Cam nodded. "I get like that, too." He looked over at her. "Do you want me to grab you a cookie while we wait for the pizza?"

"I think I can manage," she said dryly. "But thanks for your concern."

"I'm thinking of it as life preservation. I've seen you angry before."

Arching an eyebrow, she tipped her head to the side. "You haven't seen anything, pal."

Ugh that smirk. It did things to her. Things that she had no right feeling when her sons were in the room. "I'll go get some plates out," she told them. "Ready for the pizza." And to get some distance from Cam. Having him here was confusing.

"Can I do my presentation first, Mom?" Josh asked her. "I've been waiting really patiently."

She blew out a mouthful of air. "Of course, honey. I can't wait to see it."

Cam moved his right leg at the same time Michael moved his left. "You can sit here," Cam told her, patting the middle of the sofa.

"The chair is fine."

"No, go on the sofa, Mom. I want you to be able to see it all." Josh gave her a grin. "It'll be like presenting to the class if you all sit in a row."

Mia sat down in the gap Cam had made, pressing her arms tightly against her torso so no part of her body was touching his.

And then he relaxed next to her, splaying out until his thigh rubbed against hers. If she moved over, she'd be pushing herself against Michael, and she knew he'd protest.

Better to stay ramrod straight and hope that Josh spoke quickly.

"Ladies and Gentlemen," Josh announced. "Welcome to my show."

"It's a presentation, Josh," Michael murmured.

"Okay. Welcome to my presentation." Josh beamed. "I'm gonna tell you all about the human body. Blood, guts, and all. It's squelchy and it's disgusting, but somehow it all comes together in the end."

From the corner of her eye, Mia could see Cam smile. Did he have to be so good looking?

"Let's start at the beginning. With the skin. Did you know it's the body's largest organ? It's a waterproof living layer that protects us. So we should take care of it. Keep it clean, moisturize like my mom does, and try not to cut it too much."

Cam shifted his leg again. His thigh muscles felt like steel against hers.

Mia kept her eyes straight ahead as her son made his way down the body, taking particular glee at the workings of the bowel. "Did you know all that brown stuff is really just waste?" he asked them. "Our body takes out the good stuff and uses it, then bundles the rest up. It's a shame it smells so bad. Particularly Michael's."

"If you use that in your presentation, you're a dead man," Michael told him.

Josh sighed dramatically. "But it's funny. Cam told me to add in some jokes. Warm up the room."

Mia turned to look at Cam. His eyes were already focused on her. He lifted a brow as though he had no idea why she was glaring at him. She pulled her gaze away and stared resolutely at Josh.

"Okay, so that wraps up my presentation," Josh said when he'd finished, a broad grin on his face.

"You need to ask if anybody has a question," Michael prompted him.

"Oh yeah." Josh slapped his face with the palm of his hand. "I keep forgetting. Ladies and Gentlemen, do you have any questions?"

Cam put his hand up.

"Yes?" Josh grinned at him.

"What's your favorite part of the human body?" Cam asked him.

Mia bit down a smile. That was actually a good question.

Josh pressed his finger to his lips, eyes narrowing as though he was deep in thought. Then his face lit up. "The anus," he told them. "That's where all the waste goes out. If we didn't let the waste out, we'd slowly be poisoned. So that's probably the most important part of our body, and therefore my favorite."

Cam was shaking next to her, his mouth twitching in an attempt not to laugh. Mia elbowed him in the waist, wincing as her bone connected with his hard muscle.

"Ow."

Michael turned to look at them. "What's happening?"

"Your mom elbowed me," Cam told him. "It hurt."

"It hurt me more. Your body must be made of titanium or something," Mia muttered, rubbing her arm.

"Actually, Mom, bodies are made of cells," Josh pronounced. "Tiny little production factories that make us up. Isn't that cool?"

Cam leaned in closer to her. "You hurt my cells," he whispered. "My tiny little production factories might go on strike."

She shot him a look that made him grin widely. He was enjoying this.

Yeah, and maybe so was she. Just a little. It was nice having another adult here. Maybe too nice.

The doorbell rang, and Michael jumped to his feet. "It's pizza time," he said, rubbing his palms together.

"I'll get some money," Mia said, pushing herself away from Cam. She was thankful for the space. Her body needed it.

"Cam already paid with his card," Josh told her. "He ordered on the app. It's cool."

She looked at Cam who shrugged. "I'll add it to your bill," he told her, standing and rubbing the back of his neck. "Come on, let's go eat pizza."

HE LIKED WATCHING Mia when she didn't know his eyes were on her. Cam sat at the kitchen table, his long thighs crossed as he sipped on a mug of coffee. He'd tried to help clean up, but Mia had shooed him away, telling him if he was buying dinner, then he didn't get to tidy up, too.

Instead, she'd made him coffee and he'd sat down and watched as Michael rinsed the plates and Josh loaded the dishwasher.

Sam still had an old fashioned drip filter machine, the kind Cam could remember growing up with. It was surprising how good it tasted, even though his buds were more used to flat whites and Americanos than simple old fashioned drip.

"We're done," Josh said, closing the dishwasher with a loud bang. Cam smiled into his mug. He really liked Mia's kids, despite their first awkward meeting. Josh was cute and funny and always made everybody smile.

Michael was more complicated. Part of that came from his age. And some probably came from being the eldest man in the family – if you didn't count Sam. Cam could remember how his mom's death had made all the brothers grow up. It had made them more protective of Becca, too, much to her disgust.

Michael probably felt the same way about Josh.

"Can I go upstairs and finish my homework?" Michael asked.

"Sure, go ahead." Mia nodded.

"Can I go up, too?" Josh asked, always wanting to be like his big brother. "I can think about my presentation while I play on my tablet."

"Okay, but say thanks to Cam for dinner first."

"Thanks." Josh threw his arms around Cam's neck. He froze for a moment, then wrapped his arms around the little boy's body. "I love pizza so much. You made my life a better place today."

Cam looked over Josh's shoulder at Mia. She was watching them, her face expressionless.

"You're welcome, buddy. Break a leg tomorrow."

"He means good luck," Michael interjected before Josh could say anything. "Seriously, don't break anything."

Cam laughed. "Yep, no trips to the ER. Your mom would kill me."

"Thanks for your help. It looks so cool on that stand. I think I'm going to get an A."

Josh hugged him again, then ran out of the room.

Michael gave him a nod. "Thanks. The food was great."

"It's a pleasure."

Mia was leaning on the counter, her mug in her hands as she sipped at her hot coffee. As Michael left, she stayed exactly where she was, her gaze fixed on Cam. The room was loaded with silence, punctuated by her soft breaths. Her chest was rising and falling rhythmically, the sharp lines of her collarbone visible through the open neck of her cream blouse.

"You should always wear skirts," Cam told her. "Your legs look amazing."

She put her cup down on the counter. "I wasn't expecting to see you here." She didn't sound angry. More perplexed than anything.

"I wanted to help. You're busy, Michael was bitching about having to finish this project, and I know that Josh likes me. It felt like the perfect solution to come and work with him. I wasn't kidding, I know a lot about anatomy. I studied it at college. My plan was to help, then leave when you got home, but then you didn't come home and the boys were hungry, so I ordered food." Cam shrugged. "That's it. No hidden agenda. I'm not trying to rile you."

"I know." She pulled her bottom lip between her teeth. "I'm glad you were here. Josh looks so happy."

"He's a good kid."

"Michael seems to like you a bit better, too." Her lips curled. "You're obviously growing on him."

Cam sipped his coffee. "How about his mom? Am I growing on her?"

Her gaze flickered to the door. The boys were long gone. She swallowed, her delicate neck undulating. Damn, he really wanted to dip his hand beneath that silky blouse. Not touching her was a kind of torture. He knew exactly what to do to make her breath stutter and her face heat up. He wanted to part those pretty lips, and push his way inside.

"You need to stop looking at me like that." She shifted almost imperceptibly. He could see the way her thighs were squeezing together.

The memory of them wrapped around his hips made him ache.

"Like what?" He gazed at her steadily.

"Like you're about to bend me over the kitchen table."

Cam laughed loudly. "I'm not about to bend you

anywhere, Mia. I have extremely good control." He might be thinking about it, but he wasn't going to do it. "The other reason I'm here is because I need to tell you something."

"What?"

"I have to travel to Boston tomorrow. I'll be gone for the weekend."

Her face fell. "So no Saturday morning for us?"

He liked the sound of disappointment in her voice. It echoed the feeling that overwhelmed him when his agent called and told him he had a meeting at Freedom Field – no ifs, ands, or buts. The team wanted to see if he'd made any decisions, and he owed them that.

Didn't mean he wasn't pissed that he wouldn't be inside Mia this weekend.

"No Saturday for us," he confirmed. "Does that upset you?"

She glanced at him speculatively. "No, I was thinking I'd rather clean the house anyway. I just didn't know how to break it to you." The corner of her eyes crinkled.

"You always did like dirty things."

Mia shook her head. "Not dirty things. Dirty people. You." She shifted against the counter.

"I'll call you when I'm gone. Check in on how your presentation went, and Josh's."

"You don't need to do that. You're not…" She screwed her nose up. "I don't know. You don't have to if you don't want to."

"I want to." His voice was firm. "I want to talk to you."

Two pink circles heated her cheeks. "I'd like that," she said huskily.

"Why are you still standing all the way over there? Come and sit here," he suggested, patting the chair next to him. He wanted to feel the heat of her body radiating against his. To smell the soft fragrance of her shampoo. To touch her, the way his fingers were aching to.

"I can't. If I come over, I'll want to touch you." Her voice was breathy.

His lips quirked. She felt it, too. "So that's it? We have to have a six foot exclusion zone between us whenever we're in public?" he teased. "Just in case I feel the urge to strip you naked and take you in the town square."

She grinned. "It wouldn't hurt."

"How about we go outside instead? You can show me all the flowers you've planted."

"I haven't planted any... *oh!*" It took a second for the penny to drop. "Outside, yeah, that would be a good idea."

Away from the boys, and any prying eyes. He needed to see her, to touch her, be close to her.

In the hallway she slipped on a pair of sneakers, and led him toward the back door. He didn't touch her – not yet. Instead he shadowed her, his strong, hard body a breath away from hers.

The air outside was cool. Every time the wind gusted, a shower of leaves scattered over the verdant lawn, coloring it in vibrant hues.

Mia led him around the corner of the house. As soon as they were out of sight, he wrapped his hands around her waist and spun her around, pressing her back against the rough bricks as he lowered his mouth to hers.

Their kiss was needy. Days of pent up want exploded as he devoured her with his lips, stroked her tongue with his, dug his fingers into her hips, and pressed his body against hers.

She wrapped her arms around his neck, sighing against his lips. "I've missed you."

"Missed you, too." He kissed her neck, then slid his lips to that open vee of her blouse, kissing a line along her collarbone. "I've changed my mind. You need to stop dressing like this. It's inappropriate."

"I'm wearing a blouse and skirt. There's nothing more appropriate."

"But it's bringing up all my older woman fantasies. Teachers with rulers, slapping them against their palms." He kissed the swell of her breast. "Librarians with glasses and sensible skirts." Nudging his nose against the top of her bra, he brushed his lips against her cleavage, then brought his hand up to cover her soft breast. "You do things to me with these clothes."

"If you ask to call me mommy, I'm leaving," she warned, then tensed as he pushed her bra down and tugged her nipple between his lips.

"Cam… not here." She sounded torn. "We can't."

"I know." He flicked her with his tongue. "But fuck, I want to."

"Me, too." She ran her fingers through his hair. God, that felt good. But then every time she touched him it felt amazing.

"I don't think I can last another week without my balls exploding," he told her, pulling his face reluctantly away from her chest. He buttoned up her blouse until her collar was tight against her neck. "There, that's better. Now I'm not thinking dirty thoughts about your breasts."

"You aren't?" She grinned at him.

"Okay, I still am, but I always am. There's only one option left, this week we'll have to resort to online therapy."

"Is that what we're still calling it?" Her voice was playful.

"It's what it is." He nodded seriously. "It's another step in your rehab process. How's your dirty talking game?"

"Non existent." She blushed. "I've never done that on the phone."

"Never?" His brows lifted. "Jesus, Mia, we have some

work to do. This is going to take extra sessions." He leaned in closer, brushing her cheek with his lips. "Tonight you need to be naked and in bed by ten. When I call, you answer, no questions."

"You're bossy."

"And you love it."

The smile on her face told him that she did. And he loved it, too. The way she responded to him every time he touched her. The way her breath quickened as he sucked her nipple into his mouth.

The way she touched him like she really cared.

Whoa! Where did that thought come from?

"I guess I should go," he said, raking his fingers through his hair. "You have your presentation to work on."

"When will you be back from Boston?" she asked him.

"I'm not sure. Early next week, I hope. Don't worry, I won't cancel on you twice."

"Is it important? Your meeting?"

He shrugged. "Just routine stuff." Lies, all lies. But he didn't want her sympathy. Not when he could have her body.

"Okay, then. Be safe."

"I will. And you, too." He took a step back. "Good luck tomorrow."

"Thanks." Cam lifted a hand in goodbye.

He was almost at the gate when she called out. "Hey!"

He turned to look at her. Her eyes were bright, her head tipped to the side. "Yeah?" he asked. Damn he really didn't want to leave her right now. She looked too good for that.

"Good luck in Boston."

He grinned. "Thanks."

Yeah, he'd take that. Because he had a feeling he was going to need it.

CHAPTER TWENTY

"Hey, Mia!" Becca called out. Mia had fifteen minutes until her meeting was due to begin, and the four walls of her office had felt like they were closing in on her. She'd decided to walk through the distillery and loosen her muscles. It was better than sitting and getting panicky.

"I'm glad I caught you." Becca ran over, her breath coming in pants. "God, I'm so out of shape. If my brothers could see me wheezing like this, they'd laugh their heads off."

Mia smiled, glad for the distraction from her presentation. "Are you okay? Do you need an inhaler or something?"

Becca laughed. "I just need to do something other than work. Like run. Anyway, the state of my lungs isn't why I wanted to talk to you. Do you have any plans on Sunday?"

"Nothing apart from church." And moping around because she couldn't see Cam this weekend.

"Great. Then you and your boys can come to my birthday party. It's on Sunday afternoon at my brother's house. I'll message you the details."

"Which brother?"

"Gray. He has the best party house. His ground floor is practically all open plan. I'm so glad you can come. Everybody will be there." Her face dropped. "Well everybody except Cam. Can you believe he had to go back to Boston on my birthday weekend? It's the first time in about twenty years he's not playing on a Sunday, and then this happens."

Mia gave her a sympathetic smile. "I'm sorry. That sucks."

"Yeah, well he'd better bring me back a nice present from Boston. That's all I'm saying."

For a second, Mia thought about messaging Cam to remind him about Becca's birthday gift. But that wasn't her job, was it? It was confusing, because this morning he sent her a long video message wishing her good luck on her presentation, the way any boyfriend would.

But he's not your boyfriend. No, he wasn't.

Even if her heart told her it would be so good.

She wouldn't send him a message about Becca. Instead she'd concentrate on this presentation and then spend some time with the boys this weekend. They'd enjoy it at Gray's house – he was one of their favorite singers, after all.

"Well I'll be bringing a gift," Mia promised her. "Is there anything else I should bring?"

"Just yourself." Becca hugged her. "I'm so glad you can come. The others will be, too."

"Mia?" A voice echoed across the large distilling room. Mia turned to see Nathan standing at the door. His usual attire of pants and a polo shirt had been replaced by a striking grey suit and navy tie. "We're ready for you now."

"Is it the big board meeting?" Becca asked. "Oh, good luck."

"Thanks." Mia smiled at her. "I'll see you on Sunday."

"LET'S TURN TO ADVERTISING," Mia said, facing the board again. It consisted of eight people – Eliana and Nathan, plus Eliana's son Daniel, whose face was on the television screen hanging from the ceiling, having dialed in from Scotland. Then there was Eliana's stepson, Lawrence and her stepdaughter Nina, both of whom had inherited shares in the company when their father died. As well as the chief financial officer, the head of production, the director of logistics, and another dial in, this time G. Scott Carter's sales director, who was currently in Japan.

"I have a mock up of some billboard ads we're planning to run, along with a two minute long form advertisement that will run in movie theaters. We'll edit it for television and streaming services. The aim is to build the brand around a personality, the way Aviation Gin was built around Ryan Reynolds, and Longbranch Bourbon was built around Matthew McConaughey."

"Don't they own the companies?" Daniel asked, his voice crackling over the speakers.

"Ryan Reynolds recently sold Aviation Gin, and Matthew McConaughey worked in collaboration with Longbranch. I'd propose we do the same with the person we choose to head up the advertising. You'll see in your packs that I've created a shortlist of potential celebrity endorsements, all of whom have indicated interest through their management companies."

"Samuel Forest," Nathan murmured. "He's a good choice. Didn't he win the Masters last year?"

Mia nodded. "He's the number one golfer in the US right now. He's successful, rich, and living the dream. That's the kind of person our target customers admire. Who they want to be."

"I like Sarah Rosewood," Daniel said. "Having a woman head the campaign feels fresh and new."

"A woman's been running this damn distillery for the past ten years," Eliana reminded him. "Nothing fresh about that."

Mia bit down a smile at their family banter. "Sarah is a bold choice," she told them. "There's a whole demographic we haven't managed to tap yet, and she could help us. Make whiskey as cool as gin. Something people want to be seen drinking. She'd add an edge to the campaign that Samuel wouldn't."

"I like the third one," Eliana said, her voice firm. "He's local, he's successful, and he's damn hot."

"Mom!" Nathan winced. "Seriously?"

"What can I say, Gray Hartson turns every woman into a cougar."

"He's also Becca's brother. Ugh, Mom." Nathan shook his head.

Gray had been Mia's first choice. She'd had to keep it under wraps. She hadn't even told Cam, let alone anybody else that they'd approached Gray's management team to gauge his interest.

Luckily, he was very interested. He wanted to know more about the blend, the rest of the marketing campaign, all of it.

"There's something very useful about him being local," Mia agreed. "We can make it about him growing up around here, falling in love with the brand. It even fits with his graveled voice."

"Arrange for him to come in next week," Eliana suggested. "Let's see how interested he is. I'll meet with him one on one."

"I bet you will," Nina muttered. Her three brothers laughed uproariously.

"He has some brothers, doesn't he?" Eliana asked, ignoring the uproar. "Since the G.Scott Carter distillery is a family run business, and his sister has worked here for a number of years, maybe we can build on that with Mr. Hartson. I'd love to see a commercial of him sharing a bottle of whiskey with his brothers and sister. Even have Becca explaining the blend to him, that might appeal to another demographic the same way Sarah Rosewood would. What do you think?" She looked straight at Mia.

"I think that would be a fantastic idea, if we could persuade them."

"I could talk to Becca?" Nathan suggested.

Eliana nodded. "Let me speak with Mr. Hartson first. Then maybe Mia can join us and we can talk about the family angle, see if he'd consider it. If that works, then we'll speak with Becca."

She looked back at Mia, her eyes warm. "Carry on," she suggested with a rare smile. "You're doing an excellent job. I'm excited to see where we can go with this."

---

*THE PRESENTATION WENT WELL. **I still have a job! I'll be able to pay you back your $10,000 without having to sell my body. M xx***

Cam's lips twitched as he read her message. He and Derek were sitting on leather easy chairs in the front office of Marty's suite of rooms, waiting to be called inside. It felt like he was back at school, waiting at the principal's office to be told off for stuffing the boys' toilets with paper.

Yeah, he and Logan had done that just to get out of taking a math test. God, they were horrible kids.

Speaking of the 10k, have you gotten an invoice from the dealership yet? M xx

Glancing up, he could see Derek deep in concentration as he scrolled on his phone, perusing Twitter like his life depended on it.

Not yet. I had to send it back to be retotaled. Shouldn't be too long. C xx

He hated lying to her. At some point he was going to have to speak with Michael and come up with a plan. Mia wouldn't be held off for much longer.

The intercom buzzed, and the secretary lifted her head up. "Marty says you can go in now."

Derek stood, stretching his arms, and nodded at Cam to go first. "You okay?"

"Yeah, I'm good." If you didn't count the knot in his stomach that was making him want to throw up breakfast. "Let's do this."

Marty Landsman's office was huge, the floor covered in expensive dark blue carpet, and the right wall lined with bespoke teak shelves, holding books and trophies, along with some signed footballs, and the Dresden porcelain that Marty collected.

The seventy-five year old owner of the Bobcats was a self-made man, born poverty-stricken in Springfield, Massachussets. His story was well known in football circles. At the age of fifteen he moved to Boston, working twelve hour days as a laborer in a waterfront warehouse, and by night he'd bus tables and studied for a long-distance college degree. By his late twenties, he'd made a fortune by gambling on the stockmarket and bought out the owners of the warehouse he worked in. By fifty, they were measuring his wealth in billions of dollars.

At heart, though, he was still that kid from Springfield, who preferred wearing sweatpants to tailored suits, and talking football rather than profit margins.

He was sitting behind his oversized desk, his bald head reflecting the light that shone in through the large windows behind him. To his left were his signature Air Force One sneakers, which he must have kicked off at some point. He suffered from gout – a horrible affliction that made him limp on occasion – so he always preferred to be stockinged and shoe free.

"Get your ass over here," Marty said gruffly, holding his arms open. His hug was surprisingly strong, though his arms barely wrapped around Cam's wide torso. "How're you doing, boy? Your head okay?"

"The headaches have lessened." Cam hugged him back.

Marty nodded, his face turning serious. "That's good." There was a knock on the door, and he shouted, "Come in." The door opened, revealing Coach Mayberry, wearing sweats and a t-shirt, plus his customary Bobcats cap.

"Sit down, all of you. Pull up some chairs," Marty rasped, pointing at the desk in front of him. "We got some things to talk about."

Coach Mayberry nodded at Cam. "You okay, son?"

"Pretty much the same. No change."

He didn't like the sympathetic smile his coach sent him. Or the silence in the room as he waited for somebody to break it.

"Okay then." Marty slapped his palm on the table. "Let's stop beating around the bush. Your head hasn't gotten any better and it's not going to anytime soon, is that right?"

There was a tightness in Cam's chest that he hadn't expected. "Yeah, that's right." They were all staring at him expectantly, like he had all the answers. Maybe he did, but he didn't know what they were.

His head was a mess. If he carried on playing it would get worse. To anybody else it would be a no-brainer – pardon the pun. But for him, it was turning his back on the only life he knew.

But what choice did he have?

He took a deep breath, his gaze meeting Marty's. "I guess

I won't be playing again." Damn if that didn't hurt. "I'm sorry it's taken me so long to get here."

"It took you a while." Marty gave him a short smile. "But yeah, you're making the right decision. Your health has to come first."

"We need to talk about managing his exit," Derek said, turning to look at Marty. "It's in all of our interests to make it as smooth as possible. Cam's been a player for the Bobcats for the past decade, we want him to go out on a high."

"We want the same." Marty nodded. "But we also have a team to run. We need to rebuild the defensive line without him. And stop the speculation. It's been running rampant."

"Cam's interested in coaching," Derek said. "He's been working with his local high school team. The Bobcats feel like the right place for him to start this new career."

Marty shot a glance at Coach Mayberry, who gave a slight shake of his head.

"I don't think that's a good idea," he told Cam brusquely. "Not yet. If we rebuild the team, we need to do it fresh. If you're around, you're gonna intimidate your replacement, as well as any new players we bring in. Maybe even make them do things exactly the way you did. Neither coach or I think that's a good thing."

"Now hang on," Derek said, his face reddening as he leaned forward. "Cam's given everything for this team. He's taken you to two superbowls, for chrissakes. Now you're gonna throw him aside and forget about him? No, I won't let that happen."

Marty held up his hand. Cam looked from the older man, to his agent, then over to Coach Mayberry who was leaning back in his chair, observing. He hated these meetings. Anything to do with the player's career or salary – they were all things Coach didn't want to be involved in.

He just wanted to play.

Or coach.

Marty held up his hand. "Hey," he said, shooting Derek a dark look. "I didn't say I was abandoning him. I just want him to get some experience in with another team first. When he's ready, there'll always be a place for him here at Freedom Field."

Cam felt his muscles relax.

"I guess we need to talk," Derek said to Cam in a low voice.

"Before you do, let me tell you one more thing. There's talk of creating an expansion team in L.A. More than talk, if I'm being honest. Money is being raised, stadiums are being appraised, and the team is starting to recruit staff." Marty shrugged. "I'm an investor and I know for a fact they haven't recruited a defensive coach yet. If I put your name forward, the job is practically yours."

"In L.A.?" Derek said. "I'd heard rumblings."

"There are more than rumblings. It's happening. They're hoping to be ready for next season." Marty looked straight at Cam. "It's a huge opportunity for somebody starting out their coaching career. The last time the league had an expansion team was in 2002. You won't get a chance like this again."

"An expansion team, though." Derek shook his head. "No chance of winning anything. Do you know the salary?" Derek asked.

Marty shook his head. "Nope. But they'll talk to you about it in time. Just say the word and I'll put you forward." He winked at Cam. "Use it as a chance to hone your skills. Learn to manage players from the sideline. Experience the difference between a rookie and an experienced player from the other side. Do that for three years, and I'll give you a job here." His smile was soft. "We really want you to come home, son."

"Can I think about it?" Sure, L.A. sounded amazing. But this whole offer was completely out of the blue. He'd be much further away from his family, his friends, his team.

And a whole world away from Mia Devlin.

He wanted to laugh at himself. She'd be fine without him. All his teasing about her rehab was just that. What they had was nothing more than some fun. If he left, she'd be fine. Probably date somebody else.

That thought felt like a punch to his stomach.

"You can do better than think. I want you to fly out there in a couple of weeks. Meet the new owners, the head coach, get a feel for the place. They're building something good, I know you'd fit in there." Marty fixed his eyes on Cam. "It's time to move forward, son."

It was. But Cam had a feeling they weren't talking about the same thing.

CHAPTER TWENTY-ONE

$\mathcal{M}$ia rapped her knuckles on the oversized oak front door, and glanced back at the boys. Josh could barely contain his excitement. He was doing the same kind of dance he used to do when he was little and potty training, except she knew he didn't need to use the bathroom because she'd made him go before they left.

Michael was leaning on the wooden railing that circled the house, a bored expression on his face.

"Do you think there'll be party games, Mom?" Josh asked. He was holding the gift she'd wrapped for Becca. A beautiful scarf she'd found at Laura's Dress Shop in town. It was made from the softest grey cashmere, with yellow birds printed all over. It suited Becca's bright personality perfectly.

"Of course there won't be party games, doofus," Michael shook his head. "It's an adult birthday. Grown ups don't play games."

"Michael." Mia lifted a brow at him. "Don't call your brother names."

"Sorry." He gave her a tight smile. She could tell from his

expression he was nervous. She felt the same way. Gray Hartson was a big deal.

The door opened, and Mia immediately recognized Maddie, Gray's partner. She was holding one of her twin boys in her arms, the other clinging to her leg. "You made it! Hi!" She grinned down at the boys. "I'm so glad you two are here. Gray has the Xbox out and they're playing winner stays on, I'm hoping you guys can defeat him."

An unexpected smile played at Michael's lips. "What are they playing?"

"Some football game." She glanced at Mia. "It's all PG, I promise. Apart from the guys' swearing. But you two can tell them off if they do that, right?"

Josh nodded, his face serious. "Mom makes us put money in a jar if we swear. I can be in charge of it."

Maddie laughed. "That's a great idea. You'll probably make a million dollars. Come on inside, I'll show you where the den is." She grinned at Mia. "The girls are all in the kitchen. Grab a prosecco and join them."

Carrying Becca's gift, Mia walked into the kitchen, smiling as the aroma of pizza and cake wafted over her. Maybe adult birthdays weren't so different to kids ones after all. Michael seemed to have cheered up as soon as the Xbox was mentioned, and Josh, as always, was excited to be out of the house.

"Mia!" Becca called out, running across the kitchen in her bare feet. She was holding a glass in her hand, and on her head was a huge plastic tiara with 'Birthday Girl' spelled out in silver. "I'm so happy you're here. Everybody, you know Mia, right?"

A chorus of hellos echoed through the huge room.

Mia passed her the gift. "Happy birthday."

Becca grinned, her eyes sparkling as she ripped the paper open, then squealed when she saw what was inside. "I love it!" she said, wrapping the scarf around her neck. "I saw this in the window of Laura's the other day and had scarf envy."

"I saw it and thought of you," Mia said, smiling at her friend's reaction.

"You know me so well already." Becca hugged her tight. "Let's go and join the others." She passed a fresh glass of prosecco to Mia and led her over to a huge cream leather sofa. "You know Courtney, of course."

Along with Courtney, there was Van, Tanner's wife, as well as Courtney's best friend, Lainey. As soon as Mia sat down with them, the conversation picked up, as they gossiped about work, Van and Tanner's drive-in movie theater, and what movies they were planning to show that year. Then the talk turned to the brothers, as Maddie – who'd returned from the den – regaled them with a story of how Tanner wouldn't accept that Gray had beaten him at the football game, and the two of them had ended up rolling on the floor, play fighting each other like kids.

"If only Cam was here," Becca said, shaking her head. "He'd whoop all their asses in an instant."

At the mention of Cam's name, Mia found herself looking up. What would they think of her if they knew what was happening between them? Not that she'd ever say. Cam wasn't planning on staying around for good, after all. Soon he'd be back at work, and she'd still be here.

"Logan's been on edge all weekend," Courtney said. "He's so worried that Cam might want to play again."

"Surely he wouldn't do that." Maddie frowned. "It could kill him."

Mia's head snapped up. *What?*

Courtney pressed her lips together. "I know. But Logan says that football is Cam's life. He has no idea what to do when he's off the field."

"What's wrong with Cam?" Mia found herself asking. "I

thought he was taking a break because of a bad tackle."

Becca sighed. "It's a bit more than that." She glanced around at the women sitting with them. "This goes no further than this house, okay?"

They all nodded.

"He has post concussion syndrome. Not just from the tackle he took a few weeks ago, but from the build up of brain trauma over the years. There are lesions on his brain that won't ever heal, but he can still lead a normal life if he stops playing." Becca's voice was low.

"The problem is, if he carries on playing, it could make things worse. Much worse." Courtney bit her lip. "Have you heard of CTE?"

Mia shook her head.

"It's a degenerative disease of the brain due to excessive trauma. It starts with headaches, which is what Cam has. The more concussions he gets, the worse it will get. CTE can cause personality changes and forgetfulness, as well as extreme aggression and depression. I hate the idea of Cam ending up like that," Courtney told them.

"Not to mention suicidal thoughts," Maddie added, grimacing. "It's all horrific. He needs to give up football *now*."

Cam had a brain injury? The words were still sinking into Mia's own mind. He'd never mentioned it, not once. And he had time to mention it. When she was in his arms, telling him about her broken marriage and separation. He could have said something then.

She was torn between sympathy and annoyance at him not telling her. Sure, they were casual, but she was a caring person. She could have helped or at least listened to his worries.

"It's okay," Becca said, rubbing Mia's arm. "He's going to be all right."

"I'm the one who should be comforting you." Mia shook

her head at the whole situation. "You're his sister, after all."

"We've had a bit of time to come to terms with things," Becca said with a shrug.

"So has Cam, but he's still fighting it," Maddie added.

Mia shifted uncomfortably on her seat. She liked these women, and she hated that she was hiding something from them. But what was she supposed to do? Tell them that she and Cam had a secret fling going on?

She wasn't a solution to his problems. She had enough of her own. Not to mention Josh and Michael's lives to consider. But it hurt to know he was hiding this every time they saw each other.

"You know what?" Maddie said, clapping her hands together. "This is supposed to be a birthday party, not a wake for Cam's career. We need more wine, and more music. What do you say?"

"I think we should go get the guys and make them dance with us," Courtney said, the corners of her eyes wrinkling up. "Before they end up giving each other black eyes."

"Good idea." Van nodded, shifting one of Maddie's twins on her knee. "I'll tackle Tanner, you two take Gray and Logan. Becca and Mia, you put on some loud music. I really want to dance."

"Sounds like a plan." Mia smiled at them, happy the subject was changing. If they were dancing, they wouldn't be talking which was a good thing. Because right now she had a lot to think about.

———

NOBODY WAS ANSWERING the front door. Cam rapped again, but all he could hear was loud music. He turned the doorknob, but it was locked.

He could've called Gray or Logan and ask them to let him

in, but instead he opted for hopping the high fence that separated Gray's driveway from his backyard, landing steadily on his feet. He walked around to the back of the house where no doubt his family would be celebrating in the kitchen.

He could hear them before he saw them, the sound of music mixing in with the laughter and low buzz of conversation. It made the corners of his lips curl up. Weird how much he'd wanted to fly home rather than stay in Boston and watch the game.

Now that he knew his future wasn't with the Bobcats, not for now at least, he wanted to be far away from the team he'd been a part of for so long. Yeah, last night he'd gone over to Dan Motion's house and hung out with the quarterback and the rest of the team. But it felt more like a school reunion twenty years after he'd left. They had football in common, but little else.

The official press release confirming his retirement would come out tomorrow, so it didn't overshadow the Bobcat's game today. But the rest of the players already knew – Coach Mayberry had informed them – and one by one they'd hugged Cam tightly and wished him well.

And now he would have to build that kind of camaraderie all over again with a new team. Wherever that ended up being.

"It's a good offer," Derek had said quietly about the L.A. team as they'd left Marty's office on Friday. "I'll put feelers out to find out more about their plans, but my gut tells me you should grab this by the balls."

Cam had nodded, but said nothing. Derek was right, it was a good offer. But L.A. felt so far away. Sure, he had friends there, the same way he had friends all over the country. It's what happened when you were in the public eye.

He didn't know why he was in such a funk about it. He should feel relieved that his future was almost secured. He'd still be part of the game, part of something bigger. And sure it would take time to build up a new team like that, but he was never phased by challenges before.

Maybe it was because he'd actually been enjoying spending time with his family for once. For the past decade, his brothers had been scattered all over. Gray in L.A., Tanner running his own business in New York, and Logan with him in Boston.

One by one they came home. Found love and happiness in the same town they grew up in.

There was a little part of him that envied them for that.

Through the kitchen window, he could see his family doing what they always did – goofing around together and having fun. Tanner and Van were doing some kind of complicated twist that resulted in her stumbling against the breakfast counter as Tanner tumbled on top of her. Gray and Maddie were moving smoothly, their bodies so accustomed to music and rhythm that their grace was innate. And then there was Logan and Courtney, holding George in their arms as they boogied together, making their baby giggle and clap his hands with glee.

Cam's mouth dried when he saw *her*. Mia was dancing with Josh, her blonde hair flying out behind her as Josh held her hands and spun them round and round. Her eyes were sparkling, her head tipped back with a giggle that made Josh twist her faster.

Even Michael was grinning, sitting at the breakfast bar with his phone held up as he videoed them all.

Taking a deep breath, Cam rapped on the window, painting a smile on his face when they all looked over to see him in the backyard.

"Cam!" Becca squealed, her voice audible through the closed windows. She ran to the sliding glass doors and yanked them open. "You came."

"Happy birthday." He kissed her and squeezed her tight. "Your gift is in my car."

"It is? Can I come and see?"

Over Becca's shoulder he could see Mia looking at him. Seeing her made his muscles relax. He wanted to hold her. To touch her without sending the sirens off throughout Hartson's Creek.

He was sick of hiding this thing between them. Sure, the sex was amazing. But he wanted more than being a dirty secret.

"Come on," Becca said, tugging his hand. She practically dragged him around the house to the driveway, not letting go until they were at his car. The others had followed, and were standing by the house, watching with amusement.

Including Mia. His gaze met hers, and damn if he didn't feel it right down to his feet. That was the moment he knew he couldn't go to L.A. Not when *she* was here in Hartson's Creek. The thought of being without her made his chest ache.

He wanted her.

He wanted everything.

Taking a deep breath, he opened the car and pulled out the oversized box that took up the entire passenger seat. With a huge grin on her face, Becca pulled off the wrapping, then gave a little scream when she saw what was inside.

"You bought me a Kitchen Aid!" she said, her eyes wide. "I've wanted one of those for years."

"I know."

"Okay, you're officially forgiven for almost missing my party." Becca hugged him again. "Now, let's go inside. It's freezing."

He noticed Mia lingering at the back as the others rushed around the house. Cam locked his car and carried Becca's gift to the porch. He'd walk around and bring it in later.

Then he clambered down the steps to where Mia was still standing.

"You okay?" he asked her. His fingers twitched with the need to touch her.

"I thought you weren't coming back until tomorrow," she said softly.

"Yeah. I was supposed to watch the game at Freedom Field. But I couldn't wait to get out of Boston." Couldn't wait to see her.

"How was the meeting?"

"It was okay. Lots to think about." He hadn't processed it all yet. Especially the thought about not going to L.A. He needed to be alone for that.

"Your family told me about your head injury. I'm so sorry." Her brow crinkled. "I didn't know it was so bad. I can't imagine how hard that must be for you."

Cam looked at her for a minute, running his tongue along his bottom lip. "It sucks. But it is what it is. Hopefully they caught it before it got bad. It means I can't play again, but I can still live a normal life." And right now that didn't sound so bad. Yeah, football had been his life until now.

But what if there was another life for him here?

"Cam!" a voice called out. "You're up on the Xbox. Come show these losers how it's done."

"I guess we should go in," she said softly.

"Yeah, we should. You doing okay?"

"I missed you this weekend." Her smile was small, but damn did it hit him where he liked it.

"I missed you, too. Next Saturday still free?"

"Yep." Her lips curled up.

"Good." He winked at her. Maybe then he'd tell her how he felt. Because he couldn't keep fighting these feelings. Not when his heart felt like mush every time she was close.

CHAPTER TWENTY-TWO

The junior varsity league played on Wednesday evenings, using the same mini-stadium as the varsity team. It was a much more subdued atmosphere, though. The bleachers weren't full the way they were on Fridays, and only one of the refreshment stand registers was open. The small crowd of spectators was mostly made up of families of the players, and those from the opposite team.

Not that Mia minded. Michael was so excited about playing for JV that she was beaming with joy. Even the appearance of her almost-ex-husband and his girlfriend couldn't dampen her happiness.

Niall walked over to the sidelines and hugged Michael, who looked delighted that his father had arrived. Her heart clenched at how easy it was for him to walk back into their childrens' lives without a care for how they'd been the past year.

But if he hurt them again… he'd know about it. He got this one chance with them and that was it.

"Mom, can I go see Dad?" Josh asked, his eyes wide with excitement. "Do you think he'll want to sit with us?"

Mia shook her head. "I don't think he will, sweetheart. But of course you can go see him."

Josh ran down the metal steps, his feet clanging against the treads, and launched himself to the sidelines, where Niall and Michael were still talking. She looked around for Cam – he coached this team, too, after all. But there was no sign of him.

Maybe that was a good thing. She didn't need the two sides of her life clashing tonight. This was all supposed to be about Michael.

"You okay?" a soft voice whispered in her ear. Mia jumped about two feet off the bleacher.

"Dear lord, you shocked me." She pressed her palm to her chest. "How the hell did you sneak up here without me seeing you?"

Cam grinned. "It's my svelte body. I'm like a ninja."

"A two hundred and fifty pound ninja."

"Two-twenty, thank you very much." He gave her a lopsided grin. "I work hard to keep myself trim."

She found herself glancing down at his body. He was wearing his usual game night attire of sweats and a tight athletic shirt, his muscles bulging through the shiny fabric.

"I'm not complaining," Mia told him. "I get the benefit of it."

"Yeah you do." He gave her an appraising look. "By the way, do you want me to go punch your ex?"

His abrupt change of subject made her giggle. "I do want you to," she told him. "But please don't. Michael's so excited he's here, and Josh is, too. I'm just trying to be happy for them."

"You're way too good, you know that?" Cam murmured, tipping his head to the side. "He deserves a hard punch after what he did to you."

It was weird, because a few weeks ago, she would have

agreed. But now he seemed insignificant. The boys were happy, and so was she. Niall would always be part of her sons' lives, but he wasn't part of hers.

He was just somebody she used to know.

"How good?" she asked with a smile.

Cam's eyes dipped, taking in the open neck of her shirt, and the tight jeans she was wearing. His pupils darkened, as though he liked what he saw. "Too good," he said softly.

"Does that mean I'm nearly finished with rehab?"

A smile pulled at the corner of his lips. "Not yet. I'll need to do a full body assessment first. You should probably come over naked this weekend. That'll save us some time."

She raised an eyebrow. "That'll get the neighbors talking."

"You shouting my name multiple times will get the neighbors talking," he said, his voice low. "The rest is just window dressing."

"Mom, can I sit with dad?" Josh asked, panting from running back up the steps.

Cam immediately pulled back. Mia glanced at her son to see if he'd heard a word of their conversation. From the expression on his face, he had no idea what was going on.

Thank the Lord it was Josh and not Michael who'd snuck up on them.

"Of course, honey."

"He's here for a few days. He told us he and Gemma want to take us away for the weekend. There's this hotel with a waterpark inside it. Can we go?"

Mia blinked. Of course he'd want to spend more than an evening with them. He'd driven all the way from Wichita, after all.

"Let me talk to your dad later. You'll miss football practice if you're not here on Saturday."

"I know, but I really want to go. Noah says the waterpark

is amazing. There's this giant bucket that empties water all over everybody."

She glanced at Cam. He was watching them with interest, a tic popping on his jaw.

"I'm pretty sure you can go," Mia told him. "I just need to hash out some details with your dad, okay?"

"Okay!" Josh grinned widely. "Thank you, Mom." He ran back down the steps, to the front bench, where Niall and his girlfriend had taken a seat. Josh sat beside his dad, talking rapidly to him. Niall turned his head and looked up at where Mia was sitting.

She took a breath and raised her hand to wave at him. Niall blinked and waved back.

There, that wasn't so bad. Maybe he'd actually stick around long enough to spend some time with his kids.

"So you're free all weekend," Cam murmured. "That's interesting."

"It is?"

"Yeah, it is. Forget about the naked rehab, let's go away somewhere."

"Away?" Mia blinked. "Where?"

"Somewhere that definitely doesn't have a giant bucket that dumps water over everybody," he told her, his face serious. "Though I can't promise you won't get wet."

"Why do I think this is a bad idea?" she murmured, shaking her head.

"It's the best idea." His eyes softened. "Two whole days together. *Naked.*" He gave her a crooked grin. "If you prefer, you can stay at my place, though if your car's parked in my driveway overnight people will definitely talk."

"What if I don't come at all?"

"Not an option. I promise I'll always make you come."

She laughed softly. "You're a goof, you know that?"

"I'm a goof for you."

Her heart did a little leap. "Shut up and go coach the team."

Cam looked over his shoulder, as though he'd forgotten all about the football game. "Shit, yeah, I should go."

"I hope you weren't this uncommitted when you played pro," she said with a grin.

"Luckily for the Bobcats, I didn't know *you* then." He stood, his strong body towering above her. "I'll send you our travel details tomorrow."

Our travel details. A fizz of excitement shot through her.

Forty-eight hours alone with Cam Hartson. She wasn't sure either of them would survive it.

———

"Okay, you two need to go pack for your weekend. Your father's picking you up right after school." Mia took their empty plates. "Josh, I've laid out all your clothes on your bed. You just need to put them in your duffle bag and add any toys or books you want to take."

"Have you packed for me, too?" Michael asked with a grin.

"Nope. I don't dare rifle through your closet. I'm scared something might bite me." She carried the plates to the sink, rinsing them.

"Where is it you're going again?" Sam asked the boys. It was one of his rare evenings off. Which was good, because she hadn't told him yet that she wasn't going to be around this weekend either. She'd tell him once Michael and Josh were upstairs.

Sliding the plates into the dishwasher, she bit down a smile as she thought about Cam's message.

Our flight is at ten on Friday night. We're going somewhere warm. Bring a bikini and sunscreen. C xx

So you're not telling me where we're going? You realize I'll find out as soon as we check in at the airport, right? M xx

Yeah, I know that. But I like to keep you guessing. C xx

You haven't told me to bring my passport, so it has to be in the US. And there aren't that many places where I could wear a bikini right now. Is it Miami? M xx

Nope. C

Savannah? M

Still no. C

You're driving me crazy, you know that? M

That's what I'm here for. Now leave me alone. I'm trying to get my body beach ready. C xx

"Mom?" Josh asked, crouching down beside her in front of the dishwasher.

"Yes, sweetie?"

"If I take my Nintendo Switch do you think it'll get wet?"

"Not if you don't take it into the waterpark."

"But the whole hotel is a waterpark, right?" He frowned. "Doesn't that mean the bedrooms are, too?"

She bit down a grin. "No, honey, the bedrooms will be dry. You don't sleep in the waterpark itself. The hotel is just attached to it."

"Oh." Josh's face fell. "I didn't know that."

"It's okay. I'd have thought the same." She ruffled his hair. "Are you looking forward to going?"

"Yeah, I think so. Michael seems excited. And Dad says we'll have fun."

"You definitely will. It'll do you good to spend time with your dad."

"And Gemma, too," Josh added. "She seems nice."

"That's good. Now go pack, okay? You need to get a good night's sleep. You won't get to the hotel until late tomorrow, and the weekend will be full of fun. So get all the rest you can."

"Okay." Josh nodded. There was still something on his mind. She could see it from the way his brows were crunched together. "Mom?"

"Yes?"

"Will you be lonely without us?"

Her throat tightened. "No, my darling. I'll miss you, but I'll be fine. I just want you to have a good time."

"We could ask Dad if you can come?" he said hopefully. "You like waterparks, don't you?"

"You're very sweet." She kissed the top of his head. "But I think you'll have a lot of fun without me there. Maybe we can go another time."

"Sure. Okay. I love you, Mom." He threw his arms around her neck, hugging her tight.

"I love you too, bud. So much."

———

IT WAS ALMOST ten by the time the house was quiet and the boys had gone to bed. Half the evening had been taken up with Josh trying to find the charger for his Nintendo, which they finally found beneath his bed, along with a stash of candy wrappers and half a dozen unmatched socks.

Michael was calmer on the exterior, but she could tell he was excited, too. She was pleased he was. That made her life easier.

Maybe co-parenting would be a good thing. Though she was still skeptical that Niall would really step up to the mark beyond this weekend.

He'd messaged her this evening to confirm what time he'd be picking the boys up, and for the first time she'd seen some humility in his words. He thanked her for letting him back into the boys' lives, and apologized that he hadn't been around for the past few months.

She noticed he didn't apologize for leaving, or for taking everything they owned. But she wasn't expecting miracles.

And anyway, she had other things to think about. Things like airplanes and bikinis and a weekend away with the hottest guy in Hartson's Creek.

"So, I'm going away this weekend, too," she told Sam, as she walked back into the living room. He was watching an old war documentary, and lifted the remote to pause it.

"Anywhere nice?" he asked her.

"Just to see a friend. I thought I'd take advantage of having some free time." She sat in the chair beside the fireplace. "I know I'd planned on painting the kitchen on Sunday, but I'll do it next week if that's okay."

Sam waved his hand. "That kitchen hasn't seen a lick of paint in twenty years. Another week won't hurt. And you've done more than enough to this place. I feel like I'm taking advantage."

"You gave us a home when we had nowhere to go," Mia said softly. "If anybody's taking advantage it's me."

"But things are better now that you have your job."

Yeah, they were. But there was still the money she owed Cam. She frowned, remembering that he still hadn't given her the invoice.

"The job is great. And I'm managing to save some money. In a few months I'll have a good deposit, and we can move out and give you some peace."

"There's no rush. I kind of like having you all here. Even if Josh does eat all the cookies." He cleared his throat. "So this friend, is it anybody I know?"

"Um, I don't think so."

"So it's not a certain ex-football player who gives you googly eyes whenever he sees you?"

Mia froze. "What?"

Sam cleared his throat. "Don't look so worried. I won't

say anything. I just see a lot more than people think, that's all. And I saw your car parked in his driveway a couple of weeks ago when your boys were at Saturday football."

Mia slumped back in her chair. "Does everybody know?"

"Nope. But people aren't stupid. They'll put two and two together eventually." His watery eyes met Mia's. "Is it serious between you?"

"No," she said softly. "He's just made me smile again, that's all."

"That's a good thing." Sam nodded. "I've noticed how much more relaxed you've been recently."

She swallowed down a splutter. Hopefully he had no idea how relaxed Cam made her.

"You go have fun," Sam told her. "You deserve it. You've carried your family for months, but you're still young. You have your whole life ahead of you."

Her throat felt tickly. "You're a sweet man, do you know that?"

"Don't tell anybody," he whispered. "It's our secret."

She mimed pulling a zip across her lips. "It's safe with me."

———

"You can't think about pulling out now," Derek said, his voice thick with irritation. "First you took way too long thinking about retiring, and now you're having second thoughts about L.A.? It's a small industry, Cam, and reputations get made and ruined on the turn of a dime. Marty pulled strings to get you this meeting. You can't throw that back in his face."

Cam ran his hand through his short hair, glancing at his suitcase from the corner of his eye. "Isn't it just as bad if I go meet everybody in L.A. with no intention of signing? Honesty has to be the best policy, right?"

"No." Derek huffed. "Having a plan is the best policy. Thinking things through is the best policy. Not messing up your career because you're having too much fun running around with your brothers is the best policy."

Cam had twenty minutes before he had to leave for the airport. Mia had insisted on meeting him there. It grated him, but he understood why. Being seen climbing into his car with a suitcase was asking for gossip to begin. And right now she thought they were a casual thing.

Yeah, well it was time to persuade her otherwise. Starting with saying no to L.A.

"I'm not changing my mind because of my brothers. I have a lot of reasons to stay east, that's all."

"You should think about things when you're in L.A. Even better, you can do it around a swimming pool surrounded by models and actresses. The sun always shines in L.A. I promise you that. No more snow. No more rain. Just sweet blue sky every day. Why would you turn that down?"

"You seem really keen on me taking this job," Cam pointed out. "It's an expansion team. The bottom rung. It'll take years for them to win anything, if they ever do. Maybe we should wait and see if there are any other positions opening closer to home."

"If you turn this down, Marty just has to put out the word and nobody will touch you with a ten foot pole," Derek told him. "I'm not telling you this as your agent, but as your friend. Seriously, you're making a really bad decision turning this down. Your next step is crucial. You told me yourself, football is your life. Do you want to throw that all away?" Derek clicked his tongue. "Just do me one favor, okay? Fly out to L.A., meet me there, and we'll see how you feel after that. If you really feel it's not for you, okay, we'll make a different plan. But at least give it a chance."

Cam sighed. Flying to L.A. was pointless, but he hated letting Marty down. He didn't think the Bobcats owner would cause him any problems if he turned a coaching job down, but the least he could do was be willing to meet Derek halfway.

"I'll go, but I'm pretty sure I won't change my mind." He was certain, but no need to give Derek a fit.

"Okay. Good. Brian's already booked your flight and hotel for next weekend." Derek sounded suddenly upbeat. "I've got a good feeling about this."

"I gotta go," Cam said, checking his watch again. He wanted to be parked before Mia arrived. He'd booked them both into the VIP lot, and from there they'd be taken into the first class lounge. Right now, all he wanted to do was be with her.

"What's got you so busy on a Friday night?" Derek asked.

"None of your business."

His agent laughed. It was a strange, almost forced sound. "Keep your nose clean and don't go breaking any hearts, okay?"

Yeah, well, he wasn't planning on it. This weekend was about spending time with the woman he couldn't get out of his mind. Preferably naked time.

"I'll speak to you later," Cam said, lifting the phone from his ear. Just before he swiped it, Derek replied.

"I'll see you in L.A. next week."

CHAPTER TWENTY-THREE

"We're here."

Mia slowly opened her eyes, smiling when she felt Cam's lips brush against her brow.

"We are?" She looked up at him with sleepy eyes. "I guess I fell asleep, huh?"

"You were asleep before we'd even left the airport service road." He brushed a tendril of hair from her cheek. "Which is good, because you're going to need your energy tonight."

"What time is it?" It was too dark to see her watch.

"Almost midnight. We're going straight to our bungalow. We'll need to get out of the car and into a golf cart."

"Can't we walk?" she asked him, hoping the fresh air might wake her up.

He chuckled. "The resort covers three acres. We could walk, but it would take a while. Maybe we'll walk in the morning."

Three acres? Feeling more awake, she craned her head to look at the surrounding scenery. The road leading to the resort was lined with oak trees, their huge leafy canopies forming an archway that blocked out the moonlight. When they emerged from the quasi-tunnel, the driver keeping to the twenty-mile-per-hour limit, she could see a beautiful white hotel in front of them, surrounded by vast lawns and trees, along with the tell-tale sign of little red flags in the greens of the three golf courses that formed part of the resort.

"What made you decide on Hilton Head?" Mia murmured. Even in the dark of night, the resort looked beautiful. The trees were strung with lights that sparkled between the leaves, looking like lightning bugs in summer. Dotted in among them were small white bungalows, each far enough away from the next to provide privacy. From the looks of the size of them, along with the enclosed private swimming pool behind each building, they had to cost a small fortune to rent.

"It's warm enough to sunbathe naked." Cam kissed her again. So softly she could barely feel it.

"It can't be that warm. I know we're in South Carolina, but still…"

"The forecast predicts high seventies. You might get a few goosebumps, but I can live with that."

"Can you?" She lifted a brow, smiling up at him. She liked the way he was holding her. Like she was something delicate, that needed to be protected.

"Yeah. I've got a few ideas of how to keep you warm." He pressed his lips to hers. They were warm and demanding, and sent delicious tingles through her nerve endings. He cupped her head with his palm, sliding his tongue against hers. "Would you rather go to a waterpark hotel?" he asked when he pulled away.

"And get drenched by a giant bucket of water?" She wrinkled her nose. "I think I prefer this place."

Damn, he was such a good kisser. All the tiredness she'd felt only minutes ago seemed to disappear. He slid his hand down her thigh, hooking it beneath her knee until he could pull her leg over his body.

The driver cleared his throat. "We're here. The bellhop will assist you now."

Cam lifted his head, a smile ghosting his lips. "Later," he mouthed, sliding her leg from his. "Thank you," he told the driver. It was annoying how little he appeared to be affected by their kiss. Mia was still panting like a damned dog. "We'll see you on Sunday."

There were actually two carts waiting for them. The first driver took their luggage and drove ahead, while Mia and Cam climbed into the backseat of the second, which took off along the small winding pathways, past the deserted golf courses and expansive trees.

"Welcome back, Mr. Hartson. And welcome for the first time, Ms. Devlin. We're delighted you chose the Evoque Resort for your stay." The driver glanced over his shoulder, then back at the path ahead. Their way was lit by old fashioned lampposts casting golden pools across the gravel.

"Welcome back?" Mia said, arching a brow. "Do you bring all your women here?"

Cam laughed, shaking his head. "I came here for a golf tournament once. Pro-Celeb."

"I'm guessing you're the celeb?"

"So they told me." He shrugged. "I only came for the free golf and food."

She bit down a smile. "That's pretty much why I'm here."

Cam arched an eyebrow, sliding his arm around her waist. "The only sport I'm planning on playing involves being naked," he whispered into her ear.

"That's because you're scared I'd whoop your ass."

He kissed her neck, sending shivers down her spine. "Do you play golf?"

"No. But it looks fairly simple."

She felt his laughter vibrating against her skin. "Oh baby, now I really want to play you. Do you think they'll let us on the course without clothes?"

"You seem really fixed on this naked thing," she pointed out.

He slid his lips along her jaw. "Yeah, I'm pretty set on that."

Maybe she was, too. The thought of almost two days ahead of them felt enticing. No children, no cooking, no work to worry about. Just being naked with this man who knew exactly how to touch her, along with warm sunshine and a cool pool to dip into.

"We're here," the bell boy told them, hopping out of the cart. "Your luggage is in your room, and there's food waiting for you in the kitchen, along with a complementary bottle of champagne. Your breakfast will be delivered at nine-thirty tomorrow morning, as you ordered. In the meantime, is there anything else I can get for you?"

Cam swung his long legs out of the golf cart, then held his hand out to Mia. She climbed out, a grin on her face as she took it all in.

"We're good," Cam told him, slipping him a few bills. He was good at that. Clearly had way too much practice.

"Enjoy your stay. And if you need anything at all, just call reception. We're staffed twenty-four hours for your needs."

Sliding his hand into hers, Cam nodded at the bell hop. "Thanks," he said, his thumb caressing her wrist. "But right now I have everything I need."

———

MIA WOKE the next morning to the glorious sight of a naked Cam Hartson carrying a tray laden with breakfast food into the bedroom. She was naked, too – their clothes were almost certainly still scattered over the living room – her bare legs twisted into the cool white sheets.

"Did you go outside to get that tray?" she asked him.

"Yeah. They left it on the porch." Cam put the tray on the nightstand, picking up a croissant and taking a bite.

"You left the bungalow naked?" She watched as he poured two cups of coffee. "Careful, you wouldn't want to scald any… delicate parts."

He grinned. "It's Naked Saturday, remember?"

"I don't remember giving it a name."

"Well I did. It's Naked Saturday. No clothes allowed."

"What if I want to explore the island?" she asked him as he passed her a coffee mug.

"Same rules. You'll have to do it naked. Or wait until Boring Clothes Sunday."

She burst out laughing. She liked the goofy side of him as much as she liked the part of him that always played to win. "Boring Clothes Sunday. You're really selling it to me."

He shrugged. "I tried to make it Naked Sunday, but the airline put in a complaint."

Passing her a plate of pastries and fruit, he sat down on the bed next to her. "Actually, we'll probably need to get dressed tonight, too. I've booked us reservations at the restaurant here."

"No naked restaurant?" She sighed loudly. "You wound me."

"I knew you'd like Naked Saturday."

She pulled her lip between her teeth, her eyes softening. "I like being with you."

He swallowed, his neck undulating. "Yeah, well I like being with you, too." He took a deep breath, his sculpted chest rising. "I kind of wanted to talk to you about that."

"You did?" She put her half eaten pastry back on her plate, giving him an interested look. "Okay then.

"Remember my meeting in Boston last week?"

She nodded.

"They want me to go for a coaching position with a new expansion team in L.A. I'm supposed to fly out there next week, but I don't want to take it."

Her breath caught in her throat. L.A.? That was on the other side of the country. "Why not?"

"Because I want to stay in Hartson's Creek with you." He ran his tongue along his bottom lip, his eyes meeting hers. She could see the vulnerability there. It touched her.

"Oh." She breathed out raggedly. "You do?"

He took her hand, tracing the lines of her palm with his finger. "How would you feel about that?"

"I'd feel…" She took a deep breath. The thought of him staying around for her made her skin flush. She could feel the warmth of his gaze as he watched her, the teasing touch of his finger as he drew patterns on her palm. "I'd feel pretty good about that," she admitted, her lips curling. "But I'd need to know more. What do you mean by staying around? Do you want to keep on the way we are? Because Sam's already noticed and it's only a matter of time before everybody else does. And I can't have the boys dealing with that."

He shook his head. "No, that's not what I want." His eyes were hooded. "I want more. I don't want to hide how I feel about you anymore."

Her hand was shaking in his. "How do you feel?" she whispered.

Cam took the plate from her lap, putting it on the bedside table, then put her mug of coffee beside it. He slid his arms around her waist, turning them both until she was straddling his thighs, her chest pressed to his. "I think better when we're touching," he told her. "In fact, everything's better when we're touching."

She pressed her lips against his. "It really is."

"And as for how I feel?" He shook his head. "I'm not good at this stuff. I can talk for hours about a game or a play, but this stuff?" He pointed at her chest, then his. "You and me? I end up talking like a kindergartener."

"I can speak kindergarten, too," she told him. "I'm well practiced."

He slid his hand down her back, pressing his lips against her shoulder. "I'm falling for you. This isn't just about sex for me. I don't think it has been for a while now. Life makes sense when you're around. And when you're not it's just shit."

She ran her palm over his cropped hair, her fingers curling around his neck. "But you understand this isn't just about me, right? I come as a package deal with the boys. You know that."

"Yeah." He nodded. "And I'm good with that. I like them. I think they like me."

"They might not like you so much when they find out there's something going on between us."

"When?" He looked at her through thick lashes. "Not if?"

She swallowed hard. "Maybe you're not the only one who's fallen."

His lips curled up. "Of course I'm not. It's classic Nightingale Syndrome."

"What?"

"Falling in love with your doctor. It's a classic thing." He grinned.

"You're *not* my doctor," she pointed out.

"I *am* your doctor. I put you through rehab." He slid his hands down her hips, his fingers leaving a trail of fire on her skin. "It's only natural you'd fall for me."

"The Love Doctor?" She bit down a giggle. "Is that what you think you are?"

"I like that." He nodded. "Yeah, just call me Doctor Love

from now on." He nuzzled her neck. "Have you really fallen for me?"

"I have. But now I'm seriously reconsidering it."

"Damn. That's harsh." He curled his hands around her waist, lifting her back onto the mattress. "I think you need another rehab session to remind you who you're talking to." He hooked his thigh around hers, kissing her hard and fast.

"What about breakfast?" she asked, curling her hands around his neck.

He cupped her breast with his rough palm, his thumb brushing against her nipple. "Breakfast can wait."

———

"I'D REALLY LIKE to tour the island tomorrow," Mia told him, as they drank their cocktails on the restaurant deck, over-looking the ocean. "Not that I didn't enjoy Naked Saturday."

"I noticed you taking to it like a duck to water." Cam lifted an eyebrow. "Maybe it could catch on."

They'd spent the morning in bed, followed by a long hot shower together in the oversized luxury bathroom. After finally eating, they'd laid out by the pool – naked of course – then gone for a long, delicious swim.

One thing had led to another – as it always did when he was around – and they'd ended up spending the second half of the afternoon in bed. Only climbing out to get ready for dinner. She'd almost been sad to put on clothes. Being naked with Cam Hartson wasn't exactly a hardship.

"I'm not sure it'd be the same in Hartson's Creek," she said, giving a mock shiver. "It's too cold there."

"Good thing I have good heating in my house." He lifted his glass to hers. "Here's to us. And making Naked Saturday Morning a regular thing."

She clinked her glass against his, smiling. "To us."

The sun had gone down behind them, leaving behind a palette of purple and pink slashed across the sky, with dark palm trees silhouetting the line between the grassy lawn of the hotel and the sandy dunes of the beach.

There were a few people out there, flying kites and walking along the ocean's edge. It was the first time she'd seen other tourists. Even tonight, the golf cart driver had brought them straight to their table, bypassing reception and the Maître D'.

"We could head to Main Street Village for lunch tomorrow," Cam suggested. "And maybe go for a walk along the beach before that. Our flight is at three, but we have plenty of time as long as you don't oversleep again."

"I didn't oversleep." She grinned at him. "You wore me out, that's all."

"Nobody told you rehab was easy."

"I thought it wasn't rehab anymore." She looked at him from the corner of her eye. "Doctor Love."

He rolled his eyes. "Of course it isn't rehab. And for the record, I'm getting used to your snoring. It's kind of like listening to white noise, only louder."

"I don't snore," she protested.

"Yeah, you do. It's like being in bed with an old dog."

"Less of the old."

"Sorry. It's like being in bed with a really sexy, lithe, gorgeous dog who I want to…" He shook his head. "No, that doesn't work. Can we forget this whole conversation?"

She nodded, her eyes sparkling. "I think it's for the best."

"I told you I have the vocab of a kindergartener."

"You'll fit right in at my place." She took a sip of her cocktail. This was so heavenly, sitting by the beach at sunset with this gorgeous man. "Speaking of which, I think we need to take it slow with the boys. Let them get used to you. No public displays of affection. Michael's at a weird age and I really want him to feel comfortable about this. Are you willing to take your time?"

"I'm willing to do whatever it takes to be with you." He took her hand, folding it in his own. "I'm all in here, Mia."

She took a deep breath. "And you need to take it easy with me, too. I'm still technically married."

"When will the divorce be final?" he asked, his expression serious.

She shook her head. "Within the next few weeks." She traced the rim of her cocktail glass with her free hand. "And whatever we do, I want to pay my way. I can't have you paying and me taking all the time. It doesn't feel right."

He tipped his head to the side, his eyes taking her in. "This weekend is on me. No discussions."

"Okay. But you can't do this all the time. I earn my own money. My independence is really important to me. And you still need to give me the invoice for the damage to your car. I'll be paying it."

"No. It's not important."

Her jaw tightened. "It's important to me. When Niall left, I had nothing. I won't put me or the boys through that again. I've worked too hard to be brought that low again."

"I get that. But I'm not that kind of guy."

Her smile was sad. "I hope not. But I can't live without knowing I'll be fine without you. Financially, at least. So please give me the damn invoice and I'll work out a way to pay you. If we're going to do this, I want us to be equals."

He pulled his gaze from hers, staring down at the ground as though there was something really interesting laying there in the dirt. "Okay." He nodded. "I'll get it to you next week. And I understand why you need security. But I'm not Niall, I don't treat people badly. And I can't promise that I won't want to spoil you and the kids sometimes."

"Spoiling is fine," she told him, squeezing his hand tightly. "Just not all the time."

He nodded. "Understood. So we take it slow, I make you pay me money I don't need and you don't have, and then we'll be good?"

She bit down a smile. "Pretty much."

He shrugged. "If it means that much to you, then we'll do it your way."

"Thank you." She pressed her lips against his cheek. "I appreciate it."

"I still have to go to L.A. next week," he told her. "I promised my agent I'd meet the owners, even though I know I don't want the job. When I get back, maybe I can come over for dinner. Let Michael and Josh get used to having me around?"

Let them get used to having him around.

She played the words over in her mind. Maybe she'd need some time to get used to it, too. In a good way, because being with him felt so easy. When he was around, she felt as though she could breathe. Could be herself, the person she used to be before life pulled her along and made her breathless.

She liked who she was when Cam was around. And she adored being with him.

"Yeah, I'd like that." She smiled at him. "Just be yourself and they'll get used to it."

He slid his hand around her neck, pulling her in for a kiss. "You make me happy," he whispered as he pulled away. "So damn happy."

She smiled softly at him. "Ditto."

CHAPTER TWENTY-FOUR

"Hey, sweetie," Mia said, lifting her phone to her ear. Cam crossed his legs and picked up his coffee mug, watching her as she talked to her boys.

They were sitting at a coffee shop in Main Street Village. Mia had insisted they get up at eight – though he'd managed to persuade her to come in the shower with him. By nine they'd walked along the beach, then taken a taxi into the village, which was full of quaint old low country buildings and pretty boutiques.

Now they were sitting at the café, while she chatted with the boys who were still with her ex-husband. Well, her almost-ex. Cam swallowed another mouthful of coffee. Yeah, that divorce couldn't come fast enough.

"You did?" Mia said, her lips curling. "Wow, you're brave. I can't believe how grown up you sound. I'm glad you're having fun." Her eyes met Cam's. He winked at her and she blew a kiss back.

"Well, have fun, honey. And I'll see you later tonight. Is Michael still there?"

There was a pause as she waited for her eldest son to take

his phone back. Cam took the opportunity to admire her. She looked amazing, sitting in the dappled sunlight, her pale yellow sundress clinging to her skin. She'd put a change of clothes in her bag – ready to put her jeans and sweater on at the airport, and return to the cool temperatures in Hartson's Creek.

They'd head straight to the airport after this. Their bags were being handled by the hotel, and would be conveyed directly to the airline check in desk for them. The pleasures of flying first class. His money definitely made his life easier. He wanted to make Mia's life easier, too.

"Hey honey, are you having fun, too?" Mia asked, when Michael came onto the line. "You did? Great. Thank you for looking after him. He sounds like he's enjoying himself."

She picked up her coffee cup. Lifting it to her lips. "Sorry?" Her brow dipped as she listened again. "You called the landline? Why?" Pursing her lips, she blew out a mouthful of air. "I must have been in the yard and didn't hear it."

So Michael was asking questions. That wasn't a surprise. Cam knew he was protective of his mom. He'd wanted to pay back the car repairs without her knowing, after all.

That was something Cam needed to talk to him about, man to man. He'd do it this week, before he headed to L.A. Explain that he didn't feel right lying to Mia, and that Michael didn't need to come around and do chores anymore.

If they were going to do this thing, it needed to be a clean slate. No more hiding things. He was done with that.

His relationship with Mia was too important to mess up. Yeah, it had started with pure attraction, but now it was so much more. He wasn't lying yesterday when he told her he was falling for her. The fact was, he'd already fallen hard. He was laying on the ground, staring up in wonder at this woman who'd changed his life. Who'd made him feel things he'd never felt before.

"Okay, I'll see you tonight. Have fun, my darling." Mia sighed and ended the call. "He's angry because he called home and I didn't answer this morning."

"We need to tell him about us."

She nodded. "I know. But we need to do it the right way. I know Michael. He doesn't like surprises. He wants to think he's in control. Let him get used to having you around, then I'll talk with him, okay?"

Cam nodded. "You're his mom. You know him better than anybody."

"Thank you." She put her phone in her purse and reached for his hand. Their fingers slotted together perfectly. "For always being so understanding."

"I like your kids," he told her. "And I'll do whatever it takes to have you in my life." He cleared his throat. "And to make Naked Saturday a permanent thing."

She laughed, the worry melting from her face. "Why do I feel like you're being serious?"

"Because I am." He lifted her hand to his mouth, pressing her palm against his lips. "Deadly."

———

"THANK YOU," she said, rolling onto the balls of her toes to press her lips against his. "For the weekend. For being you. For everything."

Cam slid his hands to the small of her back, pressing her body to his. They'd barely been able to keep their hands off each other during the flight – much to the amusement of the flight attendants. And now they'd reached the VIP car park, and their respective cars were waiting for them – her Honda looking a little sad next to his sparkling – and undented – blue Audi.

"Thank you for being mine." He smiled at her softly,

stroking her hair. "I wish I could drive you home and spend the night with you."

"Spending the night together might take some time. But we'll get there."

"You're worth the wait. Even if Doctor Love doesn't like blue balls."

She laughed. "I like the way you've given yourself a nickname."

"I believe that pleasure was all yours." His lips lifted up.

"Well, Doctor Love, this patient needs to get home and recuperate," she said reluctantly. "And I probably have four loads of laundry to do, two boys who won't want to go to bed, and a pile of homework that neither of them has touched all weekend."

"Are you trying to put me off?"

"I'm just keeping it real. If you're all in, this will be part of your life, too." She shrugged.

He dipped his face, breathing in her hair. "I can't think of anything I want more."

"I keep waiting for you to run away screaming," she admitted. "I'm a lot to deal with."

"You forget I come from a big family. I'm used to the craziness. I kind of missed it when I left home." He gave a half shrug. "And I'm not running anywhere."

Mia's eyes widened. "Speaking of your family, I forgot to tell you. Gray's coming to the Distillery next week to talk about an ad campaign. It might end up affecting you, too. My boss is really keen on having your family be part of the launch of the new whiskey blend. She wants to persuade him to get you all involved."

"All of us?" Cam looked genuinely surprised.

"Yeah. It's a family whiskey company, and they want a successful family to promote it. Your brothers and Becca. It's still in the early stages, but I wanted you to hear it from me first." She gave him a small smile. "But you don't have to be involved if you don't want. What's happening between us has no bearing on that. It's between you and your brothers."

"I guess I'll see what Gray says."

She smiled, relief washing over her. "Thank you. I should have mentioned it before. I wasn't hiding it on purpose. It's just a bit hush hush." Sliding her hand down his chest, she glanced up at him. "I don't want any secrets between us."

Cam swallowed hard. "Me either."

"Can I call you later? When the boys are in bed?"

He traced the line of her jaw with his finger. "If you don't, then I'll be calling you."

"You'd better be naked when I call, Doctor Love."

He lifted an eyebrow. "I'm never going to shake off that name, am I?"

"Why would you want to? It's an amazing name."

He pressed his lips against her brow. "I'll come up with one for you."

"Other than MILF?"

He laughed. "You're not a MILF. Your're a MIF."

"A MIF?"

"Mom I fu—"

She put her finger across his lips. "Now stop that."

"You started it."

Mia shook her head. "Yeah, I did. And now I'm finishing it. Go home and unpack and I'll talk to you later."

He slid his fingers into her hair, cupping her face with his other hand, and molded his lips against hers. "Okay, Mom. Whatever you say."

―――――

"Mom, I can't find my toothbrush," Josh yelled out, while Mia was putting the first load of laundry into the washer. "Mike, did you steal it?"

"What would I want with your gunky toothbrush?" Michael called out. He was leaning over his homework at the kitchen table, muttering under his breath as he tried to finish his math assignment. "Look in the front zip of your backpack."

"Found it!"

Michael shook his head at Mia. "Kids."

"Have you nearly finished your homework?" she asked him. "It's almost bed time."

"Dad let us stay up until midnight," Michael said, giving her a sly glance.

"That's nice." She knew exactly what he was trying to do, and it wouldn't work. She was still too high from her weekend with Cam to let it get to her. "I'm glad you had a good time."

"We did," Michael said. His expression softened. "Did you have a nice weekend, too?"

Mia swallowed, and turned her face from his. "Yeah, it was fine."

"Maybe Dad will take us away another time, give you a break."

"Maybe." She smiled at him. "But I don't need a break from you guys. I like being around you."

Josh ran into the kitchen, wearing only his pajama bottoms. "I'm ready for bed," he announced.

"Where's your top?" Mia asked him, looking at the pile of laundry. No sign of a plaid t-shirt in there.

"I don't wear it anymore. Big guys just wear bottoms. Isn't that right, Mikey?"

"Dad told him to take it off at the hotel. It was too hot in the bedrooms." Michael shrugged.

"You don't have to be topless to be a big guy," Mia said, ruffling his hair. "It's cold in this house."

"I'm fine," Josh said. "I don't feel the cold."

Michael shook his head and turned back to his math.

"Mom, do you think you'll find a boyfriend? Like Dad has Gemma?" Josh's question was innocent, but at that moment it had her heart racing.

Mia closed the washer lid, grateful that they couldn't see her expression. "What makes you ask that?"

"Dad had a talk with us. Explained that he and Gemma would be getting married. I asked him what about you, and he said you'd probably get a boyfriend."

She feigned nonchalance. "Maybe."

Michael glanced over at his brother and rolled his eyes. "Mom won't date. She doesn't have time."

Mia ignored the pang of guilt in her chest. "If you've both finished sorting out my love life, I'll take Josh up to bed. You have twenty minutes," she warned Michael. "And then you need to jump in the shower. I can still smell the chlorine on you."

"Had to get that last swim in." Michael winked at her. "You know what it's like."

Weirdly, she did. Not that she was planning to tell him about her trip to Hilton Head. Biting down a smile, Mia followed Josh up the stairs.

"If you do get a boyfriend, I hope he likes waterparks," Josh said, making his way to his bedroom.

Mia laughed. "I'll make sure that's on the top of my requirements."

CHAPTER TWENTY-FIVE

"You sent him flowers?" Joanna asked, her voice dipping as she gave a little laugh. "I love that. It's so girl power. He does something nice, you send him a bouquet. Did he like them?"

"He loved them. He said nobody had ever sent him flowers before."

Joanna giggled. "And I can't believe you're calling him Doctor Love. That's hilarious."

"He doesn't find it quite so funny." Mia grinned as she remembered the message she wrote on the card.

To Doctor Love. **Thank you for the rehab weekend. Especially Naked Saturday. Love Mia (Your MIF) xx**

"Ah, the guy's falling for you. I bet he finds everything you do funny." Joanna sighed. "This is like one of those romance novels. I'm feeling faint just talking about it. And I can't tell you how jealous I am that he whisked you away for the weekend."

Mia leaned back on her office chair and gave a little sigh. "It *was* romantic," she admitted. And hot as hell, too. Her skin tingled at the memory of how good Cam Hartson looked in the buff, his strong defined muscles covered by taut, smooth skin.

"How do you think the boys will take it when you tell them?" Joanna asked.

"I don't know. Josh will be okay, I think. He likes Cam and he's young enough to accept him. Michael… I'm not so sure."

"He'll get used to it. He went away with his dad and Gemma, after all."

"Yeah, he did." Maybe Joanna was right.

"And he knows Cam. He's his coach. He must respect him. I know they got off to a bad start with the car." Joanna gave a little laugh. "But that's all ancient history."

"Yeah, he hasn't mentioned it for weeks."

"There you go. It'll be fine." Jo's voice softened. "I'm so happy for you. You deserve this after all you've been through. And maybe I can get some free tickets to a football game."

Mia laughed. "Maybe."

"Seriously, I want to meet him some time."

"I'd like that." Mia rolled her lip between her teeth. "He's important to me."

"I kind of got that impression," Joanna teased. "I know this is all going to work out. It has to."

"I hope so." Mia smiled softly. Everything felt so different since they'd agreed to make things official between them. She felt like she was walking around in a haze. "I should go. I have a ton of work to do before I pick Josh up."

"Okay, sweets. I'll speak to you soon. Oh and Mia?"

"Yeah?"

"I watched one of his old games last night and he has so much BDE it made me hot."

"BDE?" Mia said, her brow dipping in confusion.

"Big Dick Energy. Google it. He's pretty much the poster boy."

"Bye, Jo." Mia pulled the phone from her cheek and pressed her finger to end the call, not waiting for her cousin to reply. No doubt she'd call later, or send a dozen inappropriate texts.

With a glance at her closed office door, she opened up Safari and quickly typed into the search bar.

Big Dick Energy.

Her eyes widened as she read the definition.

It's confidence without cockiness. It is never misplaced and it cannot be simulated. It is the sexual equivalent of writing a check for $10k knowing you got it in the bank account.

She burst out laughing, because it was so on the mark, the ten thousand dollars included.

Cam Hartson definitely had Big Dick Energy. Though she'd never admit that to Joanna.

———

"You heading home?" Cam asked, as Michael walked out of practice, his sports bag slung over his shoulder.

Michael shrugged. "Yeah. Gonna catch a ride with one of the guys."

"I could give you a ride. There's something I want to talk to you about. Maybe we can head to my place and grab a drink or something?"

Michael frowned. "What kind of thing?" He pulled his duffle from his shoulder and let it fall to the ground with a thud. "Is there something wrong?"

"Nothing at all. It's nothing sinister. I just thought we

should talk about the work you're doing for me. Only if you have time." Cam kept his voice even. No need to alarm Michael. It was pretty simple. Tell Michael he didn't feel comfortable in letting him lie to his mom without getting him all riled up. Then after he came back from L.A., the boys would slowly get used to him. They didn't need to rush anything, but he wanted this clean slate.

His relationship with Mia was too important to start it with a lie hanging over his head.

"Okay." Michael shrugged, opening the door of Cam's Audi and throwing his bag in the back. Then he turned to Leon and pointed at the car. "No need for a ride, I'm covered."

Leon nodded. "Okay. See you tomorrow."

Climbing into the passenger seat, Michael fastened his seatbelt and turned to Cam. "That was a good practice today."

Cam turned on the engine and backed the car out. "You guys are really coming together as a team. You gotta work on a few plays, but I think you have a chance of winning this week."

"Not if Ben keeps fumbling the damn ball." Michael sighed. "The guy dropped more than he caught today."

"We all have off days." Cam glanced at Michael from the corner of his eye. He really wanted the kid to like him. Yeah, part of that was because it would make things with Mia so much easier, but it was more than wanting to be with Michael's mom. He genuinely liked him. He might be a bit pissy occasionally, and cocky when he didn't need to be, but what teenage football player wasn't? Cam cringed when he thought about the young thug he had been when he'd captained the team. He thought he was the king of Hartson's Creek.

Michael would grow into his skills. And maybe he'd even

get a sports scholarship. That was something else Cam could help him with – he had connections and knew what the scouts were looking for.

Pulling up outside his house, Cam climbed out of the car and pointed at Michael's bag. "You can leave that here. I'll give you a ride home when we're done."

"I live five minutes away. I can walk." Michael gave him a confused look.

Yeah, but if he timed it right, giving Michael a ride home meant Cam might get a glimpse of Mia. And he was all about that. He'd been thinking about her and their weekend together all day. The memory of her naked body curled into his had been seared into his mind.

And then she'd sent him flowers in a complete twist of normal conventions. He'd laughed like crazy when he read her message.

He wanted to be with her again. And soon.

"How was your trip to the waterpark?" Cam asked Michael as he opened his front door.

"You know about that?" His voice rose up.

Cam blinked. "Yeah. I heard Josh telling your mom about it."

Michael glanced at him from the corner of his eye. "It was good. Thanks."

Damn. He needed to be more careful. At least for the next couple of weeks. His face felt hot – he needed to splash some water on it. "You go on into the kitchen. Grab yourself a soda or something. I just need to do something really quick."

Michael shrugged. "Okay." He sloped off down the hallway to the kitchen. He'd been here enough times to know where everything was. Taking one last glance at his back, Cam turned and headed upstairs, wanting to put some space between them.

In the bathroom, he filled his cupped hands with cold

water and splashed it onto his cheeks. Looking up at his reflection in the mirror, he took a long, slow inhale.

There was no way he could mess this up. He didn't want to make things between him and Michael difficult.

"Just go talk to him, asshole," he muttered. "Get this over with."

Why was he so on edge? If he was going to be spending more time with these kids, he needed to learn how to deal with them. Maybe he needed to talk to his brothers for advice.

Nah, Mia was the one who could help. He'd talk to her when he was back from L.A. Tell her about this stupid arrangement with Michael and throw himself at her mercy.

Grabbing a fresh towel from the rack on the wall, he dried his face and blew out another mouthful of air. Time to tell Michael their little agreement was over.

Cam strode to the kitchen, determined to do this quickly. Michael had his back to him, leaning over the breakfast bar, a little white card in his hands. Cam swallowed hard, looking at the floral arrangement that was still in the cardboard delivery vase, right in front of where the kid was standing.

"Michael?"

Slowly, Michael turned his head, the card still clutched between his fingers. He glanced down at it again, his lips moving as though he was re-reading the words.

To Doctor Love. Thank you for the rehab weekend. Especially Naked Saturday. Love Mia (your MIF) xx

Glancing up from the card, Michael's gaze met Cam's. He blinked, his jaw popping as though he was gritting his teeth. "What the hell is this?" he asked, his voice tight.

Cam walked forward to grab the card, but Michael wouldn't release it. "It's not what you think," he said, his heart pounding against his ribcage. "Let me explain."

"Are these from my mom?"

Cam blew out a mouthful of air. "Michael, you need to give me that card."

Michael shook his head, as though he was trying to understand. "No. You need to tell me if this is from my mom." His eyes met Cam's again, the air between them filled with heavy silence. "What does MIF mean?" Michael asked.

"Nothing. It means nothing."

"It's like MILF, right? Mom I'd like to fuck." Michael spat the last word out. "Are you fucking my mom?"

Cam frowned. "Michael…"

"Are you?" Michael leaned forward until his face was only inches from Cam's. He could see the anger flashing in the boy's eyes. "Are you having sex with my mom, *Doctor Love*?"

When the hell did Michael grow to be so big? He was only a few inches shorter than Cam, and all the drills and gym work they'd been doing with the team made him look broader and stronger than Cam had remembered.

He was a man. One with a boy's anger. Cam swallowed hard.

"You need to talk to your mom," Cam said quietly. "I can't talk to you about this without her here."

A low growling sound escaped from Michael's lips. Then his hands were on Cam's chest, barreling him over until he landed on the kitchen tiles. Michael straddled his body, pushing and pummelling him.

"You asshole. You said you were my friend. You pretended to like me to get to my mom." His eyes were welling up, and Cam tried to reach out for him to stop the rage, but Michael batted his hands away. "You're having sex with my mom, you bastard." He hit him again. The blows landed heavily, but Cam didn't move to stop him again. He had no idea what to say to the boy.

"I hate you. I goddamned hate you." The tears were

flowing down his cheeks now. "Everybody's going to find out. The whole team. They're going to laugh at me."

Cam finally captured Michael's wrists between his strong palms. The boy didn't put up much resistance. His tears were too strong, the shaking of his chest too steady. He'd done this. He'd made an almost-grown boy cry, because he was too damn stupid to hide those flowers away.

"Nobody's going to laugh at you," Cam said, keeping his voice soft. "We'll make it right."

"*We?* You and me? Go fuck yourself." Michael screwed his face up. "And stop seeing my mom. You're disgusting. I could get you fired."

Damn that kid was apoplectic. "Michael…"

"Don't talk to me," Michael warned. "Don't say anything." He yanked his hands from Cam's, leaning back on his haunches. "Just leave us alone. We don't want you."

Jumping to his feet, Michael backed up, his lips pressed tightly together.

"We need to talk about this." Cam pushed himself up, dusting off his jeans as he looked at the boy.

"We don't need to do anything. Just stay away from my mom or you'll regret it."

"I can't," Cam told him.

Michael glared at him. "Why not?"

Cam inhaled raggedly. "Because I'm in love with her."

"The hell you are. Don't go near her. Or me. Or Josh." He pushed Cam again, as though to emphasize the point. Cam took it without responding. Michael was a boy. An angry, strong boy, but a child still the same. "And don't talk to me again. I hate the sight of you." He walked toward the kitchen door, his shoulders slumped.

"Michael…"

He didn't answer, just stomped down the hallway and

yanked open the front door. Cam stared at the card laying crumpled on the floor. He needed to call Mia.

But then he remembered Michael's bag, still in his car. He'd drive it around to her place. Try to reason with the kid. Work out how to make it all okay.

Because he couldn't lose her. Not because of a stupid bunch of flowers. They'd come too far for that.

CHAPTER TWENTY-SIX

Mia slung her purse over her shoulder and slid her key into the front door, smiling as Josh continued to unleash a constant stream of chatter about his day.

"And then Noah laughed so hard he started to choke. The teacher was so scared she sent him to the nurse. So he got out of getting in trouble."

"That's good." Mia smiled down at him, her brain full of thoughts. She needed to put dinner on, get Josh to do his homework, do some work of her own. Maybe if she was really lucky, she'd get to speak to Cam tonight.

"Yeah. I'm gonna try that next time. It was so cool. He went as red as a strawberry."

The sound of feet pounding against the pavement made her look over Josh's head. She frowned when she saw Michael running down the road, his own face red, his chest heaving.

Had he run all the way from football practice?

Before she could call out to him, the roar of an engine cut through the quiet of the neighborhood, Cam's blue Audi swinging around the corner like it was on rails.

Michael glanced at the car and ran faster, right as Cam climbed out and lifted what looked like Michael's duffle. Mia's brows knitted together as she watched him swallow hard and walk toward the house.

What the hell was going on?

"Cam?"

"Mom!" Michael shouted, his breath coming in harsh pants. "Get inside."

"What?" She shook her head, trying to understand.

"Don't talk to him," he yelled, his eyes wide and crazy.

"Cam!" Josh called out, his face brightening as he spotted the football player half-running across the road. He barreled down the steps, throwing himself at Cam's stomach. "I got an 'A' on my project. How cool is that? It's all thanks to you."

Michael stopped in front of Cam and Josh, his eyes narrowing as he continued to pant. "Get your goddamned dirty hands off my brother," he growled.

"Michael!" Mia called out, running down the steps. "What's come over you? Don't swear."

"He doesn't care about your project," Michael continued, pulling at Josh's shoulder. Josh released his hold on Cam, and looked up at Mia, a hurt expression on his face. "He's using you, Josh. To get to Mom."

"He isn't." Josh's lip trembled. "You're my friend, aren't you, Cam?"

Cam ruffled his head. "Sure I am, buddy."

"Don't make me hit you again," Michael said, his voice thick. "Take your hands off my brother. *Now.*"

"Sweetie, can you go inside?" Mia said, looking down at her youngest son. His eyes were tearing up, like he was about to let out a sob. "Go and get some potatoes out from the cupboard. I need to peel them."

"But what about Cam? Why's Michael being so mean?"

It felt like déjà vu. The first day she'd met Cam all over again. Another argument on the doorstep, another attempt to keep the peace. But this time she had no idea what was going on. "Just go in, okay? I'll come in in a moment."

"Okay." Josh nodded. "I'll go."

When the door closed behind him, she turned to look at Cam and Michael. Her son was staring at the older man, his gaze full of venom. "What the hell is going on here?" she asked through gritted teeth. "Why did you make Josh cry?"

"Maybe you should ask 'Doctor Love'," Michael spat out.

Her chest tightened as she lifted her gaze to Cam's. His eyes were soft as they caught hers. "He knows."

"I know you're an asshole who takes advantage of married women," Michael spat out. "That's what *I* know."

She wanted the ground to swallow her up. Instead, she took a deep breath and reached for Michael's arm. "Honey, he didn't take advantage."

"So you fucked him willingly?"

Her jaw set tight. "Don't talk to me like that. And don't let me hear you use that word again. It's disgusting."

Michael rolled his eyes. "Not as disgusting as him."

"Whatever you think happened between the two of us, you're wrong. Now can we go inside and talk about this like adults? Because right now we're giving the whole street a performance they'll talk about for weeks."

"That asshole's not coming in my house." Michael glanced at Cam, shaking his head. "Not now and not ever."

"It isn't your house," Mia reminded him.

"Oh I know that. You dragged me away from *my* house. The one in Kansas City. I get no damn choices over my own life. Because it's all about you and dad, isn't it? You messed up each others' lives and now you're messing up mine."

"Michael…" Cam's voice was soft. "We don't want to mess up your life."

"Do you love him?" Michael asked her, his nostrils flaring. "Sweetie, I…"

"Because he loves you. Or so he says. But we both know he's full of shit."

He loved her? Mia's hands started to shake. When she looked at Cam she could see it. The softness, the light shining out of him. A tiny gasp left her lips.

He loved her. Oh god, she loved him, too.

"That isn't any of your business," she told Michael. There was no way she was going to declare her feelings here and now.

"But you love *me*, right?" His lip trembled.

"Of course I do." She stroked his hair, but he recoiled from her. "So much."

"If you love me, you'll stop seeing him. Right now. Tell him it's over."

His words felt like a mack truck hitting her head on. She turned to her son. He was staring at her with a question in his eyes. Did she love him enough to make Cam leave?

Or was she going to turn out like Niall, and put her love life before her children? There was no question about her choice, but it hurt so damn much. She inhaled raggedly, looking at both the boy and the man she loved.

"Cam…" She tried to find the words, but her brain was a mess of emotions.

"It's okay," Cam said, his voice cracking. "I'm leaving."

That's when the tears started rolling down her face.

———

"It can't be over," Joanna said, her voice low. "There has to be a way to make this work. Maybe give Michael some time.

He'll get used to having Cam around. You can't sacrifice your happiness for your children."

Mia squeezed her eyes closed. "Of course I can. That's what moms do. And what's the alternative? Be with Cam and break Michael's trust in me forever? He already had one parent desert him, I can't do the same."

She leaned back on the bed, feeling light headed. The evening had been fraught, and more than once she'd thought she was going to throw up. Josh had been so upset when she'd walked back into the house, wanting to know why Michael was so angry and hated Cam. He'd cried as she explained it was an adult thing, but they all still loved Josh and that's what mattered.

By the time he went to bed, he'd perked up a little. Hopefully by the morning he'd be back to his usual chirpy self.

Which was more than she could say for Michael. He barely spoke all evening. Didn't eat his dinner, or hang around in the kitchen to do his homework. Instead, he'd disappeared to his room and told her to go away when she knocked.

Time. He needed time. Maybe that would help him get over this.

As for her? Everything inside of her felt broken. If you shook her, she'd rattle. The little shards of her heart that Cam had helped her glue back together had been crushed all over again.

"What about if you two cool it for now? Try again in a few months. Michael's at such a difficult age." Joanna was grasping at straws. "I mean, what if he does this to every guy you date? You'll be a lonely old woman."

"I don't think I'm going to date again." Mia's voice was monotone. She couldn't imagine ever wanting to be with anybody but Cam. He was the first man to make her feel alive. To make her feel like she could take on the world with him by her side.

The only man she cared about.

"Jo…" her voice cracked, a sob escaping her lips. Hot tears rolled down her face. "I've messed everything up. I don't know what to do."

"Oh sweetie. Just breathe. It's okay," Joanna crooned. "You haven't messed anything up. This isn't your fault. You're allowed to fall in love. It's what makes the world go around. One day, Michael will regret hurting you like this."

Mia could taste the salt of her tears on her lips. "I never should've sent those flowers."

"And Cam shouldn't have let Michael in his house while they were there, but neither of you expected this to happen. I thought the flowers were a cute touch, for what it's worth." Joanna sighed. "I still don't think you should give up."

"What do you think I should do?" Mia asked, desperate for hope.

"You should ask him to wait for you."

"No. I can't do that." Mia shook her head even though her cousin couldn't see her. "I can't leave him hanging when there's a chance Michael won't change his mind. It's not fair on him."

She could hear Joanna's soft breathing echoing down the phone. "So you're done?"

"I don't know." Mia pressed her hand to her brow, blinking back the tears. There was no other way. Not unless she wanted to alienate Michael forever. Her head was pounding like somebody was hitting it with a sledgehammer. "But I can't hurt Michael any more than he's been hurt. I don't see us coming back from this."

"Oh honey."

"I know. I know."

CHAPTER TWENTY-SEVEN

Cam pulled into the school parking lot and switched off the ignition, sighing loudly as he slumped in the driver's seat. His head was pounding, and his eyes felt as dry as the Sahara, thanks to a night of sleeplessness. Instead he'd tossed and turned, thinking about the anger in Michael's eyes, and the horror in Mia's.

This was all his fault, and he had no idea how to make it better.

At midnight he'd tried calling her, but her phone was off. So he typed and deleted about a hundred different messages, before sending a simple *'I'm sorry.'*

And now he had to go in and coach the varsity team, and pretend that everything was okay. At least it wasn't JV – so Michael wouldn't be there. But he'd have to face him eventually.

Face the fact that the kid hated his guts.

It was stupid how much that hurt. But it was nowhere near as powerful as the excruciating pain in his chest every time he thought of *her*.

Yesterday, when they were standing outside her house,

she was going to tell him it was over. He could see it in her eyes. And yeah, he'd handled it for her by walking away, but her rejection still felt like a knife to the heart. She was right to choose her son. He wouldn't have expected anything else from her.

So why was it so damn hard to breathe?

"Hey, can we have a word in my office?" Coach Hawkins asked when Cam made his way to the gym. "Something weird is going on and I'm hoping you can shed some light on it."

"Sure." Cam nodded, following the coach into the closet that masqueraded as his office. It was just large enough for a small desk with enough of a gap for the coach to squeeze around so he could sit in his chair. Cam took a seat opposite. The only light in here was from the strip hanging on the ceiling. The windowless space felt like it was lacking oxygen. It also smelled bad, like teenagers who hadn't remembered to shower.

The coach steepled his hands together, looking at Cam over his fingertips. "Michael Devlin came to see me today."

Cam took a deep breath. "What did he say?" He could guess. But he wanted to hear it from somebody else.

"He quit the team."

Cam blinked. "What? He can't do that. You just promoted him."

"That's what I told him. But he was clear. He won't play football at Columbus as long as you're a coach. So my question is, what's going on?"

"I made him angry. A personal thing." Cam wasn't sure how much Michael had shared. And he didn't want to make the kid's life any harder by spilling his guts to Coach Hawkins. "I'll talk to him. He'll change his mind."

Coach's eyes flashed. "There's no such thing as a personal thing. This is a school, and you're a coach. It's my job to protect the kids, so I'll ask you again. What happened between you and Michael?"

Cam closed his eyes for a brief moment. The mess kept getting bigger. "I was in a relationship with his mom. Michael found out and got angry." He opened his eyes and glanced at the coach. "I'd appreciate it if this didn't go any further."

Coach Hawkins sighed. "Was? That means it's over?"

Hearing it out loud made Cam's gut ache. "Pretty much, yes." He blew out a mouthful of air. "Let me speak to Michael, see if I can get him back on the team. He has too much talent not to play."

"No. I don't think that's wise. Michael was pretty adamant. And I don't like angst in my football team. The two of you working together isn't a good idea."

Cam shook his head. "You're right." There was no way he wanted to make this worse. Not for Michael or Mia, or even himself.

"So you'll stop coaching JV." It wasn't a question.

"Yeah," Cam agreed. "I will." He glanced at the ground. "I should stop coaching Varsity, too. It's only a matter of time before Michael's ready to start training with the main team. And he won't do it if I'm here."

Coach gave him a sad smile. "I think that might be for the best. For Michael's sake. I'll be sad to see you go."

Another rejection. Sure, it was gentle, but he still added it to the pile. The Bobcats, Michael, and now the school football team.

And Mia. The one that hurt more than the others combined together.

"I should go." Cam stood, glancing back at the coach. "Will you tell them I've left?"

"Yeah."

"I have a meeting about a coaching job in L.A. this week. Maybe use that in way of explanation."

The coach nodded. "I'll make it vague." He stood and shook Cam's outstretched hand. "Thank you for all your hard work. On behalf of the whole team. We have the best defense we've had in years thanks to you."

Cam gave him a nod and got the hell out of there, not stopping until he made it to his car.

There was only one thing for it. He needed some brotherly advice.

———

HIS THREE BROTHERS looked at him with open mouths. "Mia Devlin?" Logan finally said. "Why didn't I know about this?"

Cam had called his twin from the car, and told him he needed to talk. Logan must have taken that as the apocalypse coming, because before he knew it, all three of his brothers were assembled in Gray's kitchen, waiting for him to drive over and throw his heart on the goddamn floor. Becca would probably be here too, if she wasn't stuck at work.

Thank god she was. Right now she was such a big reminder of Mia it hurt.

"I guess I wasn't sure where it was going. And once I was, I needed to keep my mouth shut because we had the whole issue of telling her boys." He shook his head. "But I messed that up, too, didn't I? Like everything I touch turns to shit."

"Yeah, like your nine years of playing NFL football. That's been terrible." Tanner let out a snort. "Catastrophize much?"

"I don't remember you laughing when Van ended things with you," Logan murmured. "Give the guy a break. We all know what heartbreak feels like."

Their nickname had never felt so apt.

"So what are you gonna do?" Gray asked, leaning forward on the breakfast bar.

"I'm going to L.A. and hope to God I get the job." Cam looked down at the counter, his eyes tracing patterns in the stone. "Because I can't stay around here and not be with her."

"You're leaving? But you just got here." Tanner frowned. "Dude, don't make any rash decisions."

"I hate to say it, but Tanner's right." Logan shrugged.

"Bingo!" Tanner clapped his hands together. "I knew I'd be right eventually."

"A stopped clock is right twice a day," Gray murmured, shaking his head at his brothers. He looked up at Cam, his eyes full of sympathy. "Did you know I flew to L.A. when Maddie and I broke up?"

"Is that when she hit that guy who released the video?" Cam could remember seeing it all over social media. Gray had confronted the guy who'd spread an indecent video of Maddie when she'd been at college, and Maddie had ended up with her fist in the guy's face. The internet had gone crazy for her.

"Yeah, that's right. But when I flew there, I did it because I was fighting for her. Not because I was running away."

"I'm not running away," Cam said, his voice vehement. "I'm going because if I stay it's only going to get worse. Not just for me – I could hang around if that was the case – but for Michael and Mia. If I go, Michael will play football, and maybe he and Mia's relationship will be okay. If I stay, I'm a permanent reminder. I can't do that to them."

"When do you fly out?" Logan asked, his brows knitted together.

"On Friday. I'll be there for a few days. I'm thinking of heading back to Boston after. If I get the job I'll need to clear out the house, maybe put it on the market. I guess I'll need to learn about L.A. real estate."

"So that's it? You're done?"

"It's not like that. If it wasn't for her kids, I'd fight for her every step of the way. But it's a no-win situation. If she chose me, I wouldn't respect her. And if she chose them…" he trailed off, shaking his head. "Of course she'll choose them. Which she should. So either I hang around here like a has-been football star, or I try to work out what the hell to do next."

"But you love her," Tanner said, running the pad of his thumb along his jaw. "You can't leave her if you feel that way."

"What should I do then?" He wanted to feel some hope. But everything was too dark for that.

Tanner shifted his eyes. "I don't know," he admitted. "But there has to be an answer."

"Are you going to tell her you're going?" Logan asked him.

"Of course I am." He needed to see her one last time. Maybe then his heart wouldn't ache so much. "I'm not an asshole."

Tanner coughed into his hand. "Disagree."

"Shut up." Gray nudged Tanner in the side.

"What? Cam used to razz me constantly. And he still hasn't let me forget that I stood outside of Van's house with a boombox on my shoulder."

Cam shot a glance at Tanner. "It wasn't a boombox, it was a Bluetooth speaker. Lameness should never be forgotten."

"See? It's not just me."

Gray rolled his eyes at his brothers. "What if the kid changes his mind?"

"Then I'll be back here like a shot." Cam had no doubt about that. "But I can't stay in this town knowing she's so close yet so untouchable. It'll kill me."

Logan sighed. "Yeah, it'd kill me, too."

"I guess even the Hartson brothers can't solve every problem." Tanner blew out a mouthful of air. "It sucks."

Wasn't that the understatement of the year?

"Yeah it does." Cam nodded. "It sucks like crazy."

"Can I speak to Michael?"

Mia stared at Cam, her heart racing at his close proximity. He was the last person she'd expected to see standing on the front steps when the doorbell rang. It was unfair. She wasn't prepared. All she wanted to do was roll onto her tiptoes and press her lips against his, as though that would make everything okay.

But it would only make things a hundred times worse.

"It's not a good idea." Her hands were shaking. "He's still in a terrible mood, and isn't coming out of his room." She pulled her bottom lip between her teeth. His gaze dipped to her mouth. "Give him some time."

"I haven't got any." His words were simple, but they made her frown. "That's what I wanted to talk to him about. I wanted to…" Cam shook his head. "I don't know. Apologize, I guess. And tell him I won't be coaching him anymore. Or anybody for that matter."

"You're not going to stay at Columbus High?" Her voice was thin. She knew she had bags under her eyes that matched his.

"I'm not staying in Hartson's Creek. I can't. I'm going to take the job in L.A. if I'm offered it. And if I'm not, I'll stay in Boston for a while, work out my next move."

She wasn't surprised at the tears stinging her eyes. They felt like a constant companion since Monday. But she was shocked at how much her hands started shaking. Her body felt light, too spacey.

"You don't need to leave," she whispered.

"Yeah, I do. I can't stay around here. Not with you here, too. It's just too hard."

The tears spilled over, running hot trails down her cheeks. "Oh Cam…"

"Please don't cry, baby," he said, swallowing hard. "It makes me want to hold you, and I can't."

Wiping the stubborn trails away with the heels of her hands, she nodded, her eyes captured by his. For a moment they stared at each other. Her chest felt painful, as though her heart might explode at any moment.

"I wish…"

"I know." He nodded. "Believe me, I know."

"Will you be okay?" Her eyelashes felt wet as she blinked.

"Eventually." His smile was grim. "I'll throw myself into football. It's always worked before." He didn't sound too convinced.

"Maybe you'll find somebody out there." She attempted a smile. "Somebody with no kids to take on."

"I told you, I love your kids." He glanced down at the step. "I just wish they liked me."

A tiny sob escaped her lips, despite her best effort to stop it. She wanted to beg him to stay. To ask him to wait. But it was a selfish impulse. Michael might take years to get over this. She couldn't ask Cam to hang around, hoping her son grew up and got over himself.

Even if part of her wished he would.

"I'll work out a payment plan for your car repairs," she said. "Send it to you."

Cam shook his head. "No. That's my one request. Let me write it off. It's paid. That damn car has caused more problems than its worth. Maybe next time I'll get a minivan or something."

The smallest of laughs escaped her lips. "I'm glad you had that car. It's how I met you."

He exhaled softly. "Yeah. And I don't regret that. Not for a minute."

"Me either." She held his gaze. Was this the last time she'd see him? It was agony not to touch him. Not to reach for his hand and slide her fingers between his.

"I'm going to miss you." He tried a smile, and failed miserably. "So damn much."

She nodded, her throat full of unshed tears to say anything. Behind her, the rumble of feet on the stairs made her turn around. Michael was standing in the hallway, eyes narrowed as he realized who was at the door.

"What's he doing here?" His voice was full of anger.

"Cam came to see you. To tell you he's leaving town."

"Good." Michael turned and walked into the kitchen, slamming the door behind him, making Mia jump. She was going to have to deal with him. He couldn't keep behaving like this. She'd given him some grace, but his attitude was as bad as it had been when they arrived. But first she needed to get through this pain, because it was getting hard to breathe.

"Sorry." She turned back to Cam.

"It's not your fault." He ran his hand through his hair. "I guess I should go."

She nodded. "Okay." But it wasn't okay. None of this was. It was killing her. "But can I ask you something first?"

"Sure."

"What you said to Michael about falling in love with me, was it true?"

He swallowed hard. "Yeah, it's true."

"Because I need you to know something. I fell in love with you, too."

The pain that crossed his face was palpable. She could feel the reflection of it in her own heart. His eyes were glassy as he gave her a nod, then walked down the steps toward his car.

"Goodbye, Mia." He walked away, and she watched him, her breath catching in her throat.

He was leaving. And maybe in the end that would be a good thing.

But right now it was tearing her apart.

CHAPTER TWENTY-EIGHT

She had to pull herself out of this funk. It had been over a week since she'd last seen Cam and she was feeling worse than ever. Mia took a deep breath and tried to concentrate on the marketing plan spread across her large monitor, but nothing seemed to make sense. Her stomach rumbled, reminding her that she'd barely eaten anything substantial for days. But every time she took a bite of something, it tasted like ashes.

At least she was at work. It was a haven compared to the heavy atmosphere of home. Michael was still in the foulest of moods, made worse by her chiding and sending him to his room. Sam was mostly at the bar – he hadn't asked what had happened but she was certain he had a good idea. Either way, he was making himself conspicuously scarce, and right now she was grateful for it.

The only light in the darkness was Josh. He was still confused about the argument in the street, but she'd managed to distract him with movies and board games, and of course, football.

If only she were so easily distracted. It wasn't as though

she hadn't tried. On Saturday morning, she'd gone to a yoga class, hoping that some zen would rub off on her. But all it had done was make her miss Cam's touch. He would have laughed at the way she fell over trying to do downward facing dog.

Let the love doctor help.

She shook that thought out of her mind.

"Hey, coffee's here," Becca said, carrying two Styrofoam cups into Mia's office. She passed one to Mia and sipped at the other, sitting on the corner of Mia's desk. For a moment she stared at Mia, her eyes full of compassion. "You look like shit," she said, wrinkling her nose.

Mia almost laughed. "Thanks."

"I know it's none of my business, but Gray told me what happened between you and Cam. And I'm not asking you to talk to me about it, because I know it's all kinds of complicated with Cam being my brother. But if you ever need a friend, I'm here."

The laugh turned to tears. Mia blinked them away. She wasn't going to cry at the office.

That was the kind of reputation she definitely didn't want.

"Thank you." She gave Becca a tight nod. "I appreciate that."

"Good. So now you can tell me why I've been called to join the board meeting this afternoon."

"Gray hasn't told you?"

"Gray?" Becca blinked. "I know he's agreed to be the face of the new blend, but what's that got to do with me? Apart from being his gorgeous and perfect little sister." She took a sip of her coffee, staring at Mia over the rim.

Gray had come in as promised last week, and signed the contract on Monday. The whole board was buzzing with excitement.

Mia sighed. "I guess you're going to find out soon enough. Eliana wants you and your brothers to be part of the advertising campaign, not only Gray. She wants a long form movie commercial where you're all talking and drinking whiskey, and she wants you to narrate it."

"Me? Why?" Becca frowned.

"Because you're the lead distiller for the blend. And we want to appeal to a female demographic." Mia shrugged. "And for what it's worth, I think you'd do an amazing job."

Becca blushed. "Shut up." She looked over at the window, her brows furrowed together. "Surely Gray would be better at narrating. He's got that husky voice thing going for him. Or Logan, he's good at talking." She widened her eyes. "Will Cam be involved?"

Mia took a deep breath. "I have no idea." Part of her hoped he wouldn't. She wasn't sure she could bear to see him again. She was barely holding it together as it was.

The other part? The one that kept her dreaming as a little girl, and hoping for better as a woman... that part was desperate to see him again. Even if the impulse was masochistic.

"I hate that he's going to take the job in L.A.," Becca confided. "I was just getting used to having my whole family back again."

Another stick for Mia to beat herself with. "I'm sorry."

"Oh no, this isn't your fault. It's Cam's. He didn't have to leave, he chose to." Becca shot Mia a sympathetic glance. "You know what? I'm going to say yes. This could be fun. And maybe a chance to get back at my big brothers. I could tell all their secrets in the narration."

"Just remember, Gray's the face of the whiskey. He'll be going on talk shows and using lots of social media. He'll easily get his own back, too."

"Maybe I'll leave him out. Start with Tanner and work my

way up." Becca shrugged. "I've got years of dirt on them. It could be fun."

Mia's attempt at a smile was more successful this time. "I bet it could."

"I wish I could do something to make you feel better," Becca said, her voice soft. "I hate to see you so down. Have you been eating?"

"Not as much as I should." Mia shook her head. "But I will. I've been through heartache before. I know it's only temporary."

But it didn't feel like it was. This separation from Cam felt like a tsunami of pain compared to the breakup of her marriage. It was illogical, but true. She hadn't lost five pounds the week after Niall left. Or suffered from so many nights without sleep.

"I guess I should go. If I'm going to be an international superstar, I want to wear some makeup to this meeting. I'll see you in the boardroom."

Mia nodded. "See you there."

Putting her cup on the desk, Becca leaned forward and hugged Mia tightly. "I'm so sorry my brother broke your heart."

Mia squeezed Becca tight. "He didn't," she said, her voice muffled by Becca's shoulder. "I broke my own heart."

"Hurts just as much though, doesn't it?"

Yeah, it really did.

———

WRAPPING A TOWEL AROUND HIS NECK, Cam walked out of his home gym and toward the intercom, pressing on the button to let Brian in. Two minutes later, his assistant was knocking on the door. Cam opened it and stood aside as Brian carried a cardboard tray with two coffees and two muffins inside.

"Come in." Cam sighed. He'd been back in Boston for two days, having flown here straight after his meetings in L.A., and already he was bouncing against the walls.

"Man, you look terrible," Brian said, wrinkling his nose. "And you stink, too."

"If I'd have known you were coming over, I would have put on some makeup." Cam gave him a sardonic smile. "And I can't smell any worse than the Bobcats' locker room."

"Which is exactly why I avoid the locker room." Brian took the coffees out of the holder, then walked around to Cam's kitchen and grabbed a bottle of water from the refrigerator. "Catch," he called out, throwing it to Cam.

The bottle landed steadily in the middle of Cam's outstretched palms. At least some things didn't change.

This apartment felt less like home than ever. The kitchen was strewn with takeout boxes and dishes that Cam couldn't find the energy to clean up. Maybe tomorrow he'd give a shit about the state of the place

"You need a cleaner," Brian said, pointing at the sink. "Want me to call yours?"

"You don't work for me anymore."

"I remember." Brian grinned. "But I'm still your friend, right?"

Cam swallowed. He felt like shit. "Yeah, of course. And I'm sorry. I'm feeling a little bitchy. I worked out hard."

"I can tell that from the sweat. And by the way, if you answered your phone occasionally, I'd have arrived *after* your shower. Are you avoiding me or something?"

"Not you in particular." Cam swallowed a mouthful of water. "I'm ignoring everybody." The truth was, he'd put his phone in the hallway dresser drawer when he arrived, afraid that if he looked at it for too long he'd call or message her. He knew himself too well. He'd tell himself that one chance to hear her voice wouldn't hurt, but then he'd be hooked again. He'd want more and more and it would kill him.

Who was he kidding? He was still hooked.

"Derek asked me to check on you. He's worried about you."

"Yeah, that's because I've been avoiding him, too."

Brian leaned on the counter, eyeing Cam carefully. "I know on the outside Derek's a mean vampire of an agent, but I think he really likes you. He's worried about you. Says you were only going through the motions in L.A. I thought you'd made up your mind it's what you wanted."

"I did." Okay, so it wasn't *exactly* what he wanted, but he couldn't have that. L.A. would be second best.

"He's working really hard at getting you a top rate package. But you need to speak with him. Meet him halfway."

"I know." Cam nodded. "I'll call him."

"Today?"

"If you want."

"It's not about what *I* want," Brian said, giving him a tight smile. "It's about you. You're the talent. It's always about you. If you don't want to go to L.A., you need to tell Derek." Brian tipped his head to the side, scrutinizing Cam carefully. "Are you sure you want to leave your family? You seemed happy when you were in Hartson's Creek." Brian gave a little laugh. "I mean, you didn't call me much, because you're an asshole of a boss, but when we did talk, you sounded good."

"It was a good break," Cam said, his chest tight. "That was all."

Brian nodded. "Okay, man. So I'll call the cleaner and have her come tomorrow. And arrange for some healthy meals in your refrigerator. Where's your phone? Since you've been ignoring my calls, I imagine you've ignored everybody else's. I'll go through the messages and reply where I can."

His simple kindness made Cam feel strange. "It's in the hall dresser drawer. Along with the charger."

"Good. Now go shower. I can't concentrate with all these damn pheromones filling up the apartment."

Cam rolled his eyes. "I've kind of missed you, you know that?"

"Yeah, well. You can give me an end of contract bonus."

"You'll get more than that." Cam's face turned serious. He grabbed the keys he'd slung on the kitchen counter two days ago, pulling one off. "If you fancy a trip to Hartson's Creek, there's an Audi parked outside my house there. You pick it up, it's yours."

Brian laughed, but then when he realized Cam was serious, the smile slid from his face. "What?"

"The car's yours. Honestly, I don't want it." It was another reminder he couldn't take. "And if you go there, can you take two of the Depuis watches in my drawer with you? I want you to give them to two kids I know. I'll give you the address."

"What is this? Why are you giving away all your assets?" Brian lowered his voice. "Are you feeling suicidal?"

"No, I'm not." Cam sighed. "They're just things I don't want anymore. I want to go to L.A. with a clean slate. Leave a lot of the shit behind."

"I'll go pick up the car early tomorrow, and get you anything you need from the house. I'll even deliver those watches. But I don't want your Audi. If you really insist, sell the damn thing and buy me another car. One I can actually afford to insure."

A ghost of a smile passed Cam's lips. "It's a deal."

CHAPTER TWENTY-NINE

"Mom!" Josh came running into the kitchen, one shoe on, the other goodness only knew where. She could tell from the milk mustache that he hadn't brushed his teeth like she'd asked him to.

"You have fifteen minutes until we need to leave for breakfast club," she told him. "There's no time for running around right now."

"But Cam's here. His car just pulled in the driveway."

Mia's hand froze mid air, her coffee cup clutched in her fingers. "Cam's not here. He moved away, remember?"

"He's here. It's his car. I'm not stupid."

"Whose car?" Michael asked, sloping into the kitchen. He glanced down at Josh. "Why've you only got one shoe on?"

His mood still hadn't improved much in the last week. But at least he was being kinder to Josh. As for Mia, he was mostly ignoring her, unless she asked him a direct question. Then she'd get a grunt or a head move in response.

"Because I saw Cam pull in the driveway while I was putting them on."

"Cam's not here." Michael frowned, glancing at Mia from the corner of his eye. "Right, Mom?"

She opened her mouth to reply, but the sound of the doorbell echoed through the hallway.

"See?" said Josh, jumping excitedly. "I told you."

"He better not be here," Michael mumbled. "Or I'll whoop his ass."

"Can I answer it? Can I?" Josh asked, his energy the exact opposite of his brother's.

Mia blew out a lungful of air. "Okay."

She wasn't ready to see him. Yet a tiny pulse of excitement started to grow inside her, getting stronger as she stood and touched the back of her hair.

"I mean it," Michael warned. "I'm gonna let him have it."

"You'll do no such thing, or you'll be grounded for the next two weeks."

Michael shook his head and walked into the hallway. "Turn it the other way, doofus."

"Michael!" Mia shouted, following him out of the kitchen. "Make that three weeks."

"Mom!"

"You talk nicely to people or you pay the consequences. I'm not putting up with your attitude anymore."

Josh finally unlatched the door, jerking it open. But instead of Cam standing on the doorstep, there was a much younger man, his hair pulled into a dark ponytail that hung down his back.

For a moment, the three of them stared at the stranger. Over his shoulder, Cam's blue Audi glistened in the morning sun.

"Um, hello?" Mia said, walking forward. "Can I help you?"

"Is this the Devlin house?" the man asked. He had a bright smile on his face. "You must be Josh, right?"

Josh's face lit up at being singled out. "Yeah, I am."

"Which makes you Michael?"

Michael gave a grunt.

"My name's Brian. I have something for you both. But maybe I should give it to your Mom." He glanced at Mia. "They're pretty expensive."

"What are they?" Josh asked, noticing the shiny wooden boxes in the man's hand. He reached out to touch them.

"Watches," Mia said. "They're watches."

To be specific, Depuis watches. Valued at twenty thousand dollars each. She could remember her conversation with Cam about them. They'd been sitting in his drawer in his Boston apartment while he decided what to do with them.

"Why are you giving us watches?" Michael asked, his voice wary. "We don't even know you. And what are you doing with Cam's car?"

"These watches are from him. He wants you and Josh to have them." Brian glanced at Mia. "He says keep them or sell them, he doesn't mind. And he suggests you put them in a safety deposit box rather than letting them sit in a drawer."

Mia cleared her throat. "Please thank Mr. Hartson for us, but we can't accept them. It's too much."

Brian shrugged. "He said you'd say that. And he told me if you refuse them to leave them on the step. Either you pick them up or some lucky thief does."

"What's with that asshole?" Michael asked, throwing up his hands. "Doesn't he know how to take no for an answer?"

"Mom, can I look at the watch?" Josh asked, his eyes wide. "Is it cool?" he asked Brian.

"Here you go," Brian said, unlatching one of the wooden cases. "I'd say it's pretty cool."

The watch was huge. Way too big for Josh's little hands. Mia stared at it for a moment, wondering what the hell to do. She couldn't take forty thousand dollars worth of watches from Cam, not even if they would be used to help out with college for her boys.

But she couldn't let them sit on the step either.

"I'll take them for now," she said, reaching over Josh's shoulder. "But I'll be couriering them back as soon as I've found a safe way to do it."

"Whatever you say." Brian shrugged again. "I've done my job. The rest is up to you. I gotta go. I need to pick a few things up for Cam at his place, then head back home."

"Are you driving Cam's car?" Mia asked, looking over his shoulder at the Audi.

"Yep." Brian said. "I'm driving it back to Boston today."

So that's where Cam was. "What about L.A.?" Mia found herself asking. "I thought he was going there?"

"He is. Once he signs on the dotted line." Brian lifted his hand. "See ya later!"

As soon as she shut the door, Michael grabbed one of the watches from her. "Who the hell does he think he is, sending us watches?" he grumbled, pulling the silver bracelet from the box.

"Careful," Mia said. "Those are worth a lot."

"How much?" Josh asked, peering at the watch in Michael's hand.

She told them and Josh's mouth dropped open.

"What the heck!" Michael dropped the watch clumsily back in the box. "Why the hell is Cam giving us twenty thousand dollar watches?"

"Whoa! That's a lot of money," Josh said. "And we can sell them if we want. Can I get an Xbox with my money?"

He reached out for the box still in Mia's hand, but Michael got there first, snatching it from her grasp.

"But it's mine," Josh protested. "Give it back."

Michael held it above his head, and Josh started jumping,

trying to take it out of his hands. "It's mine," Josh shouted. "Cam gave it to me."

"He gave it to you because he wants to get in mom's pants."

Mia took the box from Michael. Damn, he had a strong grasp. "Stop it," she said. "Shut up right now. Or you'll be grounded for a month."

"Why does he want to have your pants?" Josh asked. "Doesn't he have enough of his own?"

"Idiot," Michael muttered.

That was it. She was beyond over his attitude. "Okay. You're grounded."

"Sure. Make me pay for the fact that you messed up."

Mia gritted her teeth. "Don't say one more word," she warned. "Or everything gets taken away. Your phone, your freedom. The door to your room. I'm not kidding."

"You can't take my phone."

"Yes I can."

"No you can't."

"Try me," she told him through gritted teeth.

"I hate you. I hate this place. And I hate the fact that you cry every night for a guy I detest. I wish we'd never come here. It sucks."

"That's it. You're done."

"Fuck it!"

"Michael?" Josh said, his voice small. "Don't swear."

"Shut up. I hate all of you." Michael pushed Josh out of his way, stomping up the stairs. Mia squeezed her eyes closed, her head pounding to the rhythm of Michael's footsteps.

"Mommy?" Josh said in a small voice.

"Yes, honey?"

"I'm sorry I upset Michael."

His expression made her heart ache. She reached out to cup his cheek.

"You didn't upset him, sweetie. He did that all by himself." She sighed. "Come on, we need to leave. Go find your other shoe."

———

IF SHE THOUGHT she was finding it hard to concentrate before, Mia could barely focus on the screen in front of her now. Her hands were shaking, her stomach felt like it was being eaten away by acid, and at least five different people had asked her if she was coming down with something. Maybe she should have stayed at home.

But what if she never felt better? She needed her job. After all, they needed a roof over their head and food on the table, and they couldn't stay with Sam forever.

When she'd dropped Josh off at breakfast club, his eyes were still full of tears. He'd asked her if Michael was going to leave like Cam and Niall had. If he was still mad with him. It had broken her heart to watch him walk with slumped shoulders through the school gate.

And it had taken all the maturity she had to type a simple message out to Michael.

I expect you home by three. Leave your phone on the table when you get there. We'll be having a serious talk later. Your attitude stinks. Mom.

She was going to have to leave early. She wanted to talk to her eldest before Josh got home from his after school activity. There was no way they could have a repeat of this morning. She was damned if she'd let him make Josh cry again.

Sighing, she turned back to her monitor, determined to get some work done. But then her phone started to ring, cutting through the silence of her office, and she picked it up, frowning when she saw Josh's school lighting up the screen.

Don't tell her he was sick. She wasn't sure she could cope with much more.

"Mia Devlin," she said, lifting the phone to her ear.

"Ms. Devlin, this is Shirley Mason from Hartson Elementary School. We were wondering if Josh was okay?"

A shot of alarm made Mia sit up straight. "What do you mean?" she asked. "He was okay when I dropped him off this morning. He had a little argument with his brother, but nothing more than that."

"You dropped him off?" Shirley's words were stilted. "Um, when did you do that?"

"About three hours ago. For breakfast club." Mia could feel her blood racing through her veins, adrenaline making her hands shake even harder. "Is he not at school?"

"Not according to the roll call. Let me check with his teacher again, and the breakfast club coordinator."

"Can I stay on the line?" Breathe. She needed to breathe.

"Yes, let me put you on hold."

Mia held the phone tightly against her ear, even though the hold music was blasting through the earpiece. She started rocking back and forth, her breath coming in short starts. He went to breakfast club. She saw him walk inside. It had to be a mistake.

"Ms. Devlin?" Shirley Mason said, taking her off hold. "I've spoken to both his teacher and the coordinator and neither has seen him today. Would you like me to call the police? Is there anybody that might know where he is? Your husband maybe?"

"My ex," Mia said, her voice thin. The final decree had come through yesterday. "No, he wouldn't know. He doesn't live anywhere around here. And yes. I think we should call the police."

———

MICHAEL'S FACE was ashen as he stood in the hallway of his high school and listened to his mom's panicked words.

"I haven't heard from Dad since Sunday," he said, swallowing hard. "Do you think he took Josh?" he asked Mia.

"I don't think so. But the police have to follow every angle." She glanced at the uniform officer standing with her.

"Is there anywhere else you think he could be?" the officer asked him, keeping his voice low. "Anywhere secret that only you and he know about?"

Michael shook his head. "No. He likes being at home. He's not an adventurous kid, he's a homebody. And we haven't lived here long enough for him to know of somewhere I don't." He glanced at Mia, his eyes wild with panic. "Do you think he ran away?"

"I don't know." Mia wrung her hands together.

"If he did, it's all my fault," Michael whispered. "I was such an asshole to him this morning." He looked away, his eyes shining beneath the fluorescent lights. "He'll be okay, won't he?"

"The sooner we find him, the better," the officer told him. "So if you think of anything, let us know."

"Wait!" Michael said. "You're not going, are you?"

"We need to go to Josh's school. We want to talk to his friends, and then to the parents who might have seen something."

"Let me come with you. I can help." Michael shook his head. "I can't stay here and do nothing."

He looked as frantic as she felt. Mia hugged him tightly, and Michael sobbed against her shoulder. "It's all my fault," he said again. "I hate myself."

"It's not your fault," she said, stroking his hair. "We're going to find him." She ran her tongue along her dry lips. "You could help by going home, in case he shows up. There's a policewoman there, but you're a friendly face." She gave him another hug. "I'd really appreciate that."

"Home. Yeah, that's where he'll want to be." Michael nodded. "I'll stay there until he gets back." His hands clutched at her shirt, his palms clammy through the fabric. "He'll be okay… right?"

She blew out a long mouthful of air. "He has to be, sweetheart. He has to be."

CHAPTER THIRTY

$\mathcal{C}$am had started packing up his apartment. After Brian's visit, and his gentle kick in the ass, Cam knew there really wasn't anything left for him to do but start moving on. It still hurt to think about her. Damn, it hurt to breathe. But what could he do? She'd chosen her sons and Cam was on his own.

Maybe the distance between L.A. and Hartson's Creek would give him a chance to breathe again without it hurting. To look at his bed without imagining Mia laying in it next to him.

Who was he trying to kid? It would still hurt like a bitch. But at least it would hurt in a place where the sun was shining and he had a chance at a career.

He'd almost finished sorting through his clothes – huge piles of unwanted and unworn hoodies and t-shirts were scattered on the bed. Tomorrow, when Brian was back, they'd pack them up and give them to charity. Some of the jerseys with his name on the back could probably be auctioned off.

His phone rang just after three. It took him a few

moments to find it, nestled beneath a Bobcats cap on the dresser at the far end of his bedroom.

Expecting it to be Brian, he frowned when he saw it was an unknown number. Usually, he'd hang up – he'd had his fair share of stalkerish phone calls – but something made him accept it.

"Hello?"

There was no reply. Then some heavy breathing. *Damn it.* "Listen, whoever you are, I'm not in the mood for games. I'm hanging up now."

A sob. Not in a high, female voice. But low and cracked. "Don't hang up… I need… *we* need you."

"*Michael?*" Cam ran his tongue along his dry lip. "Is that you?"

"Josh is missing."

Cam's heart skipped a beat. "What?"

"He's gone. Disappeared. It's all my fault."

Cam opened his mouth but no words came out. His chest felt so tight it was hard to breathe. "How long's he been gone? Are the police involved? How about your mom? Is she holding up?"

"She's with the police. They're following a few leads." Michael sounded frantic. "But nobody's seen him since this morning when Mom dropped him off. I don't suppose he called you?"

"No." Cam looked at his watch. His stomach turned at the thought of Josh being gone so long. "I wish he had."

"Can you come here? Help us look for him?" Michael begged. "I know I was an asshole to you. I've been an asshole to everybody. But Mom needs you. I do, too."

"Did your mom ask me to come?" Hope made his breath catch in his throat.

"No. But I know she'll want you here."

Yeah, Cam wanted to be there, too. Wanted to support the

woman he loved, help protect her children. Josh was just a kid, a tiny kid who made everybody smile. He loved playing games and drawing and throwing a ball. Where the hell could he be?

What if somebody took him? Somebody bad...

Cam swallowed the thought down. It tasted bitter on his tongue.

"I'll catch the first flight out." He glanced at the mess in his bedroom. Who gave a shit about that? "Hold on, okay? I'll be there."

"Thank you." Michael's voice was small. "And I'm sorry. For everything I said."

"It's not your fault. It's mine. And for what it's worth, I'm sorry, too. Now hang in there. Hopefully Josh will be back before I get there."

Ending the call, he threw some clothes in the bag he'd just unpacked, then grabbed his phone and wallet, shoving them into his pockets. His heart was clammering against his chest as he quickly typed out a message to Brian, who was expecting to meet him here late at night after his traveling, and grabbed an Uber to take him to Logan International Airport.

"If you make it fast, you'll get the tip of your life," he'd told the driver as he climbed into the backseat.

"Okay." The driver grinned. "I like the sound of that."

Thankfully, the roads were almost empty, and the driver knew how to put his foot down. Sitting on the backseat next to his bag, Cam messaged Logan to ask for his help, then pulled up Mia's number. He pressed the screen, holding his breath as he waited for the call to connect.

"Hello?" She was breathless. "Cam, I need to keep this line free. Josh is missing."

"I know. I'm on my way to help."

"You are?" She sounded wary. "What do you mean?"

"Michael called and told me everything. He asked me to fly back. I should get to Hartson's Creek later this evening."

She let out a ragged breath. "Okay. That's good. Thank you."

"I'll let you go. Just hold on. It'll all work out."

A sob escaped her lips. It felt like a dagger to his heart. "Please hurry."

"I will. I'll get there as fast as I can." He ended the call, looking up at the driver. "Are we nearly there yet?"

———

WHEN THE POLICEMAN pulled up outside Sam's house, Mia could see a crowd of people gathered outside. They were talking to the two officers manned at the house, who looked like they were giving out directions.

"Mia!" Becca called out, as soon as she climbed out of the car. "Logan called and told us what happened. We're all here to help. We're going to form a search party before it gets too dark."

Mia swallowed back the tears. "That's so kind of you." Over Becca's shoulder, she could see Logan and Tanner, along with Gray and Maddie. In fact, all of Cam's family was here, wearing warm clothes and carrying flashlights.

Her heart clenched, because the only one missing was the man she needed the most right now.

"Mom!" Michael came barreling down the front steps, flinging his arms around her. "Is there any news about Josh?"

She shook her head. "Not yet."

"I called Cam. He's on his way."

She nodded. "He called me. He should be here in a few hours."

"I told him I'm sorry. About everything." Michael choked

on a sob, and she hugged him tight. "I've been such an asshole."

Any other time, she'd want to know more, but right now all she could think about was Josh. It was going to be dark in a few hours, and the weather was so cool. He was wearing a jacket, but that would be no match for the night time air.

Two more cars pulled up, and more people climbed out. "We're here to help search," one of the women said. "We want to help find the little boy."

Mia's eyes stung with tears as she watched them all get directions from the officers.

"Come on, let's go inside," she said to Michael, taking his hand.

"Can't we go and help the search?"

She shook her head. "They need us here. What if Josh comes back? He'll want to see us." She glanced at her watch. "And it's almost time for dinner."

"I'm not hungry," Michael told her.

No, neither was she. There was no way she wanted to eat when Josh could be hungry somewhere.

"Then we'll wait," she told him. "Until Josh is back. Then I'll cook us all some supper."

"What if he doesn't come back?" Michael asked quietly. "What if somebody's hurt him?"

"Don't say that," Mia said quickly. "Nobody would want to hurt Josh." But that was a lie. There were bad people out there. She knew that.

Michael's phone rang. "It's dad," he said. "He knows, right?"

"He was the first person we called."

Michael nodded. He lifted the phone to his ear. "Hello." He gave a pause. "No, not yet." Mia couldn't quite hear what Niall was saying on the other end of the line. Michael glanced up and caught her eye, his brows knitting together. "You're not coming? Why not? Josh is missing."

Mia took the phone from Michael. "Niall, where are you?"

"I'm at work. I can't take more time off. If I lose this job I lose my house." He cleared his throat. "And Gemma is pregnant. You know I'd be there if I could."

"It doesn't matter," she told him, ignoring his revelation. That was his business. She couldn't even find it in herself to be angry with him. She was too scared for that. "We'll do this without you."

"But you'll let me know when he's found, right?"

She sighed. "Yeah. I will."

"Thank you." He sounded almost worried. "I hope he's okay."

"So do I." Mia ended the call without saying goodbye, and handed Michael back his phone.

She'd long since stopped expecting Niall to give a shit about his family. But from the expression on Michael's face, he wasn't quite there yet.

———

CAM'S PHONE lit up while he was in the line to buy a coffee. His plane was due to start boarding in twenty minutes. He hitched his bag onto his shoulder and swiped to accept the call. "Brian?" he said, nodding the person behind him through. "I'm at the airport. Can I call you when I've landed?"

"Um, not really." Brian cleared his throat. "Something weird has happened in the Audi."

Cam frowned. He'd forgotten all about Brian driving his car back to Boston. "What is it?" he said quickly. "If the car's got any problems, drop it at a garage. I'll cover the cost."

"It's not the car," Brian said quickly. "It's what's inside.

You know the space between the seats and the back, where there's a cover to stow bags?"

"Yeah?" Cam said impatiently. He wanted to get on that damn plane.

"There's a kid in there."

"What?"

"I just stopped to get gas. That's when I heard some shuffling. He somehow managed to get into the space and has fallen asleep. It's one of the kids I gave a watch to. The little one."

"Josh." Cam blew out a mouthful of air. "Is he okay?"

"I think so. Should I wake him up? I'm not used to kids. Is he gonna kick and bite or something?"

"He's not a damn dog," Cam growled. "Just wake him gently." He stepped back so more people could order ahead of him.

"Okay." There was some shuffling, then Brian's low voice. "Hey kid, you okay there?"

Cam heard a higher voice, and his heart about leapt out of his chest. Josh was okay. He put his hand on his ribcage, trying to breathe as the low conversation continued.

"Um, he's awake," Brian said through the phone line. "And he's okay. Apparently, he wants to see you. He told me he got in the car when I was parked outside your house in Hartson's Creek."

Cam's heart was still running a mile a minute. "Can I talk to him?"

"Sure. Hey kid, talk to Cam." Brian's voice echoed, as though he was holding out the phone.

"Hello?" Josh's voice was small. "Cam?"

"Josh, are you all right?"

"Yeah. I want to see you. Are you in Boston?"

"No. I'm on my way to see your mom and Michael. They're frantic. They have no idea where you are."

"They're both so angry. And Mom's sad. She keeps crying. I wanted to see you and ask you to come back. I don't like it when they argue."

Cam breathed out softly. "I *am* coming back, pal. And I want to see you, too. Stay with Brian, okay? We'll get you back home and I'll meet you there. Don't go anywhere without him."

"All right." There was a pause, then Josh added, "Are you mad at me, too?"

"No, bud, I'm not mad at you. I'm so happy you're okay. But I need to get you home, and I need to let your mom know you're okay. She's so upset."

Josh sobbed. "I'm sorry."

"It's okay. Everything's okay. We're gonna get you home. Can I talk to Brian again? I'll see you in a few hours, I promise."

Brian came back on the line. "So what do I do?"

"You turn around and drive back to Hartson's Creek. To the house you went to this morning. I'll meet you there."

"Shouldn't I go to a local police station or something?" Brian asked. "What if they think I've abducted him? I'm too pretty for prison."

"If you go to a police station that'll take time. Mia needs to see her son." Cam raked his hand through his hair. "Just drive carefully and within the speed limit. Josh is important to me. I'll call Mia and the police to explain."

"Okay. You're the boss."

"Yeah, I am. How long will it take you to get back to Hartson's Creek?"

"About four hours if I put my foot down," Brian told him.

"Drive carefully, Don't rush," Cam told him sharply. "Just take care of him."

"I'll treat him like he's the Vince Lombardi Trophy," Brian promised. "But please make sure I don't get arrested."

CHAPTER THIRTY-ONE

"Hello?" Mia lifted the phone to her ear. She was standing on the porch with Michael, Sam, and one of the police officers who was staying with her while everybody else searched. "Cam? Are you on the plane?"

"Just about to board. Listen, I just got a call from Brian. You met him earlier, right?"

"Your assistant?" Mia swallowed hard. This morning felt like a lifetime ago. "Yeah, he came around this morning."

"Well, he stopped for gas and found a stowaway behind the seats. Josh is with him. He's completely fine, I spoke to him, but he's worried you're all upset. Brian is turning around and driving him back to you now. He should be there by late evening."

Mia's hands started shaking uncontrollably. The tension in her chest seemed to heighten, a low sob escaping her lips. "He's okay?" she whispered, her voice wavering. "Josh is okay?"

The officer standing with her turned his head to look at her. "Ma'am?"

She covered the mouthpiece. "He's been found in the back

of my friend's car. He's fine." The officer nodded and passed along the news through her radio. Lifting her hand from the phone, Mia asked Cam, "Can I talk to him?"

"Yeah. I'll text you Brian's number. He should have his phone on Bluetooth. He's absolutely petrified he's gonna get arrested for child abduction."

"Why was Josh in the car?" Adrenaline was rushing through her like a drug. She couldn't think straight.

Cam cleared his throat. "Apparently, he wanted to see me. He wants you and Michael to stop arguing."

"Oh god." Mia covered her eyes with her free hand.

"It's okay," Cam said softly. "He's coming home. And so am I. Just hang in there, and we'll be with you before you know it. I have to board my flight in a few minutes, and I won't be able to call you until I land, but if I can buy some WiFi I'll be on messenger."

Tears were flowing down Mia's cheeks. He was okay. Her baby was coming home. "I wish you were here now."

"So do I, baby, so do I."

"Will you come straight here from the airport?"

"Wasn't planning on doing anything else. Can you talk to the police, explain about Brian and Josh? I don't want to miss my flight. I need to see you all."

She nodded. "Of course. I'll tell them now."

"Thank you." His voice was soft. "And tell Michael I'll see him soon. That I'm looking forward to catching up with him."

"I will." Her voice was thick. "Cam…"

"I know. I love you, too."

That was all she needed to hear for the tears to start flowing. All the fear and tension that had been wrapped up inside her started to escape, wracking her body and making her reach out for Michael's shoulder to stop herself from falling.

"Don't cry," Cam crooned. "It's okay. Hang in there for a

few more hours." She could hear the echo of an announcement. "I'll see you real soon."

She was still crying as he ended the call. Wiping the hot salty trails from her cheeks, she turned to Michael, who was staring at her, his eyes watering, too.

"He's really okay?"

"He really is." She gasped in some air. "He's coming home."

"Let's go inside. You can tell me everything in there," the officer suggested. "I've already let my partner know to call off the search."

"We were about to leave to start another search," Becca called out, running up the stairs, her eyes wide with hope. "Is it true what the police said? Is Josh okay?"

Mia nodded, her chest too full to say anything else. Becca threw her arms around her, pulling her close as Mia sobbed into her shoulder. "He's okay. He was in Cam's car that Brian was driving to Boston."

"How the hell did Brian not notice?" Becca muttered. "No, nix that. Brian always plays music way too loud. He's a damn metal fan. I'm surprised he isn't completely deaf already." She blew out a mouthful of air. "How far away are they?"

"Cam said a few hours." She checked her watch. How had the time gone so quickly today, and now it was only a minute since Cam hung up? She wanted time to speed up, to hold her baby in her arms.

To see Cam again. Because right now she didn't know what to do without either of them.

"Ma'am, shall we go inside?" the officer asked.

"That's a good idea." Sam nodded. "It's cold and you two need to eat something."

"I'm not hungry," Michael said, his eyes rimmed red.

"I know, son, but you need to eat. For Josh's sake. He needs you both to be strong for him."

"Do you want me to come, too?" Becca asked Mia.

"It's okay. You guys have done enough." Mia hugged her again. "Thank you for everything. All of you. You're an amazing family."

"So are you guys," Becca told her. "And you're a part of our family, too. With or without Cam."

Mia blinked back more tears. She needed to wash her face before Josh came home. She was a mess, and he didn't need to see that.

"Call me if you need anything," Becca said, walking down the steps. "Any time at all. And Logan's heading to the airport to meet Cam. All your boys will be home before you know it."

All her boys. She liked the sound of that. Liked the thought of being surrounded by the people she loved so much it hurt. And after today – or the past weeks if she was being honest – she was going to hold them all so tightly.

It was time to have her family back. That was all she wanted.

"Hello? Mia? Is there any news?"

She'd thought about not phoning Niall. Or at least delaying her call for a little while. But that wasn't her style. Even if he was being an asshole, she didn't need to stoop to his level.

"They've found Josh," she said, keeping the emotion out of her voice. "He's okay."

There was silence for a moment. "Are you sure he's okay? Where was he?"

"In a car. He'd climbed inside to try and get to Boston." She rolled her bottom lip between her teeth. "It's a long story."

She expected him to ask for more information. Because she'd be demanding it. She'd be desperate to know exactly where and why Josh had tried to get to Boston.

"Well that's good. I knew it would all be okay. I'll give him a call over the weekend."

The difference between his response and Cam's spoke for itself. And it made her heart hurt. Not for herself, but for her boys. Niall wasn't even a part time father. His role in his children's lives was a little more than a cameo part.

"Maybe you shouldn't call him." The words escaped her lips before she could think them through.

"What do you mean?" There was a frown in his voice. She remembered too late that Niall hated being told what to do. Even when she was right.

Especially when she was right.

"What I mean is you can't just flit in and out of their lives and not be there for them when they need you. Michael called you today, he was so upset. And you couldn't even be bothered to make him feel better. He needed you, Niall, and you weren't there. The same way you haven't been there for him for years."

"I only left a year ago."

Physically, sure. But emotionally? She'd been a single parent for as long as she could remember.

Mia swallowed hard. "If you want to be part of the boys' lives, then you'll need to commit to regular contact. And maybe you need to do some therapy with them."

"You can't tell me what I need to do. I have rights…"

She wanted to laugh at his rights, but she was afraid it'd come out as a hysterical scream. Right now the emotions were getting the better of her. "You do," she said, keeping her voice as even as possible. "But you also have two young men who are confused about your place in their lives, and you aren't making it any better for them. If you want to be their father, then great, I'll support you. Damn, I'll make it easy for you. But if you hurt them then I'll fight you with every breath that I have. Those boys deserve better than a father who can't be bothered when the going gets tough."

Silence blasted down the phone line. Mia inhaled a ragged breath, leaning on the kitchen counter. Michael was in the living room, thank goodness, not able to hear this call.

"I…" Niall sighed heavily. "I don't know what to say."

Say you'll be their father. Say you love them. Say you'll fight for them.

"Think about it," she suggested. "Let me know what you want."

Niall cleared his throat. "I've never been good enough, have I?"

Mia ran her fingers through her hair. "For me? No. You never were. But you're the boys' father. And you're going to be a father again. It's up to you to work out if you're good enough. Nobody else." She blew out a mouthful of air. "I need to go." She didn't want to talk to him any longer. Didn't want to beg him to be the parent that Michael and Josh needed him to be. If he walked away, they'd deal with it, the way they'd dealt with it when he left.

They'd do more than deal with it. They'd thrive, because her kids were amazing.

"Bye," Niall muttered, as though he couldn't wait for the call to end.

"Bye." She swiped the screen with her finger, and shoved her phone into her pocket. Whatever Niall decided to do didn't really matter. They'd be okay. Because she'd make sure they were.

The same way she always did.

———

THEY WERE SITTING in the living room when lights swept over the window. Even though it was dark, Mia hadn't closed the curtains. She was too desperate to keep a watch on the road outside for that. After she'd explained the situation to the police and then spoken to Niall, she'd called the number Cam sent her, her heart pounding against her chest as Brian answered, and Josh's voice echoed down the phone line.

He'd sounded so young as he kept saying sorry over and over. She hated that she couldn't hold him. Because he didn't need to be sorry – that was her job.

Michael was the first to jump up from the sofa when the headlamps hit. He had better reflexes than she did, but it was only a heartbeat later that she was joining him at the window, her breath caught in her throat as she saw Cam's blue Audi pull into the driveway. The police officer joined her, and all three of them stared out of the window.

"He's here," Michael shouted. Sam lifted his head up, blinking. He'd fallen asleep about an hour earlier.

They rushed into the hallway, Michael yanking open the door and running onto the porch, Mia right behind him, followed by the officer. Then Brian climbed out of the car, opening the rear door so Josh could hop out, and the tears started stinging at her eyes again.

Josh looked tiny next to the car. He had a bottle of water in his hand as he stared wide-eyed at the three of them standing on the porch. There was a wary expression on his face, as though he wasn't sure what his reception would be. Mia held her arms out, and his face crumpled as he ran the distance between the car and the steps, taking them two at a time.

His body collided with hers, the force winding her, but she ignored the pain and wrapped her arms around her son, hugging him tight.

"Oh my god," she whispered. "Oh Josh. You're here." It was hard to breathe.

"I'm sorry," he sobbed into her chest. "I'm so sorry."

Michael wrapped his arms around them both, his head resting on her shoulder, his hand cupping Josh's back.

"It's okay." She stroked Josh's head. "Nobody's mad at you. We were just so scared. You can't run away like that without telling anybody."

"I know. I'm sorry. Brian told me you were all really sad."

Lifting her head, she looked over Josh's shoulder at the young man. His hair was looking worse for wear, the sleek ponytail of earlier all twisted and fuzzy. He was hanging around the car, twisting his hands. He swallowed hard when he realized Mia was staring at him.

"You must be tired," she called out. "Would you like a drink?"

"Come on in," Sam called out. "I'll put some coffee on."

"I could really do with a bathroom break," Brian said, his cheeks reddening. "And then coffee would be great."

As he passed Mia, she lifted her hand from Michael's shoulders and grabbed Brian's, squeezing it tight.

"Thank you," she said, her voice low. "Thank you for bringing him back."

"Am I in trouble?" Brian asked, glancing warily at the officer.

"No trouble," the officer told him. "We can talk inside."

Sam, Brian, and the officer walked into the house, leaving Mia and Michael on the porch with Josh. She hunkered down into a squat, checking Josh over with her eyes and her soft hands. "You sure you're okay?" she asked him.

"Yeah. I'm tired, though." He yawned. "And hungry. Brian wouldn't stop for food. Told me Cam wouldn't let him."

Mia smiled with relief. She could deal with hunger and

exhaustion. She had a little of that herself. "Let's go in. I'll make you both a burger."

"Actually, I brought some food with me."

She looked up to see Cam standing at the bottom step, his duffle slung over his shoulder and two brown takeout bags in his hands. Her heart seemed to freeze in her chest for a moment, her breath catching in her throat as she took him in.

It had been less than two weeks since she'd seen him, yet it felt like a lifetime. His eyes were soft as his gaze caught hers, and she felt dizzy, as though she was falling.

"Cam!" Josh shouted. "You're here." He pulled away from Mia and threw himself at the tall, muscled man. Cam put the takeout bags on the steps and caught him easily, lifting him into his arms. "Hey, pal. You okay?"

Josh nodded, as Michael walked over and stood in front of Cam. "Hi," he said softly. "I'm glad you came."

Cam swallowed, his neck undulating. "I am, too," he said gruffly. "Thanks for calling me." He held out his hand to Michael, but instead of shaking it, Michael hugged his side. Cam met Mia's eyes over Michael's shoulder, and curled his fingers to beckon her over.

Mia walked down the steps as Cam gently put Josh down on the ground. Her heart had started up again, hammering a fast rhythm against her chest.

"Hi," she said. Her cheeks lifted in an attempt to smile.

His gaze didn't waver from hers. "You doing all right?"

She tried to nod, but her body wouldn't play ball. Instead, she swallowed a sob as she shook her head.

"Come here," he told her, wrapping his warm, strong arms around her, cradling her against his body. "It's okay." He kissed the top of her head. "Everybody's fine."

The mixture of adrenaline and fear and relief made her body feel weak. Her legs shook as he held her tightly. "Guys, you want to go in and eat?" Cam asked, nodding at the brown bags in front of him.

"I'm starving," Josh said. "What's in there?"

"Burgers and fries from Logan's place." Cam was still holding her tight.

"Come on, Josh," Michael said, sweeping the bags into his hands. "Let's go in and eat."

Mia heard the thump of their feet as they ran up the steps, then the click of the door as they walked inside. Cam didn't loosen his hold on her for a moment. She was glad. Because right now she wasn't sure her legs were strong enough to hold her up.

He tipped her chin up with his thumb, until her eyes connected with his. "What a fucking day."

She laughed for the first time in what felt like forever. "Not exactly what I planned when I got up this morning."

"I'm so sorry about Brian. I have no idea how he could've driven that far without realizing Josh was in the car." He dropped his head until his brow touched hers. She could see herself reflected in his eyes. Could feel the warmth of his breath against her cheek.

"Becca says he plays his music loud."

Cam chuckled. "Yeah, she knows him well. Where is he, anyway?"

"Sam took him inside. He needed the bathroom. I get the impression he was too scared to stop before he got here."

"Damn right he was. He was on strict instructions to get here as quickly and as safely as possible." Cam cupped her cheek with his rough hand. "When did you last eat?"

"I've no idea." Mia frowned. "Yesterday maybe?"

"There's a burger inside for you. You need to eat it now."

"Can you just hold me for a moment?" she asked, closing her eyes. All day she'd been frantic. And even surrounded by police officers and friends and family, she'd felt so damn alone.

But right now she felt okay. Not perfect. Not yet. But pretty damn close.

"Thank you for coming," she murmured.

"Wild horses couldn't have kept me away. I've missed you, Mia."

She exhaled softly. She could see the truth in his eyes, mixed with the pain of their separation. Had he felt it as much as she did?

"I've missed you, too, so much."

"Now go eat." He nodded at the door. "Before you faint."

"Come in, too. You must be hungry."

He glanced at the front door, then his gaze flickered back to hers. "I can't. Not if I have to leave again." The ghost of a smile passed his lips. "I don't think my heart could take it."

She knew all about hurt. About fear and pain. Not just from today, though that had been hard enough. But from life experiences. From losing and gaining and losing again.

But she couldn't lose him this time.

"You won't have to leave." She traced her finger along his jaw. "Stay."

"For how long?" Hope flickered in his eyes.

"For as long as you want." She bit down a smile. "Or until Sam kicks you out."

"And Michael?"

"We'll talk to him. Together. That's what I should have done from the start. I was too busy protecting him to think about how to deal with his reaction."

"And I was too sure you'd be better off without me."

Her fingertip brushed his bottom lip. "I'm so much better *with* you," she admitted. "Not because I need you, but because I *want* you. I want you in our lives. I want to start living again, with you."

"I want that, too. I want you. All of you. The boys, the craziness, all of it." He brushed his lips against hers.

She wrapped her arms around his neck as he deepened the kiss, his hands holding her steady as she melted against him.

When she pulled away, she was breathless. Sliding her hand into his, she nodded at the door. "Come on, let's go get something to eat."

"I'm all for that."

He was here. He wanted them all in his life. That was all she needed to know.

———

"Can we talk, man to man?" Michael asked Cam later, as he put their dirty plates into Sam's old dishwasher. Mia had taken an exhausted Josh to bed, and was sitting upstairs with him until he fell asleep. Sam had taken the opportunity to head for the bar. Cam got the impression that all this angst was too much for the guy.

And now Michael was standing in front of him, twisting his arms as his gaze barely met Cam's.

"Sure." Cam closed up the dishwasher. "You want to do it here?"

"Can we go outside? It's more private."

Cam nodded. "Lead the way."

The night air was cool as they walked onto the deck. Beneath the light of a single outside lamp, Cam could see that the wooden boards were slippery with moss. The table and chairs at the far end looked like they'd seen better days. Maybe in the 1970s. Michael leaned against the rail – which thankfully looked solid – and swallowed hard.

"I'm sorry for hitting you," he said, his voice small. "I shouldn't have done that."

"It's okay. I understand." Cam wanted to tell him it didn't hurt, but thought better of it.

"And for asking you to leave. I was angry and upset, but I shouldn't have done that either. I just…" Michael shook his head, as though he couldn't find the right words. "I guess nobody wants to think of their mom like that."

"You shouldn't have to. What happened between your mom and me should have stayed between us until she was ready to tell you. I messed up, too." Cam ran his palm through his hair. "Neither of us meant to hurt you. But especially not your mom. None of this is her fault. She doesn't deserve to be shouted at."

Michael looked down at the ground, his expression guilty. "I've been an idiot."

"We've all been idiots at one time or another. The secret is in how we move on from that." Cam leaned against the brick of the house, staring at the teenager in front of him. "It's good that you want to protect your mom. But maybe sometimes she doesn't need protecting."

"She's pretty kick ass." Michael nodded.

Cam's lips twitched. "Yeah, she is. Single moms usually are."

Finally, Michael lifted his eyes to Cam's. "She missed you. She cried a lot while you were gone. I hated it."

Cam hated hearing it. All he wanted to do was hold her. "I've missed her, too." He moistened his lips with his tongue. "I've missed all of you."

"Do you think…" Michael trailed off, taking a deep breath. "Do you think you could try again with her?"

Cam eyed him steadily. "I want to," he admitted. "But only if you're okay with it. You're her priority. You and Josh. You should know that. If you don't want this to happen between us then it won't."

"I think I do." Michael nodded. "Yeah, I really do."

Relief flooded Cam's chest. "I do too. But we need to see what your mom wants. If anything happens between us, we'd take it slow. We'd agreed on that. Maybe date for a while. Take you guys out to the movies or a theme park. Nothing scary."

"But you'll stay with her tonight, right?"

Cam's eyes widened. "You want me to stay here?"

Michael shrugged. "I don't want her crying all night again. It keeps me awake."

The thought of it wasn't doing much for Cam, either. "I guess it's up to your mom," he said, reaching for the handle of the back door. "Come on, let's go in. It's freezing out here."

———

"HE REALLY SAID THAT?" Mia asked, her voice low, so as not to wake the boys up. Michael had gone upstairs shortly after she came down to announce that Josh was finally asleep. He'd muttered something about an assignment due by Friday as he hugged his mom tightly. Then he'd turned to Cam and held out his hand. Cam had shaken it, impressed by how tight Michael's grip was.

"Yep." Cam nodded. "He wants me to stay the night."

She bit down a smile, glancing at him through her thick lashes. "You know the walls are paper thin, right?"

"I figured. He said he heard your crying every night."

"So we won't be able to..."

He walked forward, sliding his hands into her hair. "I'm not an animal, Mia. I think I can restrain my basic urges. And anyway, if we're gonna do this, I figure there will be nights when you're not in the mood." He brushed his lips against her brow. "Or I'm not in the mood."

"Whoa there, fella. I'm not sure I signed up for that." She pushed him playfully away. She looked so much more relaxed now that she'd had something to eat and gotten Josh to sleep. "I kind of like you being in the mood."

"Yeah, well tonight that'll lead to blue balls. So I'm gonna try really hard to think of something unsexy."

"Maybe think of Sam in bed in the room on the other side."

Cam burst into laughter. "Yep, that'll do it."

She slid her hand into his, leading him upstairs. They took turns in the bathroom, brushing their teeth and changing into pajamas, before meeting back up in Mia's bedroom.

Cam looked around, taking in the small double bed. That was going to be interesting. He hadn't slept in anything other than a king in a long time. In his apartment, he had a California king. His body liked room to breathe.

He lifted up the comforter. "So if this is my bed, where are you planning on sleeping?"

She laughed. "This is my territory, Hartson. Play nice or you'll be sleeping on the floor."

Once they were under the covers, Cam's body taking up more than his fair share of space, Mia snuggled into him, her cotton pajama top brushing against his bare chest. She splayed her fingers on his pectorals, smiling at him.

He smiled back. "You sure you're okay with this?"

"You starfishing in my bed?" She arched an eyebrow. "I'll put up with it for now, but you're going to have to learn to share."

"I'll buy you a bigger bed," he muttered. "And no, I didn't mean the starfishing. I meant us. This." He stroked her cheek with his thumb. "The last time I saw you it was to say goodbye."

She pressed her lips to his chest, kissing him softly. It was a force of will to divert the blood from shooting straight to his groin. "I never stopped wanting you. Seeing you walk away was the hardest thing I did. So yeah, I'm good with you being here." She lifted her head to look at him. "In fact, I'm great with it. But how do you feel? You had the full gamut today. A teenager with crazy mood swings. A little kid who makes the worst decisions. And their mom..." she trailed off, shaking her head. "Their mom who fell to pieces."

"You didn't fall to pieces," he whispered, kissing her head. "You were strong as hell. I don't know how you did it."

"I did it because I had to."

He traced a lazy line down her spine with his fingers, pushing them inside her pajama top until his palm met her skin. "You don't have to do it on your own anymore," he told her.

She inhaled sharply as he traced the waistband of her pants. "I like the sound of that."

"And you three really need to move in with me. I have a dishwasher that works, a bed that can fit us all in it, and a yard that won't make you wince. Hell, you can bring Sam if you want."

"Where?" she asked.

"Where what?" He frowned, not understanding.

"Where will you be living?"

"Here in Hartson's Creek, of course. Where else would I be?"

She traced the line of his stomach. Damn, she knew how to tease him. "You told me you were moving to L.A."

"Yeah, well I'll tell my agent to stop the negotiations in the morning. I'm not going anywhere." He caught her hand before it could dip beneath his waistband, lifting it to kiss her palm. "You're killing me, smalls."

Caressing his jaw with her hand, she leaned up to brush her lips against his. "Sorry. My head says no, but my body says hell yes."

"When they're both in agreement, we'll revisit," he promised her.

"Won't your agent be angry at you turning down the coaching job?" she asked him.

"Probably. But he'll get over it." Cam shrugged, pulling her closer to him. This time when their lips met, it was hot and hard. He slid his hands to her ass, pulling her against him, smiling when she let out a little moan.

"Not fair."

"Hey, what comes around goes around."

She shook her head. "I kind of miss Doctor Love," she teased.

Cam chuckled. "He's still here. But his attending hours have changed."

"Maybe I can book in with him." She shook her head. "Anyway, what are you going to do if you don't take the coaching job?"

He shrugged, her head lifting against his chest with the movement. "I guess I'll concentrate on your rehab. Play games with the boys. Repair Sam's dishwasher."

"You'll be bored to death."

His eyes were soft. "I don't think so." It was strange, because his life had been mapped out for as long as he could remember. School, college, draft, then the NFL. For the first time in forever, his life stretched out before him with endless possibilities. "Maybe I'm not in a hurry to make my next move," he told her. "And anyway, last I heard I'm gonna be an advertising superstar. Selling some crappy whiskey this girl I know represents."

"Shut up." She grinned up at him. "Our whiskey is the best."

"I know." He cupped the back of her neck, inclining his head to kiss her again. "Everything about you is the best." Damn, she tasted good. Lying here with her in his arms felt like coming home. She fit against him perfectly, even if her bed creaked and groaned with their every move.

"When are the boys going back to school?" he asked her.

"I'll keep them home tomorrow. Then we'll be back to normal. I need to get back to work."

"But you have a lunch break, right?"

She gave him a confused smile. "Yeah…"

"Good. In that case, Doctor Love can fit you in at twelve."

She shook her head. "You're an idiot, you know that?"

"That's Doctor Idiot to you," he said, kissing her again. "And by the way, this idiot is crazy in love with you."

She slid her hands to his cheeks, a smile curling her lips. "The feeling is so very mutual."

"You okay?" Cam asked, sliding his arms around Mia's waist as he pulled her against his chest. The warmth of his breath tickled her ear as he brushed his lips against her.

"I will be when this is over." She leaned her head on him, surveying the scene in front of them. Gray, Logan, and Tanner were sitting in arm chairs in Gray's backyard, surrounded by lighting equipment and cameras. The three of them were goofing – as usual – even though the director had told them to save it for the cameras. They just couldn't help themselves. This was how they always were.

That was something she'd learned from spending so much time around the Hartson siblings. They played off each other. Gave one another life.

And now she was part of it all, along with Michael and Josh – and even Sam when he was available to go over to Gray's for Sunday dinner. In the five months since Cam had moved back to Hartson's Creek for good, her boys had accepted him with open arms. She loved how easily he'd fit into their family, not as a father figure, but as a friend, and sometimes a guide.

And a coach, maybe. Which was what he was on Saturday mornings, for the pee wee team, much to Josh's delight. He'd introduced Cam to everybody as his friend, and loved getting a ride to practice in Cam's Audi. At least this time he sat in the seat.

Naked Saturdays would have to wait for a while. And she was good with that.

Cam hadn't gone back to coaching Michael at the high school. The two of them had some kind of unspoken agreement where Cam helped him with football privately. Cam's voice would be low as the two of them watched a play on Cam's oversize television, discussing the play. He'd learned – sometimes the hard way – to gently steer Michael rather than tell him exactly what moves to make. And Michael blossomed under his tutelage. It warmed her to watch the two of them sitting on Cam's oversized sofas, talking on Sunday afternoons.

In these few months, he'd turned out to be more of a father to them than Niall had ever been. Sure, her ex-husband had attended two therapy sessions with Michael and Josh, and they'd agreed on a visitation schedule of two week-long trips to stay with him each year, but he wasn't who the boys turned to for fatherly needs.

Cam was their real dad in everything but name. And the boys loved him as much as Cam adored them.

"How long do you think this will take?" Cam asked, his lips moving against her skin.

"A lot longer if you don't sit down and do as the director tells you," Mia said, biting down a smile. Trying to wrangle the brothers was like trying to tame a herd of lions. They talked over each other, laughed loudly, and kept looking at the camera when they weren't supposed to. The only one they listened to was Becca.

Mia had to bite down a smile when the whirlwind of a woman let her brothers have it about twenty minutes earlier.

"If you don't stop goofing around, I'm gonna whoop all of your asses," she'd hissed, when Tanner had started tickling her. "I'm serious."

That's when the director had called a break. And now they were all back again, ready for another take.

"Go sit down and stop winding Becca up," Mia said, turning her head to smile at Cam. She'd been grinning all day. Thank goodness she'd thought ahead and booked the crew for two days.

She knew this family well.

"We can't help it. It's in our blood." Cam gave her a grin. "Anyway, she gives as good as she gets."

"Just remember she'll be doing the voiceover," Mia reminded him. "So she'll have the last word."

"But we get approval, right?" Two tiny lines formed in Cam's brow. "I swear it said that in the contract."

"You get to see it. Not approve it." Mia wanted to laugh at his expression. "It's okay. I won't let you come across as a complete asshole."

It had been her idea to film the Hartson siblings without a script. Give them topics to talk about while being filmed, that could be cut to make both a long form movie advertisement, as well as a shorter one for television. They all held a glass of the international blend as they spoke, occasionally sipping it, which she was certain wasn't helping their general behavior.

Once this part was filmed, it would be interspersed with shots of the distilleries here in Virginia, Scotland, and Tokyo. Then Becca would record the voice over, explaining that G. Scott Carter's blend was about family, international cooperation, and being yourself in a world where too much could be expected of you. She'd talk about her own family, as well as her experience of creating the blend. Mia was excited to see how it would turn out.

"Okay, we're ready for the next take," the assistant director called out. "Can you all take your seats?"

Cam gave her a quick squeeze, then ambled over to the group of chairs.

From the corner of her eye, Mia could see Becca come out of the house. She looked beautiful, her long hair shining in the spring sun, her skin glowing from a fresh application of make up. She was wearing a blue and white dress that brought out the color of her eyes, the soft fabric clinging to her curves in a way that made her brothers' eyes narrow.

"You sure you're not cold?" Gray asked as she sat down with them. "Maybe you should put a sweater on."

Mia had to cover her mouth to stop a giggle from exploding. Poor Becca. No wonder she never brought guys home. Or barely dated. Having four growling older brothers had to be such a pain.

"Okay. So now we're going to talk about your individual families," the director reminded them. "Gray, maybe you can start off by talking about your twins. We'll go on from there."

When the assistant called for the cameras to run, Gray leaned back on the chair and took a sip of whiskey. "I guess things have changed, huh? We're all grown up now."

"It's not often we get to talk without being surrounded by kids," Tanner agreed. He smiled at his wife, Van, who was watching them talk.

Maddie was inside the house with her boys. They'd watched the recording for a while, but the rambunctious twins kept tugging at her arms, desperate to join their dad and uncles. In the end, she'd taken them back to the kitchen and put on a TV show to keep them quiet.

"So I hear you and Van want to start a family," Logan said to his youngest brother. "You want any words of advice?"

"Not really." Tanner grinned. "I think I'll be fine."

All three of his brothers started laughing.

"What?" Tanner asked. "How hard can a having a family be?"

"Come talk to me when you're knee deep in diapers," Gray suggested. "You can tell me then."

"How about you?" Tanner asked, turning to Cam. "You're kind of a dad already, right?"

"I'm a friend. That's better than being a dad." Cam grinned, his eyes glancing at Mia. "But yeah, I'd like to think I'm a parent figure, too. Or I will be."

"When will you be?" Gray asked, his eyes dancing with interest.

Cam slid something out of his pocket. "When Mia agrees to put this ring on her finger."

"Whoa." Tanner leaned over to look at the box in Cam's huge hands. "That's big."

Mia froze as everybody turned to look at her. She waited for the director to call for a cut, but instead he was looking at her, too.

"Should we stop recording?" she asked, her voice thin.

The director grinned. "We're kind of in on this whole thing.."

"I'm catching it all," Van said, holding her phone out in front, recording Mia as she stared at Cam.

From the corner of her eye she saw Michael and Josh standing in the doorway of the house, along with Maddie and her twins. They were all grinning at her.

Cam stood and walked over to where Mia was frozen in place, dropping to his knee in front of her. "I've been carrying this ring around for two months," he told her. "Waiting for the right time."

Mia's breath caught in her throat. Tanner was right, it was huge. The square cut diamond glistened in the sunlight. She opened her mouth to say something, but Cam shook his head. "I'm not finished yet."

"He's turning into a blabbermouth like you," Tanner told Logan.

"Shut up."

Cam smiled up at Mia, his eyes full of love. "From the moment you came into my life, I knew everything had changed. You're everything I've ever needed. Everything I didn't know was missing from my life. And I want to spend the rest of it with you. You and the boys." He glanced over at Michael and Josh, sending them a wink. "They helped me pick the ring. In Josh's words, it needed to be 'the biggest ring you've ever seen'."

It was pretty close, that was for sure.

"Will you marry me? Be my wife. The mother of my children. The ones we already have, and the ones we haven't made yet?"

She pulled her bottom lip between her teeth. They'd already talked about a family. She was still young, and she knew that Josh was desperate for another sibling.

Michael had even said he'd be *okay* with it. Which was pretty enthusiastic for him.

"Yes," she nodded, tears pricking her eyes. "Yes, I will."

Cam leapt to his feet, picking her up and swinging her around as everybody started to cheer around them. When he put her back down, he pressed his lips against hers. "Damn, I love you."

"I love you, too." She smiled up at him, not even caring that everybody was still watching them. She wanted them all to share in their joy.

"About the baby thing. When can we start?" he asked

softly, sliding his hand down her stomach, caressing her with his fingers. "I'm so ready to be a stay at home dad."

She laughed, because he was deadly serious. They'd already talked about that, too. Right now he was picking and choosing some jobs. He'd done the occasional commentary for The Sports Network, and a few endorsements like this. But more than anything, he loved being with her and the boys. Helping them with homework and throwing balls with them in the street.

It suited her. Plus she loved her job and wanted to keep working for G.Scott Carter.

"How about tonight?" she suggested, sliding her arms around his waist.

"What about the boys?"

"Josh is going to Noah's, and Michael is sleeping at Ben's."

Cam pressed his lip against her ear. "I'm gonna rehab you so hard you'll need another ten sessions."

She bit down a smile. "Is that right, Doctor Love?"

"Yep. Every word."

"In that case, you'd better go back to your chair and start behaving. We have a commercial to make."

Reluctantly, he stepped away, giving her a sexy grin before walking back to the chairs where he sat down with his brothers. Becca squealed and hugged him hard, blowing a kiss over his shoulder at Mia.

Within moments, Courtney and Van were at her side, talking excitedly as they looked at the ring. A minute later, Michael and Josh joined them.

Mia felt a warm glow envelop her. They were all family now. Something she never thought she'd have again. And as the director called for the cameras to roll once again, and the brothers started talking, it felt like the start of something wonderful.

Cam grinned at her from his seat. She blew him a kiss back.

It was good to be independent. But it was even better to be loved. For the first time in forever, she finally had it all.

And she never wanted it to end.

DEAR READER

Thank you so much for reading Cam and Mia's story. If you enjoyed it and you get a chance, I'd be so grateful if you can leave a review. And don't forget to keep an eye out for **WHEN WE TOUCH**, the fifth book in the Heartbreak Brothers series.

ABOUT THE AUTHOR

Carrie Elks writes contemporary romance with a sizzling edge. Her first book, *Fix You*, has been translated into eight languages and made a surprise appearance on *Big Brother* in Brazil. Luckily for her, it wasn't voted out.

Carrie lives with her husband, two lovely children and a larger-than-life black pug called Plato. When she isn't writing or reading, she can be found baking, drinking an occasional (!) glass of wine, or chatting on social media.

You can find Carrie in all these places
www.carrieelks.com
carrie.elks@mail.com

A heartwarming small town beach series, full of best friends, hot guys and happily-ever-afters.

Let Me Burn

She's Like the Wind

Sweet Little Lies

Just A Kiss

Baby I'm Yours

Pieces Of Us

Chasing The Sun

Heart And Soul

Lost In Him

THE SHAKESPEARE SISTERS SERIES

An epic series about four strong yet vulnerable sisters, and the alpha men who steal their hearts.

Summer's Lease

A Winter's Tale

Absent in the Spring

By Virtue Fall

THE LOVE IN LONDON SERIES

Three books about strong and sassy women finding love in the big city.

Coming Down

Broken Chords

Canada Square

STANDALONE

Fix You

An epic romance that spans the decades. Breathtaking and angsty and all the things in between.

ACKNOWLEDGMENTS

Writing a book like this is always a labor of love, and like the other kind of labor, I couldn't do it alone. Thanks as always to my beautiful family. Ash, Ella, Olly and Plato the Pug. You guys are my reason. Special thanks to Olly who was so patient with all my questions about the NFL and footballers!

Meire Dias is my fabulous agent and friend. Her support is everything. I wouldn't be a writer without her.

To my editor Rose David, and my proofreader Mich - thank you for all your help and for the comments that make me smile. You're the best.

Kirsty Ann Still is an amazing designer and made this cover SO PRETTY. Thank you, lady!

And to the newest member of my team - Amanda Walker. Thank you for putting up with my often illegible requests. You understand me more than I do on some days.

Finally, to you the reader. Thank you for taking my characters into your hearts, and for being as invested in their journeys as I am. I love hearing from you - whether it be by email, social media, replying to my newsletters or in my Facebook group. Thank you for all the support you give me.

Until the next time! Carrie xx